The Laws of Attraction

Books by Mary Connealy

From Bethany House Publishers

WYOMING SUNRISE
BOOK 2

The Laws of Attraction

MARY CONNEALY

BETHANYHOUSE
a division of Baker Publishing Group
Minneapolis, Minnesota

© 2023 by Mary Connealy

Published by Bethany House Publishers
Minneapolis, Minnesota
www.bethanyhouse.com

Bethany House Publishers is a division of
Baker Publishing Group, Grand Rapids, Michigan

Printed in the United States of America

Library of Congress Cataloging-in-Publication Data
Names: Connealy, Mary, author.
Title: The laws of attraction / Mary Connealy.
Description: Minneapolis, Minnesota : Bethany House, a division of Baker
    Publishing Group, [2023] | Series: Wyoming sunrise ; 2
Identifiers: LCCN 2022055232 | ISBN 9780764241833 (casebound) | ISBN
    9780764241147 (paperback) | ISBN 9781493442140 (ebook)
Subjects: LCGFT: Western fiction. | Romance fiction. | Novels.
Classification: LCC PS3603.O544 L39 2023 | DDC 813/.6—dc23/eng/20230103
LC record available at https://lccn.loc.gov/2022055232

Scripture quotations are from the King James Version of the Bible.

Cover design by James Hall
Cover model by Richard Jenkins Photography

Author is represented by the Natasha Kern Literary Agency.

Baker Publishing Group publications use paper produced from sustainable forestry practices and post-consumer waste whenever possible.

23 24 25 26 27 28 29   7 6 5 4 3 2 1

To my mom, Dorothy Moore

This is my first chance to dedicate a book to my mom since she passed away. Mom, the best encourager. The best at making a daughter, trying to write a book, feel like it was possible. A woman of great faith, so I know she's in a better place. But I miss her. I love you, Mom.

1

If I have to make one more pair of chaps . . ." Nell Armstrong heard her own voice. Good grief, thinking about chaps had her talking to herself again. She badly wanted to make dresses and bonnets, ribbons and ruffles. "Would it kill someone in this town to want a few yards of lace?"

Irritated, she snapped her teeth together to shut herself up. Then she thought of all the men in Pine Valley and knew it *would* probably kill them. The front door to her dress shop—dress shop? She almost snorted aloud but then managed to control herself—crashed open, and a little boy dashed in and slammed the door closed. The boy looked her in the eye, looked left and right, saw the counter to her right, took two running steps and dove behind it.

From behind the counter, she heard a quavering voice whisper, "Don't tell."

Heavy boots thudded on the boardwalk that fronted her shop. Through her small windows she saw a man dash past and keep running. Her shop was the last one on this side of the street. The thudding stopped.

The man shouted, "Sam, you get back here!"

Nell recognized the voice. Brandon Nolte. A homesteader she barely knew. But the general shape of him in the glimpse she'd gotten through the windows matched the voice, though she'd never heard him shout before. She'd hardly ever heard him speak before.

But it was him.

The thudding started again, coming straight for her shop.

He thrust open the door. "Sam, are you in here?"

The whisper came again. "Don't tell."

She did *not* want to get in the middle of a fight between a man and his runaway son.

"Can I help you, Mr. Nolte?"

He was looking all over, and when she spoke, he almost stumbled. As if he were surprised there was a person in the room. She sat behind a worktable, putting iron rivets in chaps. Her friend Mariah had made the rivets for her.

"I'm looking for Sam."

She'd heard he had a family, but she didn't know much about who lived on the homestead with him. Obviously he had at least one child. "You've misplaced your son?"

"I'm not a boy!" The voice wasn't quavery then so much as it was the high-pitched voice of a girl.

Brand wheeled around to glare at the counter. He gave Nell a narrow-eyed look with a pair of cool blue eyes.

"You come out of there. Right now."

The little—Nell quickly shifted her thinking—little *girl* popped up from behind the counter. Short hair. Not shorn exactly, but a crop of unruly brown hair that looked boyish to Nell, sticking out from under a slouchy broad-brimmed hat. Blue eyes that gleamed with fury and unshed tears. The girl looked a whole lot like her dark-haired, blue-eyed pa. They even had nearly the same haircut. She wore a plaid flannel shirt and overalls. What was more, now that the girl was in view and glaring at her pa, she wasn't all that little. Possibly a young lady, fourteen or fifteen maybe. Hard to tell, what with the shapeless clothes.

"I'm not going into that general store dressed like this. You go on and drag the rest of my poor sisters in and humiliate them if you've a mind. But no one in town is gonna see me dressed like this. I won't be going to church neither, nor to school. You just go on while I start the hike home."

"I told you, Sam, you need to get over being shy."

Sam didn't look that shy to Nell. She looked embarrassed to death, and furious.

"Is the problem your clothes?" Nell asked.

Both whipped their heads around and glared at her like she was an unwanted intrusion.

Well, too bad. They should have picked another place for their argument than her shop. *They* were the intruders.

"Because making proper dresses for girls is what I do here." In theory anyway. Fact was, she mostly made chaps, as well as trousers and flannel shirts. "Do you need a dress for church and school? And what is your name?"

"It's Samantha. He always calls me Sam. It's dreadful."

"All right. Mr. Nolte, do you really want your daughter,

a young woman she seems like to me, to parade around town in britches? Does that seem proper to you?"

Brand, still staring daggers at Nell, said, "It's all she's got, and all I know how to make."

"Can you afford the material for dresses for your daughters?"

Brand's expression softened a bit. "Not really. We've been getting by with little or no cash money for a while now. We got to Pine Valley at a poor time of year last fall. I've got a small flock of chickens for eggs and a couple of cows that provide us milk. I didn't grow so much as a single potato to get us through the winter. I can't be buying dresses. What little I have . . ." His voice faltered.

Nell noticed a flush high on his cheeks, as if he were ashamed of being poor.

"What I have went to laying in supplies for the long, cold winter we just survived. What I got left over is for more supplies and seed. I don't have cash for much else. None of the girls like wearing britches, and I let the winter provide an excuse to never attend church, nor to bring the girls into town for school. But that is over now."

Nell quit watching a grown man blush and turned to the girl. A girl. A real live girl in need of a dress. Nell was tempted to grab her and run. Keep her forever.

"You have another daughter?"

"Three. Cassie and Mick."

"Cassandra and Michaela," Samantha said with scorn. "Their names are Cassandra and Michaela, and I'm Samantha. You don't even know we're girls, Pa."

Brand studied his defiant young daughter. "I reckon

the others are young enough they don't feel so bad about how I dress them."

"Yes, they do."

His shoulders slumped. He looked purely demoralized. Then he swept one hand toward the door. "Walk on home. I'll pick you up along the trail when I've finished with my ordering."

The defiance drained out of Samantha, and she darted around the counter and threw herself into Brand's arms. "Pa, don't feel so bad. I just want to stay home. Maybe in a year we'll be able to buy some material and get dresses made up for us girls. But I *can't* go to church or school dressed like this. I can't. I just can't." Samantha wailed her last few words, let go of her pa, and ran for the door.

"Stop. Right. There." Nell had a voice that cracked like a whip. She didn't use it often, but her late husband had taught her a lot about how to go about surviving on the frontier, and one of the things she knew how to do, when it was called for, was to take command of a situation.

Samantha whirled to face her. Brand crossed his arms and glared again. He might not like it, but he wasn't talking.

"I am a woman who makes pretty dresses for a living. I will make three dresses."

Brand started shaking his head.

Nell plunged onward before he could say no. "*In exchange* for the three of them coming in to work for me after school each day. Mr. Nolte, you can simply wait to fetch them until two hours after the normal end of the school day. They will earn a dime a day apiece, and I will wait to pay them until they've earned the value of their dresses. That will take about a month of their labor. After that, if they want to continue working for me, I'll pay cash money. Or they can earn a bonnet or a second dress, whichever one interests them."

No one really knew how much money she'd made making chaps. Honestly, it was so much that she was probably the richest person in town. But making chaps was a huge bore. She was so completely tired of them! She'd pay the girls for nothing more than coming in to talk to her. And she'd make them all the dresses they wanted for free because she had bolts of material on hand she'd brought west with her, thinking fabric would be hard to come by in a place like Wyoming.

She'd pretty much accepted that she was never going to turn the fabric into dresses. Honestly, she'd pay their father if she could get the girls to come into her shop after school and stay for a spell. She was almost giddy about the prospect. But remembering the father's embarrassment, she knew his pride wouldn't allow taking the dresses as a gift.

"Do you girls know how to sew?"

Samantha shook her head. Nell saw the hope in her eyes. Samantha didn't make a sound, as if afraid one wrong word might sway her father away from the offer.

"Then I'll teach you. It will be like training my employees." Almost dizzy with what felt like a diabolical plot, Nell wondered if she could teach the girls to make chaps. She'd leave out the cost of the leather and give the girls the rest of what they'd earn. She tried not to giggle. "I'll teach you to make chaps, too. If you show skill at it, I may have to raise your salary. For now, though, we'll start with a dime."

She really had no idea what proper wages were. Maybe a dime was miserly. Maybe it was a fortune. "I'll make the dresses for you before next Sunday. That way you can go to church dressed properly." She looked at Brand and arched one brow. "Does that sound all right to you?"

Brand's jaw clenched. He turned to look at his daughter and must have seen the hope shining in her pretty blue eyes.

He nodded silently.

Samantha shrieked and flung herself into her father's arms for the second time. But this time it was with unbridled joy.

"Mr. Nolte"—Nell tried to sound stern so he'd take her seriously, when she wanted to shriek and hug him just like his daughter had—"would you go to your other daughters, who are no doubt waiting in your wagon, and send them into my shop? I'll take their measurements, and they'll be ready to ride home with you when you've finished at the general store. It's Monday, so if you can get back to town on Saturday, I'll have the dresses done, and you can bring the girls here so we can try them on."

She could just send the dresses with him, but she wanted to make the girls feel pretty in the new dresses. She couldn't wait to see each of the girls wearing them.

"Samantha, you stay here with me while your pa gets Cassandra and Michaela." She wasn't asking permission. She was, in fact, throwing Pa out and keeping the girl. There was no sense running off with her. Nell had nowhere to hide.

But she could come close.

Brand gave Nell a frustrated look, then looked down at

Samantha, jerked his head in a nod, and stomped out of the shop. He slammed the door behind him. That might be a manly pride thing, too. Nell had seen a prideful man kicking up a fuss over things she couldn't understand many times. Her late husband had more than his share of stubborn pride.

Once he was out of sight, Nell looked at Samantha, who ran into her arms just like she had her pa's and squealed. Nell couldn't help but join in the ruckus.

2

Brand thought he'd heard a squeal coming from inside the dress shop. He wasn't sure, but Sam was tough—she could handle the seamstress woman just fine. His girls were only half a block away, sitting in his wagon outside the general store, so he kept walking.

He could see them crouched in the back, peeking over the wagon box. Yep, they were embarrassed too, only they were too young still to be openly defiant like Sam. She'd be sixteen in a couple of months.

He reached them and said, "I'm getting dresses made for you, but you're going to have to—"

The end of his short speech was lost in the excited leaping. He muttered, ". . . earn them."

"Dresses, Pa?" Cassie—Cassandra, that is—leapt over the side of the wagon and ran in the direction he'd come from. Cassandra was the most comfortable in her trousers. His tomboy. His buddy. Thirteen years old, so maybe she hadn't yet taken to womanly notions.

"Yep, dress shop down there. I left Sam inside." He

pointed and then had to hustle to keep up. So maybe a few womanly notions. Cass wanted the dress.

He walked with Micky, holding the girl's hand. He didn't want her running off ahead of him. He saw Cass open the door to the dress shop, and then she was gone inside with a slam.

"Can we afford new dresses, Pa?" Micky asked. "I don't need one if it's too costly."

He squeezed his littlest girl's hand. Seven years old. Blond like her ma instead of dark-haired like him and her sisters. He noticed her hair had gotten a little long and he had no notion of what to do with long hair. Time for a trim for everyone.

Micky was a quieter soul than the other two. And a worrier. He didn't like knowing he'd loaded his money worries on the girls. He needed to do better. He'd failed his girls without Pamela to take care of them. He missed her as if he'd had his arm cut off. The pain part and the clumsiness part.

"You're gonna have to do some chores for Mrs. Armstrong, the . . . the dress lady." Seamstress? Dressmaker? Needler?

"She's going to whip up three dresses for you before Sunday, then you'll have to go to her shop and work for her after school." He glanced down at his little Michaela. She smiled up at him, but a furrow of worry still drew a line between her eyes. "She said she'd teach you how to sew, and you'd earn out your dresses in work."

"So it won't cost you nothin'?"

"Nope, it's all just fine. We always manage, don't we, little darling?"

The furrow eased.

He wasn't sure how Mrs. Armstrong's deal was exactly fair. She obviously ran her own shop herself and probably didn't need the help. Which meant it was charity. But then maybe she had work for the girls. He'd have to be sure of that or he'd need to scrape together the cash money to pay her, somehow. The trip to the general store would leave him close to flat broke. Still, he had enough for garden seed. He shook off the fretting that he wasn't hiding well enough from his girls as they reached the shop.

Through the window he saw Cassie and Samantha chattering with Mrs. Armstrong. He was struck by the fact that Samantha was almost as tall as her. Of course, Mrs. Armstrong wasn't an overly tall woman. Maybe five and a half feet tall. And she had a delicate look about her. Blond hair done up all pretty. His girls should probably have their hair looking like that. Yet there wasn't too much fussiness about Mrs. Armstrong. She was wearing a pretty pink shirtwaist and what looked like a riding skirt. So maybe she wouldn't bury his girls in frills they couldn't work in.

He opened the door and the chattering stopped. Mrs. Armstrong gave a beaming smile. She didn't seem one bit put upon over this arrangement. In fact, she looked thrilled.

"Here's Michaela. And did Cassandra tell you her name?"

Mrs. Armstrong smiled down at Cass. "Yes, she did. You've got three beautiful girls. How I envy you."

Envy him? A mostly penniless widower with three girls he wasn't raising right? She oughta stop envying him right now. "I'll leave you three girls in Mrs. Armstrong's care while I fill my order at the general store. I'll stop back for you soon."

He tugged on the brim of his hat, looked between the girls, all four of them, then ducked back outside. He got the distinct impression he was neither wanted nor needed.

An impression that made his heart ache. His girls had found someone they wanted to be with more than him, and after just two minutes' acquaintance.

Nell clasped her hands together and squeaked. Grinning, she said, "Let's get started."

She waved the girls over to the counter, where Samantha had been hiding earlier. "I've got a tape measure and notepad here. I'll write down how long to make the skirts and how wide the shoulders and how narrow the waists. Samantha, you first."

Samantha just stood there. A girl who'd never gotten measured before. Nell didn't mind teaching her things.

"Do you want Cass and me to work for you now, Mrs. Armstrong? We could sweep up or something while you work on Sam."

"Start calling me Samantha, Michaela. I want a woman's name. I'm done with Sam."

A furrow appeared on Michaela's smooth brow. Working quickly, because she didn't expect Brand to be gone long, Nell said, "I just came up with the idea of having you help me. But I'm so busy I can use all three of you."

Nell stretched her tape measure around Samantha's slender waist. She'd make sure to put in plenty of fabric to be let out as the girls grew. It wasn't only legs that grew on a child. "You'll earn your dresses, never fear. But I won't be at this long enough to show you much today." As Nell worked, she asked the girls, "Do you three know what I make the very most of here?"

"Dresses?" Cassandra guessed.

"Bonnets?" Samantha turned when Nell gestured for her to.

Michaela shrugged.

Nell pulled an exaggerated face as she finished with Samantha, jotted down the measurements, then said, "Cassandra, you're next."

Cassandra stepped up, and Samantha moved away.

"I make chaps," Nell answered.

All three girls fell silent. They had matching looks of confusion on their faces.

"I thought you said you made dresses, ma'am." Samantha walked to the table where Nell had been sitting when Samantha burst in. She studied the leather spread out on the table.

"I do make dresses, if anyone would ever order one. I made only four this year. Four." With a disgusted snort, she went to measuring the middle girl. She had the same tousled mess of brown curls as her big sister did. And the same bright blue eyes that they shared with their pa. Such a pretty girl under her boyish, ill-fitting clothes.

"But chaps! I get a new order for chaps nearly once a week. A man once asked me if I knew how to make them. I said no. He had a pair that was worn clean out and he begged for me to help him. He said he'd bring a pair in, and I could copy them. Well, I've worked some with leather, and he even said he'd bring me in a nicely tanned cowhide to practice on. I reluctantly said yes. After that, it was like the floodgates opened."

Nell finished with Cassandra and said, "You're next, Michaela."

Cassandra wandered over to the table to study what was clearly a pair of nearly finished chaps.

"So I've been making nothing but chaps, not counting those four dresses, for a whole year. And one of the dresses was for me, and I didn't even need one. I made one for Mrs. Roberts, the town blacksmith. I nearly forced one on Miss Pruitt, who owns the Idee Ranch."

"It's a huge spread," Samantha said, running a hand gently over the leather. Well, if busting broncs didn't hurt chaps, then a young woman could do no harm. "It's straight east of town on past our place. I think Pa's dream is to be a big rancher like that. But we're just barely making do with a few cows and chickens and one hundred and sixty acres."

"You're getting a good start," Nell said. "You can grow as big as you want out here. Wyoming is a rich land with plenty for everyone. Men and women both. That's why my friend can be a blacksmith. It's not a man's job, now, is it?"

Cassandra seemed to really be paying attention since she'd said "men and women both."

Nell finished measuring Michaela. "Now come on over and look at the mountain of pretty fabric I've got. Fabric I never, ever use."

"You said four dresses. One for the blacksmith, one for the lady rancher. One for you." Samantha seemed to do most of the speaking for the group. "Who's the fourth?"

Nell shook her head. "Another one I forced on someone.

Parson Blodgett's wife had a new baby last year, late in the fall. I made a dress for her, a new dress that wasn't big as a house, like the dresses she usually wears. It was a Christmas gift I gave her very early."

Samantha giggled. "Did the blacksmith and the rancher pay for the dresses?"

"No."

All three girls giggled. Shy little Michaela said, "So you made four dresses and gave all four of them away. You didn't sell a single dress all year?" Then more quietly she added, "And now you're giving three more dresses away?"

Nell ran a hand over Michaela's slightly longer hair. She wondered how Michaela's blond curls had escaped the chopping block.

"I am a desperate woman. I love making dresses. And I hate making chaps, though the pay is fine indeed." Nell ran her hand up a stack of calico fabric, some flowered and some plain. She couldn't wait to put ruffles and lace on these things. But she'd surprise them with the finer details.

"Pick a color, girls. I've got all this fabric I brought along to open my dress shop. My brother and I came out to Pine Valley together after my husband died. Then he wanted to move on west, and I told him I'd moved for the last time."

"Can we really pick any color, ma'am?" Samantha's hand reached for a bright blue sprigged with small pink-and-white flowers with a pretty vine of greenery worked around here and there.

"You most certainly can. But I am not giving these away. I genuinely would love some help. I'd love the company, too." She tugged the bright blue color, a match for Samantha's eyes, out of the stack. "This color for you then?"

Samantha nodded.

Cassandra picked a delicate yellow calico scattered with blue-and-pink flowers with green leaves.

Nell smiled. "That is going to be so pretty this summer. Excellent choice, Cassandra."

Michaela reached one hesitant finger and pointed to a light pink, a solid color that would work up into something beautiful. Nell could already see it with white lace and a ruffled neck.

"That is going to be so perfect with your blond hair. Oh, I can't wait to get to work on these."

"What about the chaps?" Michaela sounded worried again.

"I've got orders for chaps reaching into next winter. All kinds of orders. Men who are wearing perfectly fine chaps right now but who like mine better. Trust me, every single one of them will wait. I charge a lot for them and still the orders flood in. I could only dream they'd be impatient and take their business elsewhere. And with you three helping me, I'll get their orders out even faster. So, making these dresses in exchange for you working for me won't delay me a bit."

Each one of the girls picked up the bolt of cloth she'd chosen. She watched them stare at the pretty fabric, hug it. Oh, she just couldn't wait.

The rattle of a wagon sounded outside, and she turned to see their hopelessly inept father pull up.

Nell caught herself. That was unkind. There'd been no mention of it, but there must not be a mother in their lives. As a widow she could easily understand a family losing someone. And the girls were healthy and clean. Their teeth were a bright white. He was a good father . . . just perhaps inept in something he readily admitted was beyond him.

"Leave the fabric and run out to your pa. Don't make him climb down."

The girls obeyed instantly and ran for the door. Samantha was last in line. She looked back with longing at the blue fabric. "You won't forget which color I want, will you, Mrs. Armstrong?"

Nell laughed. "No, I most surely won't. The dresses will be ready before you need them for Sunday services."

Samantha grinned and dashed out the door after her sisters, slamming it shut.

Nell let the slamming go and chalked it up to excitement. But maybe she'd teach the girls a few things about ladylike manners, along with how to make chaps.

3

Brand slapped the reins against his team's backs. It was a long half hour out to his homestead, riding in the wagon. He could do it in about half the time on horseback, especially since he could leave the well-cleared trail and cut some distance off.

He planned to take the girls to school on horseback and get to church that way, too. They were all good riders. Good farmhands. They worked so hard and were such fine young women, and he'd gone and humiliated them by making them wear britches to town.

As he drove out of town, he looked at his three girls. So animated, smiling and whispering to each other. Happier than he'd seen them in a long time. Maybe since Pamela had died over seven years ago.

"I didn't realize how much you girls wanted dresses. I'm sorry. I think back and I know you tried to tell me. But it just didn't seem important when we were going through so much."

"It didn't seem that important to me either, Pa." Sam

was on the far end of the wagon seat. Cass was between him and Sam. Micky was on both girls' laps, straddling one knee apiece. They were wedged in, and it was another surprise. They'd always sat three across with Micky on someone's lap, but those days were coming to an end as his girls grew up. Brand thought Sam might already be taller than Pamela had been.

"Not when you think of Ma dying, then Grandma Nolte, then Grandma Drexler," she went on. "Then selling out back east, then catching on with a wagon train."

"And we had dresses back then, but once we were on the wagon train, remember one of the families said their youngest son had grown out of his overalls? He was a little older than Sam, and when they offered them to us, Sam, you liked them, didn't you?"

Nodding, Sam said, "I did. I thought it was fun. Britches were comfortable, and climbing in and out of the wagon and handling the horses and herding the cows were a lot easier. When I grew out of my dress and handed it down to Cassie, she was grumpy about it."

"I wanted britches, too. By the time we heard of land to homestead up here and split off from the wagon train, we were all wearing overalls and boys' shirts handed down to us. You even sewed a pair or two."

"So you haven't been miserable the whole time, then?"

Sam leaned forward to look around Micky. "Nope, I liked when you gave us a haircut, too. No more braids. No more hair in my face or scolding Micky to sit still while I got a comb through her snarls."

Micky elbowed her big sister. "It hurts!"

Sam hugged her. "I know. I'm sorry. I'm bad at it."

25

Micky patted Sam on her knee.

"It just hit me hard when you took us to town today. We've hardly ever *been* to town. Only that day last autumn when you went to the land office and checked about homesteads. Then we went out and scouted around and picked a spot. You left us with the cattle and wagon while you rode in and signed up for a claim. You came back, we built the cabin and barn, tended the horses, cattle, and chickens, then settled in for the winter. Nope, the overalls are warmer than dresses and probably safer. I'll keep wearing them at home. But I can't go to town dressed in britches. I just can't."

Nodding silently for a while, Brand thought about it. "And your names. I've been calling you nicknames all your lives. It never struck me that the names are boyish. I'll stop doing that. I think you're the prettiest girls alive. I don't mean to treat you wrong. I'm just a lunkhead about things like this. It was Ma's job to know things such as how to do up a girl's hair. And then when she passed, I never learned it. I just dumped the job on the grandmas, then on you, Sam . . . Samantha, I mean."

"We do it too, Pa. Call ourselves by the same nicknames you use." Cassie tilted her head and rested it on Brand's shoulder. "I like Cassie. I think it's a girl name, enough of one. I want you to keep calling me that. But Sam and Micky." Raising her head, Cassie shook it. "Nothing girlish about those names. You'd better stop it."

"I'm used to it, Pa. But I'm changing. Cassie can keep her name, but Michaela's not going to be Micky anymore, okay?" Sam twisted around to look at the littlest of them. "I'm going to call you Michaela. It's a pretty name."

"I like it. It goes better with the new dress." Her words did something to the girls. Suddenly the single bench seat could hardly hold the suppressed excitement.

"Tell me what Mrs. Armstrong said." Brand figured he'd better let them talk before they exploded.

"She measured us." Cassie gripped his arm and hugged it. She explained being measured for a dress. "Then Mrs. Armstrong let us each pick out our own color." Samantha's legs started swinging. "She had a big stack of cloth, all so pretty, and she said she's only made four dresses all year. She started complaining about chaps. She said all anyone ever wants her to make are chaps, but she wants to make *dresses*."

The girls just plain chattered. It was like a flock of chirping birds had landed beside him. Chaps were boring. Four dresses all given away. Mrs. Armstrong this, and Mrs. Armstrong that. It all kept them happy and talking the whole drive home.

As they finally approached the homestead, the girls kept talking. Brand had listened as best he could, but he figured they'd now talked about three times longer than they talked even with the dress lady.

He curved around an outcropping of boulders that was sprouted with trees and saw his cabin. He'd done a good job of it. It was much nicer than the bare minimum required of a homestead cabin. Well, *much* might be a little strong. It had a front room that took up the entire length of the cabin, a bedroom behind it, and a kitchen beside that bedroom. He'd made it tall enough that the girls could climb up a ladder and have a loft room almost as big as the whole house under the eaves. Yet it wasn't going to be tall enough much longer if Samantha kept growing. The ceiling slanted with the roof, and she must only be able to stand up straight right in the center. For now, though, it was all right. Small enough to keep it warm in the winter, with a chimney dividing the front from the back, which opened to his bedroom and went up through the girls' room.

He had a barn that was about the same size as his house. There were two rooms in that too, along with a hayloft. One side for the cows, one broken into stalls for the horses. Large corrals to the left and right of the barn let the cattle and horses get outside and graze.

And there was a small chicken coop for his modest flock, though four of his hens were setting eggs now. He was hopeful his flock would grow enough that he could have a chicken dinner now and then without eating too many of his egg suppliers.

He'd also started breaking up the ground for a garden. He didn't intend to plant crops. The animals didn't need hay and corn, not with wild grass for grazing so plentiful. He needed the garden to help feed his girls.

He pulled the wagon right up to the front door. Hopped down and reached up for each girl. They let him help them down.

"First Cassie." He lowered her to the ground.

She smiled her tough-girl smile at him.

"Then Michaela."

She snuck in a kiss on his cheek. "I love you, Pa."

"I love all of you girls so much I don't have words big enough to explain it all. But I love you. Lastly Samantha."

She gave him a sheepish smile. "I pitched a fit in town

today, Pa. I'm sorry. I regret making such a fuss, but it seemed to be needed to get your attention and make it clear that I was saying something really important."

"Which means you don't really regret it." He placed her on the ground.

The smile brightened, and for the first time ever, he saw his ma in his girl. "Thank you for the dresses, Pa."

"You'll be earning them."

"But it was so reasonable of you to let us get them. I'm going to try to be more reasonable when I want something and just talk with you about it. Not pitch another fit." She hugged him tight, and then all three of the girls pressed in from all directions and Brand had one of his favorite things in the world: a family hug.

For one second, just one, he let himself miss Pamela and felt the bite of tears in his eyes. Their family circle wasn't as it should be. There was a huge gap where his pretty blond wife should be.

Samantha pulled back and gave him yet one *more* version of her smile. Very sassy. "I won't pitch another fit unless I really have to."

He tweaked her nose. "Let's get these supplies into the house. We've got chores."

4

Nell waited until the dust had settled down behind the Nolte family's wagon, peeking out her window, nearly bouncing with excitement. She forced herself to count to ten to make sure they were completely out of sight of town.

When her patience would hold no longer, she threw open the door, slammed it shut behind her, and ran straight for the blacksmith shop.

She rushed inside, shoving the door wide. Mariah leapt away from the burning red iron she'd been pounding with a sledge.

It was clear she'd calmed down since last fall when some men had tried to kill her. She didn't hurl the sledgehammer she held in one hand at Nell's head.

Steady nerves.

"Mariah, oh my grace. Oh, my merciful heavens. Oh, praise God." The final sentence must have cleared up Mariah's confusion about whether a fight was coming because she set the sledge aside and walked toward Nell. "You'll never guess what happened!"

Mariah arched one pretty dark-blond brow and said, "Are you asking me to guess?"

"You know how I've been offering to make you another dress?"

"Offering," Mariah said dryly. "More like nagging, pestering, outright begging. I don't need another—"

"I can't make it." Nell cut her off. "I don't have time!" Nell clutched her hands together under her chin and she might have jumped up and down a little. She'd probably have time next week, but she'd put off the nagging until then. Mariah's belly was getting round with a baby on the way. The woman definitely needed another dress.

"My guess is, considering the joy, this isn't a really big chaps order." Mariah reached behind her to untie the strings of her leather apron at the small of her back, then lifted the loop that hung the apron around her neck and dropped the apron on a nail by the front door.

"Dresses. Real live dresses for three little girls."

As Mariah pulled the leather scarf off her head, she seemed to think through everyone in town. It wasn't a big town. Parson Blodgett had a lot of youngsters, though just one girl and six sons, including a boy born last winter. "For whom?"

"You remember Brandon Nolte?"

"Sure, Nell, he was part of the search party who came hunting me when I was kidnapped last spring. A homesteader this side of Becky's place." Becky Pruitt was their friend, a lady rancher who was tougher than both Mariah and Nell put together. "His wife ordered three dresses?"

"He doesn't have a wife." Nell clapped her hands, then realized that was probably rude. "Uh, I mean, he's got three little girls and no wife."

Had he said there was no wife? But there must not be a wife. Which likely meant his wife was dead, which made the clapping more than rude. It made her appear cruel-hearted.

Still, the dress order was indeed exciting.

"That's terrible. Did she die recently?"

"I am just now realizing I know nothing about the family except that he's got three girls who never come to town with him. He forced them to come along today, and one of them, the oldest, probably a fifteen-year-old, threw an absolute fit and ran from him and hid in my shop."

"Can the man afford three dresses? A lot of homesteaders are short on funds."

"I'm making them for free."

Mariah rolled her eyes. "You need a better business model, Nell."

"I make a fortune on those chaps."

"A fortune, really?" Mariah seemed overly curious about that.

"Are you done for the day?"

"I am. And Clint should be in soon. He did the afternoon chores at home and will carry in what he can in preparation for the diner tomorrow. Then he'll come here until I'm done. But I'm ready to quit. Let's walk over to the diner and see if he's there. So, why did the little girl run?"

Nell caught Mariah's arm. "Oh, you should have seen the poor little things. Dressed like boys. Trousers and their hair cut short." Except not the little one. Probably because the older girl, Samantha, could manage to do her little sister's hair.

"And he brought them to town dressed like that?" Mariah closed the blacksmith shop doors and locked them firmly. Mariah, since the attempts on her life, was a strong proponent of high-quality locks. She'd learned to make them herself.

Nell told Mariah the whole story, including the job offer.

Mariah sounded interested in that. "You know, I was working in the blacksmith shop with Pa by the time I was fifteen. Do you think Mr. Nolte would be willing to swap child labor for some horseshoes or a bucket?"

Mariah, as the town blacksmith, farrier, and cooper, made horseshoes and shod horses, and fashioned wooden buckets and other watertight wooden things such as butter churns and washtubs. The woman kept the whole town running.

While Nell made chaps.

They saw Clint stepping out the front door of his diner. He smiled at them, then locked the diner and headed toward them.

Nell wasn't nearly done telling Mariah everything, for the second time, when Clint reached them.

"Do you want to come out to the house for supper?" Clint only made breakfast and a noon meal at the diner. He was a fine cook. A chef really. But he'd calmed down from calling the diner the Grand Restaurant, which he pronounced *Grawnd Restaurawnt*. Or something along those lines.

He'd even painted the words CLINT'S DINER over the top of the front door. The man was turning pure Western at last. But he was still cooking like his diner was a fancy eating place. No one wanted him to stop that.

"I'm sure I'd get a better meal out at your place, but I've got work to do. I've got dresses to make." She gave Mariah an impulsive hug. "I shouldn't have even come to tell you, but I couldn't control myself. I've got three dresses to sew by Saturday."

She whirled away and ran for her shop, so excited she was afraid she'd whack the fabric to ribbons with her eager scissors. Except, of course, she never would do such a thing. These dresses were going to make those girls' eyes shine.

Finding work for the girls might prove a little difficult, yet she couldn't wait for their company.

Brand couldn't believe he'd done such a stupid thing as to take charity. For dresses. He was a failure. His pride was stung until it was like a run-in with a swarm of bees.

He pulled the wagon up to the dress lady's shop, and the girls just plain vaulted out of the back of the wagon where they'd been hiding. They zipped across the short stretch of boardwalk and were inside the shop before he'd gotten the brake thrown.

Climbing down, he heard the girl talk from outside. He hesitated. He probably shouldn't go in. Would the girls be changing? But no, not right in front of the window. Should he knock?

There were so many things he was helpless about with the girls. He felt like a failure in more ways than just taking charity.

Why had God let Pamela die? Bringing into the world

that last baby had done for her. But didn't God want man to be fruitful and multiply? Prayerfully asking for wisdom as the pa and sole parent of three girls, he opened the door slowly while listening for screams. He went into an empty shop, but he heard voices coming from behind a nearby door. Apparently, Mrs. Armstrong had a changing room. Made sense.

Mulling over what to do next, Brand raised his voice just loud enough to be heard. "Should I wait out here or give you girls a chance to get gussied up?"

"You can go on for a bit, Mr. Nolte. We'll be a while getting changed."

We? He doubted the dress lady was changing. Why *we?*

"I'll go visit the parson, then. Or someone. I'll be back in a half hour or so."

"Make it an hour." Mrs. Armstrong sure didn't seem to think a pa was important right now. Probably the girls didn't think so, either. Definitely the parson, except . . . as Brand opened the door, he saw Clint walking toward the smithy.

The only person moving on the street anywhere. Then he noticed one of the Wainwright brothers standing in the open doorway of their store. Henry. Brand had found a few places in town needing a man to work now and then. Nothing steady. But the Wainwrights required help at least one day a month when the supply wagon rolled into town. And a few others would pay for help from time to time. In fact, it'd gotten him through the winter.

Strange thing about the man in the doorway was his absolute stillness. Not standing there casually as though taking a break from work, but more like he was watching.

And his watching was aimed right at Clint.

It struck Brand as peculiar. He'd worked as a deputy sheriff back in Missouri for a few years before he'd gone to digging a living out of the wild and wooded Ozark land where he'd lived. Digging up trees, fighting new ones all the time. Always at war to keep a small plot of land cleared for his humble farming.

Brand shook his head for his unkind thoughts of a neighbor and walked away from the dress shop. The movement drew Wainwright's attention.

"Howdy, Henry."

The man waved, then eased himself back into the store and closed the door behind him.

Brand jogged down the steps, took a second to see that his horse was securely tied to the hitching post, and called out, "Clint, hold up."

Clint was heading for his wife's shop, probably wishing he could stop the woman from playing with fire when a baby was on the way. He stopped and waved, waiting while Brand strode toward him.

When they were close enough not to have to holler, Clint said, "Your girls are getting new dresses, I hear."

Brand managed a smile. News traveled fast in a small town like this one. "They're so excited I had trouble keeping them in the wagon. They liked to jump out and sprint all the way to town."

"They're sure to be pretty dresses. Nell made one for Mariah, and now that my wife's getting on with a baby, Nell's after her to get another one made special for expecting women. Not sure what that'd be like, but Mariah won't hear of it. Still, Nell making dresses?" Clint lowered his voice. "Has she said the word *chaps* to you?"

Brand tried to remember. "She might've."

"Well, she has orders reaching out to the end of time." Clint shook his head. "She thinks they're boring to make, but the money is good."

"Did Nell speak of the arrangement she made with my girls to work off the cost of the dresses?"

Clint nodded. "She came running over all worked up to tell Mariah about it."

A fond smile bloomed on Clint's face. It occurred to Brand that Clint had a wife, and it seemed Nell was a good friend of his. A man who might know something about women.

"Can I ask you something?"

Clint shrugged. "Sure. I'm a little early to walk Mariah home."

Brand became aware of the banging of a hammer against an anvil.

He swallowed hard. He didn't really know Clint. He'd eaten in the diner a couple of times when he'd been working and someone else paid, but he couldn't afford it. So he had no friends and no family anywhere close by. It was asking a lot for Clint to treat him as a friend. But maybe . . . Brand decided to plunge ahead. "I'm a failure with girls." The look on Clint's face told him that'd come out wrong. "As a *father*, I mean."

Clint nodded and looked a little less shocked.

"With my wife gone, passed away that is, I don't know what I'm doing. I'm afraid I'm hurting them by not knowing nothing about how they should be taught. I can't do hair. I thought they looked fine in their trousers. I thought they liked them. I was dead wrong about that. I don't know how to treat them, and I can't tell what they're thinking. I can't see if I'm hurting their feelings unless they about pound me over the head with it."

Brand snatched his hat off and ran one hand deep into his overly long hair. "I'm afraid they're gonna grow up with only bad memories of their pa and none of the skills a woman oughta have. They're a big help with everything, but I probably ask too much of them, and all the wrong things."

"Um . . . you know what? My wife lost her ma real young."

The banging went on. Not a womanly occupation. But he knew Mariah even less than he knew Clint.

Clint kept talking. "I'd say she'd tell you her pa didn't know what to do with her, either. She might have some strange ideas about how women behave. She's got a manly job and such. And she's excited about a woman coming to Pine Valley this summer to speechify about women being allowed to vote."

"But Wyoming already has that. Why give a speech here?"

Clint shrugged. "I might've asked her that myself. Doesn't seem like she liked the question much."

Clint lowered his voice and leaned in a bit closer. "I'm not sure I know a thing more about women than you do, Brand." He then straightened away and talked normally. "But I do know my wife is a fine woman. Strong and skilled at blacksmithing and still a woman in every way. She might be ready to shut the forge down by now."

Brand realized the banging had stopped.

"Why don't you come in and ask her about your girls—how they think and how they feel and how to do their hair and such. I don't know much about those myself."

Brand felt his face heat up. "I wouldn't've told you about it if I thought you'd go carrying tales to your wife. I take no pride in being a failure."

Clint clapped him on the shoulder. "It's not a failing to not know how to do something no one's ever taught you to do. But it might be a failing to be too proud to ask for help."

And Brand felt like he'd been cornered right into doing exactly what he didn't want to do. Clint was a wily one. He walked along beside him to the smithy. Clint got the door and waved Brand inside.

Mariah was hanging up her apron and pulling the leather scarf off her head. She wore a skirt that was too narrow on her legs until it was almost a pair of britches but wasn't quite. And a dark shirtwaist that hung out of her skirt rather than tucking into it. It was necessary to give her belly plenty of room. Not the most feminine clothing in the world. But Clint was right. She was a woman all right, and no one would think different for a full minute.

Maybe she could help him.

5

"Oh, Mrs. Armstrong, it's so beautiful." Samantha almost floated off the floor, she was so happy.

Nell wanted to hug the pretty young lady. And young lady for a fact. This was no child. She more than the others needed a chemise, pantaloons, other underpinnings. And she needed her hair done nicely and grown out long. She needed something else, too. A talk about what to expect when a girl was growing up.

"How old are you, Samantha?" Nell finished buttoning up the back of Michaela's dress while she studied Samantha in her bright blue.

Nell had kept the dresses reasonably simple. She had lace tatted, which was a skill she possessed and then had no use for it. A few ruffles. She'd fought the urge to make the dresses an explosion of frills. Their father might be overcome by shock.

She'd save that for later dresses.

"I'm going to be sixteen in June."

Nell wondered how long Samantha's mother had been

gone. Had anyone talked with her about becoming a woman?

Nell needed to do it and it needed to be soon, but not in front of the other girls. But these three seemed to come as a package. She wasn't sure how to arrange a private moment with Samantha. Perhaps by enlisting Mariah or Becky to distract the other girls for a bit?

She looked at Cassandra. "Your sleeves are a bit too long. Take the dress off, please."

Cassandra hugged herself as if to fight any attempt to take the dress.

Smiling, Nell said, "Oh, you'll probably grow into those sleeves in a month. We'll leave them as they are." Then, hoping she had time, she asked, "Can I comb your hair? Let's get you all neat and tidy for your pa."

The four of them had the best time imaginable, or at least Nell couldn't imagine anything more fun. They had plenty of time. Pa Nolte didn't come back for a long time.

⁓

Mariah talked with Brandon Nolte for a surprising length of time. He confessed his failures until she got more than a little bored. Clint had wandered off and came back later with a pot of warm coffee and three cups.

"I left it on the back of the stove in the diner. I start new each morning, but if there's any left, I leave it in the pot. Just in case someone wheedles their way past my door."

He poured them all a cup. Mariah had settled into a chair she used when she was doing her cooper work. Black-smithing and farrier work was all done while standing, so she enjoyed the break. There was an extra chair because Clint came by and waited to walk home with her most nights.

Brand was shaking his head as he took the coffee. As defeated-looking as a man could be.

"You just have to do your best, Brand," Mariah said, taking a coffee cup. "It warms my heart to see how much you care about your girls. You'll do fine. I think my pa did fine, and he never seemed to give treating me in a special way one minute's thought. But I knew he loved me. And I'll be mighty surprised if your girls don't know the same about you."

"But hair!"

Mariah smiled. "Nell would be a good one to teach your girls about doing their hair."

Brand sat up straight as if startled. "B-but she's already making them dresses."

"Yes, and it sounds like they're going to be spending a couple of hours with her after school. You could ask her about hair, but I'll be surprised if she doesn't do it without being asked. Nell's good at things like that. Working with her is going to be great for your girls."

Brand looked over his shoulder as if he could see through the smithy wall all the way to where his girls were working with Nell. Nodding silently as he looked at nothing, he said, "Maybe that will work out, then. Maybe. I've left them there for too long as it is. I'd better go."

"He's coming," Cassandra hissed as if he could hear her, and she wanted to jump out and yell *surprise*.

Nell said, "Line up, girls. Let's hit him all at once with a row of girls, all of you dressed up."

If he didn't make enough of a fuss, Nell would personally find a way to make him sorry he'd been born.

The girls collided with each other, giggling and turning around to face the door. Nell rushed to grab the knob before Brand could arrive and swept the door open to let him in.

He looked at the strangely opening door, frowning. Then his eyes rose and locked on his girls.

Nell was watching him like a hawk in case she had to do something drastic. But he behaved perfectly. His eyes widened, and a smile broke out on his face. She thought, since she was watching so closely, that maybe his eyes shone a bit, as if they were filling with tears.

"You girls are so beautiful I can hardly breathe." He strode for them, his arms open wide, and they all stormed at him and hugged him tight, surrounding him.

The way they fit so perfectly together, Nell knew this was a family that'd done some hugging.

Something she didn't know much about. She closed the door and came close without interrupting a precious family moment.

The girls started talking then and giggling of course. He touched a bit of lace on a collar, said something about their pretty hair. Oh, he was just doing perfectly.

He tapped Samantha's chin and said, "Thank you for forcing me to see you needed these dresses."

Samantha grabbed him and hugged him for a second time.

He took one long moment from paying strict attention

to his girls and their blooming smiles to look at Nell. "And thank you for . . . for . . . for making this possible. Thank you."

She nodded and bit her upper lip because, for just that moment, Nell, who'd been through a lot of hard things without shedding a tear, was probably showing some shiny eyes of her own.

He looked at her as if he saw everything. She most certainly hoped not because Nell had a lot of things she kept hidden. Things that kept her from exchanging long, meaningful looks with a man for years. But this look held. There was so much there. Gratitude, but something more. Respect. Something that made her feel wise and very female.

Then Cassandra said something that drew his attention to her. Just as it should. And the little family was off and chattering again with their pa's complete attention.

6

Nell watched the sweet family roll away in their wagon, the girls' and their pa's thanks ringing in her ears. With lots of *"We'll see you at church on Sunday, Mrs. Armstrong"* thrown in for good measure.

When their dust had finally settled and all those bright, happy faces had faded from her vision, she looked around her shop. She had so many plans. Bonnets, first and foremost. Tomorrow was Palm Sunday, and the next week was Easter. Those girls needed bonnets. She'd make them with fabric to match their dresses. Then the next thing would be riding skirts for all three of them, and that meant making them all shirtwaists.

Then bonnets that could be worn with different clothes—neutral colors, not matching.

Underpinnings. Yes, she had enough fabric to make them all petticoats.

She realized she was standing there with a silly grin on her face, plotting how to get the girls dressed up properly. She laughed at herself.

Now . . . how to figure the worth of her dresses? How should she count the money they earned? The girls had done some work for her this afternoon. She'd shown each of them how to use an awl to poke holes in leather. She'd shown them how to install Mariah's decorative metal rivets—a fancy little extra she charged for, and they were selling fast.

She was sure the girls would be able to cut leather and, with a little training, make the chaps themselves. If she could make them faster, four of them working instead of one, she'd make money faster. If so, the girls deserved more than a dime a day. Yet she didn't want to do a single thing that would stomp on their pa's pride.

It was a tricky business, but she had learned well how to deal with Web, her late husband, and stubborn men like him who had ideas that weren't fair or reasonable. Web didn't like anyone, especially his wife, challenging him. She'd tried a few times and remembered a stinging slap or two. Or seven.

Web's attitude about his wife was a big part of her decision to let her brother go on west while she remained in Wyoming. Here she had the right to vote, and she was finding it easy to remain safely unmarried. As a matter of fact, the more outspoken she was about women having rights equal to any man, the more she repelled suitors. And in a town so lopsided with men, that wasn't easy.

But she was proud to say she'd managed it.

Being married to Web, Nell had learned *not* to state her opinion when it differed from his. She knew better than to hope for a discussion that might end with her husband changing his mind and deciding to do things her way. Nope, she'd learned to use her womanly wiles, apply tears where needed. True, she wasn't a crier, but her late husband hadn't known that. She'd learned to sneak, then cover her tracks, all in pursuit of having some say in how she lived her life.

She wasn't proud of that. And to stop the shame, once she'd escaped marriage through widowhood, she'd lived in a much happier, more honorable way. She was strictly honest now, and when that stepped on a man's toes, it made her smile.

Except she'd done a little manipulating with Brand, hadn't she? Now here she stood, all aflutter to make his girls bonnets and dresses. She had to wonder if she hadn't slipped back to her wiles to get her way. But who cared if she had?

Smiling, chaps notwithstanding, she turned to tidy up her workspace before retiring to her upstairs rooms for the night.

Then she heard the clatter of an approaching wagon.

Much too fast. A whiplash sounded. A man shouted, pressing his horses on.

It couldn't be Brand unless something had happened. Had one of the girls been hurt?

Nell rushed to the door and flung it open just as a different rig rounded a corner on two wheels. A buckboard, not the small wagon Brand had driven. She heaved a sigh of relief that it wasn't the girls but knew bad news was arriving. The wagon was driven by a stranger. He hauled on the reins, shouting "Whoa!" and leaning hard on the brake.

"I need a doctor!" the man shouted from the buckboard seat.

Nell dashed forward, across the street well ahead of the oncoming driver. With wild gestures and at the top of her lungs, she said, "The doctor's office is over here."

She saw the man nod, charging toward the door. She ran into the doctor's office. "Trouble coming, Doc."

Doc Preston was running by the time he came out of his back room. He'd probably been upstairs, where he lived. He was a married man, but his wife, Isabelle, was in Denver visiting her mother. Doc was a stout man with a balding head of white hair, and older, though that hadn't slowed him down much.

"What's going on?" He had to have heard the wagon skidding. Traces jingled. A horse cried out. Before they could turn to go outside, a man burst in.

"He's been shot." A man with another in his arms. "I found a stagecoach, came riding along on a trail with no notion of trouble."

Doc was at the man's side, helping bear the burden as the running man staggered under the weight of the wounded one.

"Counted six dead and figured for this one, too. But I checked each one of them closely, and even with four bullet holes in him, I still heard a heartbeat."

Doc Preston began examining the unconscious patient. "Nell, fetch the sheriff."

Nell was gone at a run before the doctor's words faded from the air. She dashed to the sheriff's office.

The jail was a few doors down and around a corner from Doc Preston's office, which was probably the only reason the sheriff hadn't responded to the commotion.

He was sitting at his desk when Nell slammed the door open. "Come quick. A man shot. Doc has him."

The sheriff was up and running before she'd finished talking. The sheriff was an older man and not slender anymore, which was the only reason Nell beat him back to the doctor's office. She wrenched the door open and let him in ahead of her.

"What's going on, Darrel?"

"Four gunshot wounds. The man's unconscious. A head wound that looks real serious." The doctor looked up at Sheriff Mast to emphasize the understatement of it. The man was shot to ribbons. Yet somehow he was still alive.

"You think it's the Deadeye Gang?" The sheriff had to have his own opinion on it.

"The man who brought him in is outside. He said he came along after the robbery was over. Everyone else was dead, and this man was left for dead."

"Sloppy," Nell said in disgust. "Two survivors now. They're getting reckless and careless. It'll be their undoing. Mariah helped us capture one of them, Key Larson."

"But Larson's dead." The sheriff stared at the wounded man, but he talked to Nell like he respected her opinion.

"No chance to question him." Nell then walked up to the sheriff to stand by his side and study the victim. "We have to make sure someone is with him every hour of the day and night. Someone tough enough to fight off any killers who come here to finish their sloppy job. Larson tried to kill Mariah four times, and that's with her not remembering a thing."

"That'll take a lot of volunteers," the doctor said, still working frantically over the man to staunch the bleeding and remove the bullets. "Hold this bandage on his head, Nell."

There was no bullet in his head, but he had a terrible cut that went deep. Ugly as it was, he might survive it, but probably not the shot in the chest, nor the one in the gut.

Nell did as she was told and kept talking. "It's more volunteers than you think because it must be two people to a shift. Not just to protect him, but because we know someone in this town is connected to those outlaws. That's the reason behind them leaving no witnesses. The witnesses might recognize them. So we can't trust any one man alone with him."

The sheriff stopped staring at the man on the operating table and turned to Nell. "You're a suspicious woman, Mrs. Armstrong. And a knowing one."

"My husband was a lawman back east. He was caught up in the trouble between Kansas and Missouri after the Civil War. That's what killed him. He used to talk a lot about the law and justice and investigating crimes. I've heard plenty, probably too much."

"Sheriff Mast, hold this bandage tight on his leg while I tie it off."

The sheriff stepped up. As soon as the bandage was fastened, Doc moved to the next wound.

The sheriff said, "Nell, I need to talk to the man who brought this fellow in. Can you handle it? Doc, is one extra set of hands enough?"

Nell said, "I've helped with plenty of doctoring, including for my husband a time or two."

"Go on." The doctor moved on from tightening a bandage on the victim's head and freed Nell to staunch the next wound.

The sheriff went out.

"Grab an apron." The doctor jabbed a finger at the wall behind her.

Nell grabbed it off a nail, then rolled up her sleeves. This was a messy, ugly business.

The doctor took quick swipes with his scalpel, snapped orders at Nell, and handed her bullets, which she took with a metal pan at the bedside.

Nell fetched and wiped. She cut stitches and pressed on wounds bleeding too fast.

Despite the man's awful wounds, he kept breathing.

They worked over him for far too long. With the sun going down, Nell lit five lanterns to keep the room bright enough for the doctor to see clearly as he made tiny decisions that might mean the difference between life and death.

The door banged open, and the sheriff strode in. "I've been out to the site where this man was shot. I've brought in six bodies. I left them with the undertaker. How's this one doing?"

Doc grunted. "Almost done. Doubt he'll make it, but for now he's hanging on. I think the bullet to his gut hit the backbone."

The sheriff didn't waste time asking more questions. "Can I help?"

"Nell's been like a rock. How are you now?" Doc Preston glanced up at her. "We've been hours working over him."

"I'm worn all the way out, Doc. But then so are you,

and I suspect the sheriff is, too. Fetching six bodies wears a man down. Did you find anything? Hoofprints? Other evidence?"

"I had men with me who are trackers. I sent for Nate at the Idee. He's about the best around. We've got some notion of how many robbers there were. Nate thought five."

The doctor battled on. The sheriff talked. Nell asked some questions that she thought might help.

Finally, the doctor fastened the last bandage on the man's leg. He'd bandaged it fast at the beginning before dealing with the more serious wounds, but even the leg was a nasty wound. The bullet had hit the bone in the man's lower leg. There was a good chance he'd lose it. A broken bone would heal, but one like this, not just broken but shattered, would suppurate and kill the man if the doctor didn't amputate.

"We'll give the leg a chance. I picked out all the tiny bone fragments I could find and splinted it. I'll check it for a few days, and if it's not infected, I'll cast it. As badly wounded as he is, amputating the leg right now would probably kill him. We'll wait on that."

"I'm going to sit with him tonight," the sheriff said. "We've got to keep watch over him day and night until he regains consciousness. He may have seen something that will make all the difference. Maybe put an end to these killings."

"They struck over near Laramie this winter." Nell took a step back from the operating table. Her back hurt so much that she almost couldn't straighten.

"Yep, and once south of here. They hit a stage carrying a payroll for Fort Bridger. Not much travel around here in the winter due to the snow. They've been around for a long time now. We think a robbery five years ago was their first."

"Have you paid much attention around town as to who was gone during those robberies? Have you asked at the surrounding ranches if any of their cowpokes took off, maybe on a good excuse, and then came back? You could compare the absentees to the times of the holdups. If they're enough afraid of anyone surviving that they leave no witnesses alive, it stands to reason it's someone we all know."

The sheriff's brows rose. "No, I haven't asked those questions. All I could do was be glad the carnage happened far away from where my area of responsibility is."

"I understand that, I do. But now that the robbery's back on our doorstep, you're back in charge of solving this."

"Mrs. Armstrong, you said your husband was a lawman and he discussed his investigations with you?"

Nell's throat dried out. Talking about Web was not something she liked to do. But she had started this when she'd mentioned him, so the sheriff would understand she had some background knowledge.

"That's right, Sheriff. Web Armstrong. We lived along the Kansas-Missouri border, and there was trouble all the time. A lot of the trouble was attacks and burned-out businesses and homes. He knew there were men all around us who might be guilty of those crimes. And he trusted very few people. He liked to talk through what had happened, and I was the one he trusted to listen."

Whatever Web's shortcomings, and they were legion, he'd been a good lawman.

The sheriff seemed to think Nell had said that to encourage him to talk. He told her and the doctor what he'd found at the site of the murders. The valuable cargo reportedly on the stage.

"So a payroll was stolen, this one headed for Fort Bridger just like before?" Nell asked.

"Near as I can tell. There's no sign of a payroll, though. No knocked-open lockbox, nothing that makes me sure. But considering the route that stage takes, it'll end up in Fort Bridger." The sheriff went on, and Nell asked questions and made a lot of suggestions.

In the end, the sheriff said he'd stay, and the doctor intended to, as well.

"I'll sit with him later, Doc," Nell offered. "You and the sheriff can maybe each get a turn to rest. Come and get me when you're ready to collapse. I've got a quiet day planned after church tomorrow and can sleep then."

The sheriff nodded. "I'll ask in church if we can get volunteers to sit with him, explain the situation."

"Do you think that's wise? We'll be telling the killers we suspect they're from here in Pine Valley. For that matter, telling everyone. It'll set off a lot of suspicion."

"It will and that's a shame. But if I'm going to go around and ask everyone their whereabouts yesterday and last winter during those robberies, the word is going to get out anyway. I'll make a point of saying how near death our patient is. A wary man might hold off trying to kill him if there's a good chance he'll die."

Nell looked at the man. Still as death even after all these hours.

"There *is* a good chance he'll die." The doctor rubbed

his hand over his head in a gesture so weary, Nell felt like she should send him to bed right now.

"Doc, be on guard. I've got to walk Mrs. Armstrong home. It's late for her to be out."

Nell opened her mouth to protest, then closed it. Quietly she said, "Only one other time I've been even a little nervous to walk the streets of Pine Valley."

The sheriff looked glum.

Doc Preston said, "I'll keep an eye out."

The sheriff made short work of delivering her to her shop with her sleeping quarters overhead.

As she washed blood off her hands and prepared for bed wearing a loose-fitting clean dress, she remembered Mariah last summer with her father and brother killed and several attempts on her life. How involved Nell had been in watching over her friend.

And then, though she'd been afraid for Mariah, she'd never really been just flat-out scared like she was now.

She remembered Becky bringing in her large, growly dog Brutus to stay with Mariah. Nell wondered what that dog was up to right now.

7

Nell was weary the next morning as she headed for church.

The sheriff had come at about four in the morning, apologizing, but the doctor had fallen asleep twice and the sheriff had caught himself waking up, which had left no one on guard. He'd shaken Doc Preston awake and come to get Nell for the second watch.

Nell and Sheriff Mast had played cards for the rest of the night to stay awake.

The doctor had reappeared just after sunrise, rested enough to survive. Nell went home, slept for two more hours, then woke up late enough that she had to hustle to get ready for church.

She forgot all about her huge triumph—well, the small victory maybe—of making dresses for the Nolte girls, until she saw them come riding into town. Samantha and Cassie were on one horse, Brand and Michaela on another.

The girls were beaming as they rode up. All her exhaustion forgotten, Nell rushed to the two girls and helped them dismount.

They were skilled riders and didn't need much help, but she adjusted their skirts as they descended so their legs didn't show overly.

"Samantha, you look beautiful." The strong blue was like a blazing Wyoming sky. Perfect and bright and feminine. Nell gave her a huge hug and loved the feeling of having it returned.

"Cassandra, let me look at you." Nell straightened a ruffle and grinned. "You look so wonderful."

Nell got another hug. She'd just let go when she was hit by a little whirlwind. Michaela was on the ground and wanted in on the hug.

"Pink is just right for you, Michaela." She looked between the girls. They all needed bonnets and at least a riding skirt and shirtwaist. But everyday dresses would also be necessary.

"And you've done your hair, all of you. Samantha, you braided Michaela's hair?"

Samantha made a gesture, quite grand, toward her pa. "He braided it. Turns out he knows how."

Nell arched a brow at him.

"Learned it braiding a horse's mane when I was a kid. I'd kinda forgotten I knew how, but Samantha showed me how to start and it came back to me."

The church bell rang its summons into the air. It was the school bell, but it worked just as well.

Nell said, "I was up late last night." She decided not to talk about the wounded man yet. Why bring that darkness into this bright moment? "I was almost late to church."

Brand smirked. "Us too."

They went in together. Nell saw Becky sitting to the right side, with Mariah and Clint beside her. She was taking a step toward them when Michaela caught her hand.

"Sit with us, Mrs. Armstrong, please."

Nell looked down at the little sweetie. "Come this way. There's room right behind my friends."

The girls huddled around her. It was a little bit of a knot since church was starting and the Noltes didn't seem to know how to file into a pew, especially when all three girls wanted to sit by Nell.

They solved it by Brand going in first, towing Cassie. Then Nell went in holding Michaela's hand. Samantha came last.

When Nell saw both older girls looking disgruntled, she sat down and pulled Michaela onto her lap. A girl on each side and one on top.

Mariah must have heard them, though the girls were quiet. She glanced back with a smile of greeting, saw Nell surrounded by the Nolte girls, and her smile widened. Her brows rose. She nudged Becky, who was politely watching Parson Blodgett open his worn Bible.

Becky glanced back at Nell, turned away, and then her head whipped around again to stare at her. Then, as the parson began to speak, Becky snapped back to facing forward.

Nell wasn't quite sure why her friends had acted quite so strangely, but this wasn't the time to question them.

They all stood to sing "All Creatures of Our God and King." Mrs. Blodgett was a piano player and had a fine soprano voice. Parson Blodgett joined in with a solid tenor.

His voice wasn't so pleasant, but he made up for it by letting his love for the Lord shine through.

The service wasn't long. Nell caught herself nodding off once. She'd thought a nap might be in her future but realized she probably needed to go take a turn watching over the wounded man and let the poor sheriff get some sleep.

Between worry for the sheriff, the patient, and her own exhaustion, only Michaela's occasional wiggles helped keep her from missing the sermon.

When they rose to leave, the parson stopped on his way out to greet Brand and the girls and welcome them to church with his usual kindly, twinkling eyes before continuing to the back to shake hands as his congregation moved out. Nell couldn't leave right away. And her friends were blocked in, so they turned around to say hello.

Just as Clint reached out a hand and said, "Brand, good to see you again," a voice interrupted, "Folks, I'm sorry I was slow getting here today, but I need to have a word with all of you." Everyone turned to see what was going on. Nell stood Michaela on the pew, and not being among the tall folk, she craned her neck to catch a glimpse of Sheriff Joe Mast, who was holding his hat, blocking the door.

"I need your help," he said, and a few folks gasped.

Maybe they thought he was going to a shootout or something.

Nell wasn't sure the man was handling this just right, but he certainly had everyone's attention.

"Sheriff Mast . . ." Nell felt like she had to say something.

"Yes, Mrs. Armstrong?"

"I wonder if the children should step outside while we talk."

Becky jabbed her in the ribs with an elbow and gave her an arch look. It was pretty clear that Nell knew more than Becky did, and that didn't suit her.

"That's a good idea. Thank you. Yes, families with small children might want to go outside. There's nothing here they can't be told, but maybe we'd all be a bit freer to talk if we don't have to watch our words so carefully. Any women who want to leave can go now, as well."

Several mothers started herding their children out. One Nell had never met stopped and looked at Nell. "I'd be glad to take your girls out, Mrs. Armstrong, if you need to stay."

Nell didn't correct her, there just wasn't time. "Go on out, girls. We won't be long."

All three girls gave her a frown. Nell wasn't sure if it was because they were confused at being claimed as Nell's children, or because they didn't want to be shuffled off when things were getting interesting. Whichever it was, they went along without a fuss, except for the small tussle it took for Cassie to get past her to the aisle.

Once the commotion of children and their mothers leaving died down, the sheriff closed the door and said in a quiet voice, but into a silence so profound that no one in the building missed a word, "The Deadeye Gang has robbed another stage."

A bigger gasp went through the room this time. Enough women were left that, when possible, they moved closer to their husbands.

"We've got six men dead. No one local, so at least we

don't have that grief, not like last summer when Mariah Roberts's pa and brother died. But I need help. And I can't promise it is completely without some danger." He briefly outlined what had happened. "I am afraid for this man's life. The Deadeye Gang is notorious for never leaving witnesses alive."

The sheriff paused, his eyes meeting Mariah's, the only witness who had ever lived. "We also believe that this gang leaves no witnesses because some of the members are local. They may be people we know. Because of that, we need to post a guard on this man. He's not regained consciousness since the shooting. Doc Preston, who is with him right now, along with my deputy, Willie, is afraid he never will. His wounds are very serious. But even unconscious, this man's life is in danger. Whoever belongs to the Deadeye Gang around here can't afford to let him wake up and say something. I need volunteers, two people standing guard at all times, because we know at least one person around here isn't trustworthy, so we can't allow just one to watch over our victim alone.

"It's my hope that the killers will hear we're posting a guard and stay away. It's very risky for them to just come into town, bullets flying. If they know there's a guard, I think putting out the word that it's done will prevent an attack. So just being there will make everyone safe."

The silence was deep for too long. Nell could think of plenty of reasons why no one would want to stand guard against a deadly gang of killers. Sheriff Mast's assurance that the very presence of watchmen would keep danger away struck Nell as overly optimistic.

Henry Wainwright raised a hand. "I'll take a watch."

His brother, Peter, spoke up. "And I will."

Clint and Mariah talked on top of each other. "We'll stand guard."

"I will too." Becky raised her hand. "And I've got a few cowpokes who'll volunteer, I'm sure. Pa might come in if I ask him."

Joshua Pruitt wasn't a churchgoing man, but he was tough. He'd be a good one to stand guard.

"I'll take a turn," Nell said, then held her breath, hoping Brand wouldn't say anything. He couldn't leave his girls out at his cabin alone for hours when there was trouble.

"I can watch him for a few hours most days." Brand's voice, smooth and goodhearted, came from behind her. "I'll need a shift while my girls are in school. I have to ride in to pick them up anyway."

More voices rang out, hands raised. Sheriff Mast was ready with a piece of paper and a pencil. "Come on by me as you walk out. I'll take down names and see if I can assign you a time right here and now."

In the sudden bustle of a small, moving crowd, Clint leaned toward Nell and said, "Come on out for dinner at my place." He reached out and clapped Brand's shoulder. "I made a big batch of . . . of beef stew."

Nell had to wonder what its real name was. Clint was giving up his fancy recipe titles but keeping the recipes. She'd heard him say once that his *coq au vin* had changed so much that he was calling it Clint's Chicken now.

"Um, well, that's real neighborly of you, Clint. I don't have a meal started at home. But are you sure? I come in a crowd of four."

Clint smiled. "I figured the girls would get to come

along. There's plenty. Yes, please come. Mariah would like to meet them."

Something was beneath the simple words, and Nell wasn't sure what. But it looked like Clint and Brand knew each other beyond just occasional greetings.

"You too, Becky."

Becky smiled. "Mariah already invited me earlier in the week. I have a large loaf of bread and a box full of cookies to share. Sure, I'll come."

Nell added, "She invited me, too. I had plans to bake a pie last night, but I was there when that wounded man was brought in. I ended up helping with surgery and—"

"You helped with surgery?" Becky cut her off. "You know how to do surgery?"

Shaking her head, Nell said, "I handed the doctor things, staunched bleeding wounds while he operated, and I held out a plate for him to drop the bullets on." She swept the story aside. "It adds up to . . . I don't have food, but I can tell you all the details. Grim details, I'm afraid, and not fit for children's ears. I was in the middle of it and sat up with the injured man for hours last night."

They all nodded thoughtfully as the aisle cleared and they made their way to the sheriff to get their names written down to stand guard over a man who would be hunted by a killer.

8

Brand was surprised to see Parson Blodgett's name on the list of sentries. His wife too, but not on the same shift.

Mrs. Blodgett, mother of seven, the youngest being about three or four months old, was a sturdy woman.

"You don't need to sit with the man five days a week, Brand," the sheriff said from across the room.

"I'll be coming into town for the girls anyway." Then Brand held up a staying hand as he looked back over the list again. "Just let me know if you need help. It's a busy time of year, so it might be more than I can handle, but I'll step in when you need me. I'll wait until your list of volunteers is complete and then give what assistance I can."

Sheriff Mast nodded. "Thanks, Brand. I know you've got your hands full with three young'uns and no wife and a homestead to make into a farm or ranch. I appreciate your willingness."

Brand shook his hand, then stepped outside and called for his girls, who were waiting patiently in the shade. It was lunchtime, the noon meal taken care of, and by a cook as skilled as Clint Roberts. Brand felt as if he was imposing, yet he couldn't resist the offer. And he wanted to get to know the folks around Pine Valley better. He and the girls had been mostly stuck out at the homestead all winter. He'd become a fair cook if he could keep things simple. He'd fry or roast meat he hunted himself because his own animals were too few. He'd boil potatoes. He'd bake biscuits, though only on special occasions—flour was scarce. There was milk and eggs and precious little else.

Eating at Clint's home was bound to be a treat. And he might find time to talk to Mariah again. He'd thought of more questions. And the girls could fuss over Nell.

The girls were so excited about their dresses, Brand couldn't help but want to thank Nell yet again.

Also, what part did the woman share with that shooting victim? At the church, he'd listened to every word Nell had said about being in the middle of it. He was shocked. Such a pretty woman, full of sweet smiles and kindness toward his girls. A woman who liked flowery cloth and ruffles. Such a woman wasn't usually quite so comfortable talking about blood and surgery and shooting.

They certainly grew them tough in Wyoming.

As they walked toward Clint's, Brand and his girls came across the rest of the party. The woman he'd heard called Becky smiled at the girls and said she'd brought a puppy over to the Roberts place. She said they'd find him on Clint's front porch but not to untie him for fear he'd run for home.

The girls dashed ahead. Once they were out of earshot, Nell told her story. He'd heard just a bit about the Deadeye Gang but hadn't realized quite how ruthless they were.

Mariah dropped back to walk alongside Brand. She touched his arm, and they slowed some until they had a bit of space.

Mariah spoke quietly. "I wish I'd told you one more thing when we talked. One thing he did wrong is, he treated me like a blacksmith and, at the same time, treated me like a woman shouldn't be a blacksmith. He let me do small jobs, nails and angle iron, things like that, but he didn't like it when I wanted to add pretty details to something we made, acting like a woman had no business doing the job—even while he let me do the job."

Brand thought of a few jobs the girls did that he considered manly chores. Had he given them that mixed-up message? Needing the help, and needing to keep an eye on the girls at the same time, had he belittled the girls' efforts and frowned over their doing the very things he'd asked them to complete?

"I don't think I do that with my girls. I don't see any unhappiness in them. What I do feel is my own sense of failure because I don't know what to do except keep them with me. And I need the help." Brand turned to Mariah. "I'm going to pay more attention to what I say and how my words affect them."

Mariah smiled. "And maybe I'll come to look back on what my pa did as a man just trying his best. I can let little things he said stay as an ache in my heart, or I can give him credit for wanting me near and his own feeling that I shouldn't just be sent home alone while he and Theo worked. That being with him was better." Nodding, Mariah said, "Yep, I might just give my pa a little more credit." As they neared the house, she added, "I thought

I'd help you out with how to treat your girls, but you may have helped me just as much."

Clint moved closer to her side. "You don't need any help, Mariah. You're perfect just as you are."

She grinned at him, and the three of them reached the porch, where Becky sat with the girls doting over a wriggly black puppy. Nell was sitting in a rocking chair, bent over and petting a big dog resting at her feet.

"What's this?" Mariah asked. "Is Brutus banished again?"

Becky smiled. "Yep, Lobo's got a new litter. She won't let him near her or the babies. Lots of growling and flattened ears. This puppy is the only one who didn't find a home last year."

Becky picked up the year-old pup. She explained to the Nolte girls, "He's the runt of the litter. Born with a game leg. It doesn't seem to hurt him much, but it's noticeable when he runs."

All three groaned at the injustice of it and redoubled their fussing over the pup.

"Hey, I wanted him." Mariah gave Becky a good-natured shove.

"Yes, you did, my friend. I wanted him to grow up a little before I brought him in. And now he's ready for a new home."

The girls beamed at Mariah.

"And Brutus came along. He can help the little guy learn how to behave around the chickens and such Clint has. A puppy can think the farm animals are a meal. If that happens, the dog can't stay."

They all looked at the puppy and gasped. Michaela hugged him so tight, Brand got ready to interfere before

67

she choked the poor critter. But Michaela released him before it turned into a fight.

"Lobo's got six new puppies. You girls are so nice with this one, how would you like one of your own? A lot younger than this one."

The girls' heads came up like they were a startled flock of chickens. Then, as if one neck controlled them all, they turned to Brand.

He said, "We don't have the money for anything right now."

Becky stood and patted him on the shoulder. "They can have their pick of the litter, no cost. I like knowing the pups have a good home, and I can see that with these girls, they certainly will. I've sold puppies in the past, but it was slower last year—not a lot of people around. It took a while to find them all homes. This year I'm giving them away. Their ma will be a while weaning them. After that, she'll like old Brutus around again. So, it'll be six weeks or so. Can you wait that long, girls?"

The girls could barely suppress their excitement.

"Can we have a puppy, Pa?" Samantha jumped up from where she sat on the porch and grabbed Brand's hand.

"Yes, I suppose we can have a puppy. I'd like one, too. A dog's good to have around the place. And I've got a sturdy pen for our chickens. Even an unruly pup won't get to them."

Nell, straightening from where she sat in the rocker, said quietly, "I wonder if Brutus and his son shouldn't spend some time at the doctor's office. They could maybe spend their nights there."

Everyone froze. A few seconds ticked by, then they all pivoted to look at Nell.

Becky said, "That's a really good idea."

"Why didn't I think of that?" Mariah crossed her arms, looking disgruntled at herself.

"You know . . ." Nell rose from her rocking chair, looking as pretty and delicate and ladylike as anyone Brand had ever seen. "I spent time listening to my husband."

"You have a husband?" Samantha seemed oddly upset by that.

"I'm a widow. My husband was a sheriff in a Missouri border town after the Civil War. He died, killed by a marauder."

"That's sad." Samantha came to sit on the floor beside her. "We're from Missouri, too. That's where our ma died."

"We've both had some sadness in our lives." Nell rested a hand on Samantha's shoulder.

Brand wondered how long it'd been.

"Anyway, Web, my husband, liked to talk over his cases. I listened and sometimes we'd consider evidence together. I learned a lot about the law. And I learned things like, well, that a man who survived an attack like the man in the doctor's office did needs to be guarded and protected."

"That was your idea?"

Nell's eyes flashed. "We had trouble last fall that put Mariah in danger, and we stood guard over her. This man is the same."

She was a delicate, beautiful woman, but she had a sharp mind, too. He needed to respect that about her— along with her sewing skills.

"Let's go in and eat. We can walk back to town with you later and take Brutus and his son to meet the sheriff."

The crime was left behind while they enjoyed Clint's unusually delicious meal. Becky's bread was well made, too.

Then they walked back to town together. Brand and his girls, along with Becky, had left their horses at the hitching post by the church.

It was time to get home and do up what chores couldn't be put off, even if it was Sunday. And then tomorrow a new life began for Brand.

His daughters were going to school. He'd be home alone. He wanted them in school, but he was going to miss them with an ache that went all the way to his heart.

9

Nell slept part of the afternoon away. Then she spent an hour making bonnets for the girls. When the sun was beginning to set, still early in the Wyoming spring, she took all three bonnets with her to the doctor's for something to pass the hours of the night.

Willie Minton and his wife, Kate, were there.

Kate was a dab hand at sewing, judging by the pretty dark-green dress she wore. She was plump and attractive. Not a likely match for Willie, who seemed disinclined to bathe regularly. Nell wondered at the strange paths that brought people together. The two were forty years old or so and had five grown children, some of whom lived in the area. Willie worked with Mariah on occasion and had gained decent skills as a blacksmith.

Mariah had said that when the baby was born, she'd turn the place over to Willie unless someone brought an order he couldn't handle. More and more, Willie was learning a good trade and gaining confidence. He was also the deputy sheriff, but in a peaceful town like Pine

Valley—Nell's eyes slid to their gunshot victim and she controlled a flinch—the job was only part-time.

If she was interested, maybe Nell could teach Kate to make chaps. After the Nolte girls earned out their new clothing, Nell would need some company.

"Hi, Kate. You and Willie got Brutus, I see."

"Yes, Mariah and Clint had the shift before us and brought the dogs in. They said Brutus and the pup can stay overnight."

"I met the puppy after church." Nell crouched down to give both dogs a good rub.

"They told us they were naming him Spike. In honor of the spikes Mariah makes at the smithy."

"Oh, well, good for you, Spike." Nell looked up at Kate and smiled. "He had no name when I met him."

Willie chuckled. "Clint and Mariah were bickering over the name when Mariah told us his name was Spike. She said she wanted him to have a strong name. Clint was teasing her about naming the dog T-bone or something about food."

They all three laughed, and then Nell rose to her feet and set the tapestry bag on the high examining table at the man's feet. She didn't want the puppy to eat her creations. She'd met a puppy or two in her life and knew they liked to chew.

Willie and Kate stayed on, visiting until Sheriff Mast came in. Then they headed for home.

Now Nell and Joe Mast were on duty. Along with Brutus and a puppy named Spike that moved with a limp, though he didn't seem to be bothered by it. He was a friendly little guy.

"What are you doing to find out the man's name?"

The sheriff settled beside her at the small table in the doctor's office. "I wired the last town along the trail. I haven't heard back. I also told them about the deceased men and that I brought them into town. Two were the stage driver and the man riding shotgun. So, three other passengers, all dead. The driver and guard ought to be known men. I'm hoping we can track down all the others on that stage so we can let their families know what happened. All of them had empty pockets, not a copper penny left. If they carried any paper to tell me their names, it's long gone."

"You can wait a week to bury them, I suppose. Not a whole lot longer." Web had been buried fast. Killed one day, buried by sunset. Nell had no idea what the longest possible time was to wait for a burial. She only knew it wasn't long.

"Our undertaker said a week is as long as he likes to wait unless it's winter. Then the bodies last longer. But once they're underground, it's a lot harder to get anyone in here to look at them and claim them."

"Our victim here is dressed in a rough Western way. Pointy-toed boots, none too new. Denim pants. A dun-colored broadcloth shirt. What were the other men wearing? That might give us a clue as to what kind of men they were."

The sheriff nodded for a time, silently. "I'll go have another look, but I'd say one was in a good-quality suit. He looked like a city fella. The second one . . ."

The sheriff talked it all through with Nell, a lot like Web used to do. But Web only wanted her to listen. The sheriff seemed really interested in her insights.

The night passed. They set aside their investigation talk, and Nell attached the brim to a bonnet. She'd been at it a while when a snore from the sheriff's chair drew her attention. The man was fast asleep.

Before she could decide whether to wake the sheriff or not, a second sound drew her to her feet, and she hurried to the patient's side.

"Sheriff, wake up. The man might be regaining consciousness." Maybe long enough to talk about what had happened. Maybe describe his attackers. Help them catch a pack of cold-blooded killers.

The sheriff was awake and on his feet instantly. Nell was on the man's right, the sheriff on his left. The man's head tossed a bit but weakly. But this was the first he'd moved. Then a dry moan escaped his throat.

"That's what I heard before. I think he's waking up." Nell raised excited eyes to the sheriff.

He nodded and leaned close. "Can you hear me? We found you injured. What's your name?"

Nell clamped her mouth shut. If this man had the energy to say a single word, she wanted that word to uncover a killer's identity. If he wasted his strength on his own name, that might set some worried wife's mind at ease later, but the killing would go on.

The man mumbled and turned his head toward Nell. "Camp."

Nell's eyes snapped up to the sheriff, who said loudly, "Your name is Camp?"

"Bell. Campbell. My name, Ian Campbell."

"You've been shot in a stage holdup, Mr. Campbell." Since he was looking at her, she asked the questions.

"Did you see anyone? Can you describe the men who shot you?"

A thump of footsteps on the stairs told Nell the doctor was awake. The sheriff's voice had been loud enough to rouse him. Just as well if his patient was awakening.

"Holdup. Four men. Tried to fight. Heard . . . payroll. Stripped bodies." The man drew in a ragged breath. "Took everything. I must've passed out before they got to me. I can't believe I survived."

It wasn't enough. They needed a description. How would they track those killers down with this? Four of them. "Can you describe any of them?"

"One in a suit." The man's forehead crinkled, and he flinched. With his head wound, that had to hurt. "Three Stetsons. Nice ones. Silver hatbands. Cold, black eyes. Man in suit. Uh . . . Yellow Boy rifle. Carved stock."

The doctor pushed the sheriff toward the foot of the bed. He had a stethoscope out and listened to the man's heart, maybe his lungs. Nell wasn't sure.

The man's eyes fell shut, his breathing deepening.

A Yellow Boy? A Winchester '66 rifle with a carved stock was an unusual gun. It was called a Yellow Boy because of the metalwork around the trigger guard, which was made of bronze and looked yellow. It was a fairly new gun, and expensive.

"He's unconscious again. If you could step back and let me have some time working with him?" The doc made it sound like a request, but it was an order.

Nell realized she and the sheriff had sort of besieged the poor man. They probably shouldn't have, and the doctor was letting them know that.

Sheriff Mast stepped away.

"Can I help with anything?" Nell asked.

"I'll let you know." The doctor didn't look away from his patient.

Nell went to where the sheriff stood. "A Yellow Boy. That's a new gun. Pretty costly too."

Nodding, the sheriff said, "'Course, they steal cash money for a living. They likely have plenty of it, especially if they spend like fools every time they get an extra fistful of bills."

"And the gun has a carved stock. I wonder how it was carved—decorations or notches from kills?" Her eyes went to the man, dissatisfied. "I wish I'd asked that. A Yellow Boy isn't that common, and a distinctively carved stock might make it one of a kind."

"Well, we now know the man's name," the sheriff said. "Ian Campbell. I'll get word out of this as soon as the telegraph office opens. It'll be waiting in every town within a hundred miles."

That sounded like a lot, but it was a wide-open country. It might reach five or six towns at most. But was it a good idea to spread this information far and wide? Who was manning the telegraph offices? Who would hear about the wounded man, supposedly hurt too badly to talk?

"Start out by just sending his name. To say more than that lets too many people know our wounded man has talked to us." Nell hesitated to share more information.

The sheriff nodded his agreement. "Good idea. I'll send his name to Fort Bridger too, and Laramie and Cheyenne maybe. Hard to know how long he'd been on the stagecoach."

Nell added, "We'll be watching for that gun here in Pine Valley. We can ask around a bit, too. About the gun."

"It could be stolen, and folks might know about it. And, Nell, I'm sorry to ask—it's an ugly thing, and if you refuse, I'll understand—but I want you to come over tomorrow and look at the bodies we brought in. You might see some things in their clothes and such that would give us an idea where to look for the missing men."

Nell snapped her fingers. "We should have asked Mr. Campbell if he knew the names of the others on the stage with him. He'd been shut up with them for a while. There's a chance he'd talked with them. Knew names, where they came from, where they were going."

"No, you should *not* have asked him that." Doc Preston was at their sides then, his face flushed with anger. "You should have come for me."

Nell gave the doctor, a man she respected and knew well, a look that seemed to freeze him in his tracks. "You're the one"—she lowered her voice—"who told us he had next to no chance to survive." She was glad the man was out cold. No sense frightening him. "We can't pass up the chance to get answers from him. Next time he awakens, and *every* time he does, we'll ask every question we can get in before he passes out again."

The doctor blinked but didn't object.

The sheriff said, "We have to stop these killers, Doc. If you think gentle treatment of this man is the difference between life and death, say so now. But we need to know what's in his head, and we need it fast, because as sure as the sunrise, someone'll come for him. Then all the gentle treatment in the world won't save him. Our real chance to save him is to find out who shot him and hang 'em high before they can kill him."

The doctor looked unhappy about it all, but he didn't scold them anymore.

"Go on back up, Doc." Nell rested her hand on his arm. "Your job is to save lives and ease suffering. We understand that. If he wakes up again, I'll call up."

The doctor looked suddenly exhausted. With nothing more to say, he turned and headed up the stairs.

Nell's eyes met the sheriff's. They listened for the doctor's door to close.

The sheriff spoke quietly. "I've got about ten more things I'd like to talk over with you, Nell. You've got an unusually clear notion of the law. Better than anything Willie can ever think of. Heaven knows I'm no investigator. I've only solved crimes by plucking the gun out of the killer's hand while it's still smoking and a body is on the ground in front of us both. And that's only happened a couple of times, and I witnessed the shouting beforehand and figured it for a fair fight. Not a lot of need for keen detective work there. It helps to talk things through."

Sickened to think of what lay ahead of her, she kept her expression stony. "I'd be glad to help any way I can." Nell glanced at Brutus, who had his head up but hadn't gotten to his feet. That energetic pup lay beside him, sleeping like the dead.

"I got a decent sleep this afternoon. Try to sleep, Sheriff. With the dogs here, one of us on watch is enough."

With a wan look on his face, the sheriff said, "But no one can be trusted, remember? That's why there must always be two of us watching."

"Risk it, Joe." Nell gave him a dry smile. "That man just woke up and looked me in the eye. He never said a word about a woman robber, nor did he see my face and start screaming."

"You're probably safe enough." The sheriff's voice was laced with kindness as he went to his chair, which Nell knew from personal experience was none too comfortable.

Sheriff Mast folded his arms on the table and laid his head down. He was snoring within minutes.

Nell studied the man and compared him to Web. Both good lawmen. Both tough frontiersmen willing to face danger to protect their towns.

But she detected no cruelty in Joe.

As for Web . . . well, the only word that fit him was *contempt.*

Web had held her in contempt. He considered her his inferior. He considered all women that. His death had set her free but had left her badly scarred. When her brother had heard she was a widow and come to see her, he was on his way west to homestead. Nell went along, eager to leave the terrible memories of her married life behind.

When Wyoming had given women the right to vote, Bob had shaken the dust of Wyoming off his boots and headed for Oregon, or maybe California. He had no destination, only a place he wanted to leave.

He'd been shocked when Nell had refused to come, clinging to this small town, the beautiful outpost in the west with its towering mountains and reflective water. Its harsh winters.

She looked out the front window of the doctor's office, and in the wash of moonlight she saw those mountain peaks. The Cirque of the Towers. A range of mountains that lined the west side of Pine Valley and seemed to stand as sentinels. A lake on this side of them reflected the moon, and the snowcapped mountains shone down even at night.

It was a beautiful sight, soothing and inspiring. Reminding her that God was a great artist. A Father who'd created a majestic world for His children.

It had all suited Nell right down to the ground, most especially the suffrage vote. In Wyoming, suffrage wasn't just the vote. It was the right to hold public office. The right to own land. Elsewhere, no matter what a woman brought into a marriage, it immediately became her husband's property. If a woman inherited money, that money was immediately her husband's. If she earned money through work, that money was her husband's, as well.

Not in Wyoming.

Wyoming suffrage was a wonderful thing.

Esther Morris had been the first woman justice of the peace in South Pass City, one of the nearest towns to Pine Valley. She'd been appointed rather than won an election, and when her appointed term was up, she hadn't run again. But she was a hero and an inspiration to Nell, and word was she was coming to Pine Valley this summer, along with Josette Mussel, a speaker on the rights of women.

Nell and Mariah and Becky were excited to listen to her.

Settling into a chair at the small table across from the sheriff, the only place to sit in Doc Preston's examining room, Nell got out her sewing. Thinking of how excited the girls would be, she shoved aside all thoughts of women's rights and the muttered witness statement of a critically wounded man and even the low snores of the sheriff, and focused on putting a tidy brim on Samantha's calico bonnet.

She wondered how observant their father was. Would he notice if she slipped a few extra clothes to the girls? While the man seemed to be not that bright, certainly not about womanly or girlish things, he did seem like the type to keep track of anything he might sniff out as charity.

A man had his pride. She knew this was a fact she had to accept despite considering it an enormous nuisance.

10

Becky met her pa for the noon meal in Clint's Diner in Pine Valley.

She didn't see him much. He wasn't a church-going man or one to invite her to Sunday dinner. He ate with his cowhands in the bunkhouse. She wasn't inclined to invite him to her place, either.

When they saw each other, it was usually by happenstance. But today she'd ridden over to his place, and because he was out riding the range as any good cattleman should be, she left a message for him, inviting him to a meal in town the next day. A drover had shown up at her place later in the day with a note from Pa asking to postpone it yet another day because of moving his herd from a distant pasture.

Here they were.

"Becky girl." Pa, Joshua Pruitt, sat down across the table from her.

Becky had already told Clint that Pa was coming. He

was out the door of the kitchen before Pa was all the way settled in his chair.

Mariah followed behind him with a pot of coffee. She smiled at Becky. "Hello, Joshua."

Pa gave her a disgruntled look, then nodded.

Becky knew Pa liked to be called Mr. Pruitt by those he thought were beneath him, especially women.

Mariah knew it too, which was why she called him Joshua.

Moving out of his house and starting her own spread was the smartest thing Becky had ever done.

"What is it, girl? You finally come to your senses and decide to give up the foolishness of running a ranch?" Pa called her *girl* a lot. She thought he liked to poke at the wound in his soul that came from not having a son. He liked to poke at her, too.

"I've got my own home and my own ranch now, Pa. I'm not moving home. I wanted to talk to you about something else."

With a grunt, Pa started in with eating his meal. The man had never accepted her moving away, and Becky was sure it was mostly because he wanted the money she'd inherited and figured if she'd stayed with him, it would have found its way into his hands.

"You've heard of the man in Doc Preston's office who was wounded in the stagecoach robbery?"

"He still alive? I heard he was gutshot and maybe got a bullet in the backbone. Figured he'd be dead by now."

Becky was a little surprised Pa knew so many details, but word seemed to spread fast here in the West. She knew her father well, and he was interested. Of course, it was the biggest thing happening around town, so why wouldn't he be? And the Deadeye Gang was a threat to everyone.

"I told Sheriff Mast I'd ask you if you and the cowhands would pitch in to stand guard over him."

"I don't have men to spare to ride in every day."

Becky nodded and began eating. "Fine then. It is a long ride."

It wasn't that long, and they both knew it. Pa and all his hands rode into town anytime they needed something, and they rode far and wide over the vast Pruitt Ranch every day.

"And it's always a busy time. I know that, too. Spring's hectic for a fact. Just be nice to keep this man alive until he can wake up and tell us what happened to him. We might get the varmints who killed John and Theo Stover."

Mariah's pa and her brother. Both good men, skilled, hardworking blacksmiths Pa had done business with and was friendly with. Not friends, however. Pa didn't have friends. But he respected John and Theo. Catching and bringing their killers, the Deadeye Gang, to justice should appeal to Pa's sense of honor, assuming he had one of those.

"And you know Key Larson was using his job at your ranch as cover. Seems like you'd want a chance to show this town you want the killing to stop."

Pa was a big man. Gray-haired with overly bushy white eyebrows. And he had brown eyes just like hers, which could narrow and look so cold they'd send a chill up Becky's spine. Another reason she'd struck out on her own when she inherited enough money from her ma's parents to start a spread.

Pa had a rough crowd at his place. Not a single woman

anywhere. Becky had been more cowhand than protected daughter, and she'd heard and seen plenty she shouldn't have. Now she had her own place, and that chill in her spine wasn't as biting as it used to be.

Then Pa surprised her.

"I'll come in myself. John Stover was a good man. And Larson was a traitor and a filthy sidewinder. Yep, I'll come in myself. I'll go check with the sheriff and see when he needs me. I could send men in too if the sheriff is short-handed. The man hasn't woken up? Not at all?"

Becky let herself smile at Pa. She could almost remember back to when she was little and she'd adored him. With Ma there to smooth things over and keep Pa happy. Becky had two little brothers who died when a fever went through. Then Ma died birthing a boy, and the boy died too, and Pa had turned hard and bitter, with no room in his stony heart for a daughter. Or maybe he'd always had a stony heart toward his daughter, but with Ma there to soften his words and protect Becky, she hadn't noticed.

Now he was doing the right thing, and she remembered. Then she thought of that terribly injured man.

"Doc Preston doesn't think he'll make it. In fact, he's sure he won't. He doubts he'll ever regain consciousness. But he needs protection as long as he's alive. Thank you, Pa. Sheriff Mast will be glad for the help."

They finished eating, talking about the spring calf crop, the winter weather, the branding time coming up. Plenty in common. Just not much in the way of the love that should be between family. Becky regretted it but took no blame for it. She knew her pa real well. And she had no hope of there ever being more.

⌒

"You heard what he said about a guard on our witness." The boss stood with his back to a rocky outcropping. He studied the four men with him.

All of them together only happened during a robbery. There was a sixth, but he never came out of hiding. Boss was making an exception because he didn't like that witness surviving.

"We just need to watch the place," Skleen said. "Pick our moment. They're watching him close right now, but they'll let down. Give them a few days."

Boss reached for his gun and wanted to start blasting. He didn't. He needed these men. He was shorthanded with having to kill Key Larson last fall. But he was finding keeping a team of bandits together to be trying. Not surprising that men who robbed stages for a living weren't the smartest bunch.

"He could wake up at any time."

The closest, Clancy, a tough man, but no one you'd rely on to add up a general-store bill, shook his head. "It sounds like he's on the verge of death. I myself put two bullets in him. One in the heart, one in the head. And he was already shot up."

"You must've missed both or he'd be dead."

"He will be, and soon. And without waking up. He was gutshot, too. Bleeding other places. No one lives long like that. I can't believe a man survived all those bullets."

Boss knew Clancy was almost for sure right. No one did survive long, not with where those bullets were placed. But would he survive long enough?

"I saw them going in this afternoon with two dogs."
Boss figured that'd shut them all up. Make them take this
seriously. "One of them that killer dog that attacked Key."

All of them frowned. No one had a response. Then
Clancy came up with something: "So we kill the dog, too."

"You're talking a bullet. The right way to get rid of the
witness is quietly. And I'm not taking that dog on with a
knife. He'd have to get too close for a knife to do any good.
And there were two dogs. Besides that brute, a puppy was
along. Not sure he's a killer, but I'll bet anything he's
mighty noisy."

They all stood there silent. In the end there was little
choice, and Boss wanted to end the meeting.

No one was out here in the dark, but if someone was,
if they were seen together, there'd be no way to explain
it. And they'd have to kill someone from right here in
Pine Valley.

Boss hadn't gone on the raid that killed Mariah Roberts's pa last fall. And her brother. Shame about that. He
might've called it off if he'd known who would be riding
in that stagecoach. Those men were talented blacksmiths,
and the town missed them. The expected payroll hadn't
been on that stage either, so they hadn't even profited off
the raid. A disaster all around.

Mariah did the blacksmithing now, but it wasn't a decent way for a woman to live, especially not a married
woman. She was shaming her husband. Grinding his pride
into the dirt.

She'd been left for dead at the robbery but was making
a surprising recovery. Key told him she'd looked him right
in the eye during the robbery, and he'd done his best to

silence her, but he failed and was now dead himself. None of the rest of them had seen her, so Boss had decided to let Mariah live.

Still, he itched to take her down a peg, help restore her husband's pride, but then who would shoe his horses and repair his wagon wheels?

"We'll keep an eye out," Boss said. "See if the guard slacks off. See if a moment presents itself to silence the man. But no direct attack, not in town. It ruins our whole goal of no witnesses. The one good thing is, I'm taking a shift guarding him."

The other men laughed, and he couldn't help but join them.

"If the other guard falls asleep, I can smother the man quietly, then wait and act surprised when he turns up dead in the morning."

Clancy slapped him on the shoulder. Boss was tempted to break his arm. He didn't like the men thinking they could be friendly with him. Yet he had to put up with it at least a little, so he didn't show how he really felt.

"Let's break this up. I don't want us seen together."

They all went their separate ways quietly—agreed, at least for now, to wait.

11

Nell saw the sheriff coming and met him at her front door.

Dread writhed in her stomach, but she didn't let it show. She was a master at keeping her thoughts from showing when she chose to. Another lesson Web had taught her well.

They were going to look at corpses.

Shot-up corpses.

All she could think of was to plaster a bland expression on her face. No smiles would be suitable, no fear or disgust. Nothing she could think of would be right.

She managed bland.

"You're sure about this, Mrs. Armstrong?"

"I am. I'd like to identify these men if we can."

"I still haven't got word back on any of them. Even the stage line isn't sure what crew they had riding that stage. But they're checking into it." Shaking his head, the sheriff stood, hat in hand, as she closed her door. The two of them strode toward the undertaker's building, which was off Main Street a few blocks for reasons of the unpleasant nature of the job.

Nell found talking too much work, so she walked in silence beside Sheriff Mast. They were soon greeted by a cadaver of a man, the undertaker himself, James Burk. Nell didn't know him well. He came to church. He had no use for chaps. He wasn't a talkative man even under the best of circumstances.

He stood at his door, donning a black suit. He wore spectacles with gold-wire rims. His head was bare save for the whisps of a monk's curve of white hair. Burk watched Nell with an odd expression. She couldn't quite define it. Not anger or resentment. Not exactly pity. All she could tell, his bland face to hers, was that he almost certainly,. with his perfect manners, didn't think it good or right for Nell to be coming to look at these bodies.

Burk opened the door, let Nell and the sheriff pass, then stepped inside and closed the door behind them. Nell had a sense of being trapped, but she trusted the sheriff, so she knew it was just her inner turmoil. The undertaker led them from the small front of the building to a larger back room, where six coffins lay. All looked newly built. Burk had been busy.

A body was stretched out in each box. She noticed they were covered with blankets, pulled up to each dead man's chin.

"I tried to cover the worst of the injuries for you, Mrs. Armstrong. It's a gruesome business for a woman to see such carnage."

"Gruesome for anyone, man or woman." She didn't bother to see if Burk reacted to her comment. Instead, she went to the first coffin with no further comment.

"This is the stage driver, I believe." The sheriff moved

to her side and pointed to another man next to the driver. "And that man was riding shotgun. I'm basing that on our finding the driver there slumped over on top of the stage, with the shotgun rider off to the side of the trail and a ways behind where the stage finally stopped. I'm guessing he was shot and fell off while the stage was still rolling."

"Sounds like you figured it about right." Nell could spend more time examining them, maybe find out a few things, but she suspected these two men would be easy to identify. She passed the shotgun rider with barely a glance and reached the next coffin. Six pine boxes filled the room up tight.

"This is the man you mentioned dressed in a suit?" She glanced up at the sheriff. She focused on the dead man's collared white shirt, string tie, and shoulders that showed a black suit coat. Tidy hair, not counting the blood spatter.

She fought a grimace . . . bland, calm. *Don't show anything or they'll put a stop to this.* And maybe it would have been better if they had.

"Yes," the sheriff replied. "The other three are more of a match for the driver. Hair overdue for a cut. Their garb had 'em looking like Westerners. All three of these other bodies, four including the man who survived, were inside the stage. Every one of them with a shot to the head, besides other wounds."

Nell thought of how Mariah had survived the stagecoach robbery last summer. No shot to the head. Maybe they were trying to be more efficient killers? Grimly, she studied the city man before her. Reluctantly, she said, "I'm going to have to pull down the blanket." She turned to the undertaker.

"I appreciate your trying to spare me the ugliness of their wounds, Mr. Burk, but the sheriff and I are hoping we can discover something about these men. We need a better look at his suit, his shoes, things that would maybe give us a clue about who the man was."

The undertaker shook his head, but he didn't forbid it, not that she'd've accepted his forbidding. He had no such authority. But she appreciated that he didn't make a fight out of it.

Nell swallowed hard, then gripped the blanket and drew it down slowly.

Black suit. White shirt. String tie. Bullet to the heart. Pulling the blanket completely away, she turned over the edges of his suit coat. "No wear on the fabric. This is a new suit. A prosperous man, or at least one who doesn't mind spending money to look prosperous." Which gave her pause. She picked up his hand and turned it over. "Look at this."

She ran her finger over his thumb and forefinger. Then she turned up the shirtsleeve where it stuck out rather far from the sleeve of the coat.

"What are you seeing, Mrs. Armstrong?"

"Look at this strange hem in the shirtsleeve and the oddly placed calluses on his fingers."

"What does that tell you?" The sheriff leaned across the man's body and examined his left hand, left sleeve. "No calluses. City hands. No strangely hemmed sleeve." The sheriff shoved the sleeve higher. "Gun up his sleeve."

Nell saw the cunning little holster strapped to the man's wrist. A spring-style holster so he could shake the little derringer out fast.

"I never even noticed that." Burk stepped closer and studied the gun. "I've never seen one that small."

The sheriff nodded. "He's a gambler, I'd say . . . or was one. The calluses alone wouldn't be a good enough clue, but that hemmed sleeve? I've heard of that. A gambler who hides cards up his sleeve. And a gun."

Nell looked up at the sheriff and gave a little shrug. "When I said he spent money to look prosperous, that's what gave me the idea. A gambler who was looking to make an impression. The sleeve hem, and the sleeves are just slightly too long. Easier to slip a card out of them. That's the biggest clue."

She studied his lower half, including his well-polished boots. On impulse she pulled one of them off, and the sheriff stepped in to help her.

"Really, ma'am, is that necessary?"

She pinned the undertaker with a gimlet eye. Much as she'd done with the doctor when he'd protested their talking with his patient. "Yes, it's necessary. We need to stop these killings. And we need to get word to the families of these men. I doubt a gambler has much for close family, but—"

Playing cards spilled out of the man's boots. And a letter.

Nell didn't bother with the cards, though the undertaker began gathering up all that had fallen.

Nell removed the letter from its envelope and unfolded it. "There's a name here. Jefferson Carson. And an address on the envelope, as well as a return address. Someone will want to know about him and his whereabouts."

She frowned thinking of the grief they'd be bringing

to someone. After handing the letter and envelope to the sheriff, she pulled the man's other boot off. She found a knife and a roll of paper money. Several hundred dollars.

"He had his boots on when he was brought to me, and he wore this suit." The undertaker sounded defensive. And a little embarrassed. "It never occurred to me to search him more thoroughly. Before you rode out to fetch the bodies, you told me to build six coffins, and I did. I had two on hand and a third one done by the time you got back. We just laid them straight into the pine boxes."

"Completely understandable, Mr. Burk. This man deliberately concealed these things. You weren't meant to find them."

She spent a bit more time examining the man's clothes before she went on to the next dead man. She did find a man's name etched into the leather of his belt. That set Sheriff Mast and Mr. Burk to searching the others' belts and removing all their shoes.

Nothing more came to light, however.

Sheriff Mast scowled. "We've got more than we had before. I'll wire the names to some other towns in the area. If we narrow down even a couple of the riders, it might lead to the next one and the next one."

Nell nodded, then thanked James Burk. He seemed easily upset for a man who prepared bodies for burial.

The sheriff walked beside Nell. He held all they'd gathered, including the one man's belt, and headed with them toward the jailhouse.

"Can we talk for a few minutes before we go back to the doctor's office?" she asked.

The sheriff gave her a hard look, then nodded. "Come

inside. Did you notice something you think will lead to the killers?"

"Possibly," she answered. "South Pass City is to the east of us, the closest town. The stage that was robbed was found south of town. And there isn't a town nearby, so you're going to find they came from that direction. Because things stay closed up on Sundays, you should send your wires again and focus on the towns to the south."

The sheriff nodded. Nothing she was saying seemed to be news to him.

"As to those bullet wounds, the bullets we took out of Ian Campbell—he said someone had a Yellow Boy rifle. The bullets were .44 caliber rimfire bullets. We could dig out the bullets from the rest of the men who died, and maybe we should. But multiple killers with multiple weapons, that makes sense."

Nell looked up at Sheriff Mast, feeling so grim she couldn't keep the expression off her face. "The head shots. I went to John's and Theo's funerals, and they weren't shot in the head, and Mariah certainly wasn't."

"But she was pinned under the stage. They thought she'd been killed. Even so, they shot her once just to be sure of it."

Nodding, Nell went on. "You might check to see if all the folks killed had that ugly head wound. I'm afraid that because Mariah lived last year, they've come up with a more deliberate way to make sure everyone is left dead. Which means our killers are more deadly than ever."

"And that doesn't help us catch them."

"The stage line needs armed escorts, at least until the killers are caught. I wonder if the cavalry could be persuaded to get involved, to ride along with each stage. Things are quiet here these days. No sign of a war anywhere. Now that women have the vote, I'm hoping there'll never be another war again."

"That still doesn't help us catch them."

Nell shook her head. "No. It doesn't. It only gives us a reason to be more frightened than ever."

Nell left the jailhouse to go get her gun, which she didn't always wear, but now decided to start doing so. Maybe she should hide a little gun up her sleeve. It stood to reason that they wouldn't bury that gambler with that derringer on him. Jefferson Carson.

Nell knew that somewhere, despite his wayward life, a gambler and a cheat at that, someone had cared enough about Carson to send him a letter. And he'd cared for that person enough to keep the letter with him.

Her investigating was going to break someone's heart.

12

"Mrs. Armstrong?"

Nell had left her stupid table with the stupid chaps and gone upstairs for a break. Now she hurried down, surprised to hear Brand Nolte calling her name.

She couldn't help but smile at the poor man, standing there so awkwardly. The saying *bull in a china shop* flitted through her mind. But the man couldn't break fabric nor leather.

He stood with his hat in hand, smiling up at her. "I'm in town to sit for a shift with Doc Preston." He twisted the brim of his hat a little. "I just thought I'd stop in and say hello. The girls will be here soon for their first day of work. They'll walk over after school."

Then he quit twisting, and his brow furrowed. "What's wrong?"

Nell touched her face. She'd done her best to be welcoming, smiling, open. What did he see?

Some odd urge to confide in someone shook loose some

words. "Earlier today I went to inspect the bodies of the men who'd been brought in dead from the stagecoach holdup. I suppose I'm still upset from that."

"If you'd rather I didn't let the girls come to—"

"No, please don't do that. I can't blame you for not wanting them around me when I've seen such ugliness. I thought I was acting correctly, but if it's so noticeable to you, then I'm not handling it well. I'll get firm control of myself." She walked toward him, ready to beg.

"It's not that, Nell. I just don't want you to have something else piled on an already hard day."

"I can't wait to see the girls. Having them here will help me put this morning aside." She realized she'd clutched her hands to her chest, like she was praying . . . or begging.

"If you're sure, I'd like to let them come here. It'll be good for them to learn any sewing you can teach them."

"I-I never got a chance to apologize for the misunderstanding at church, that the girls were mine. I didn't mean to leave such an impression, but I didn't want to go to fussing right in front of the girls."

"Don't worry about it." Brand's hands seemed to relax, and he quit torturing his hat. Nell should probably make him a new one. She shuddered to think of what mayhem that might create in her career if word got out she could make hats.

"Were the girls upset being sent out of the church? I could see Samantha didn't like it."

Brand shrugged. "I didn't tell them much, just that the sheriff was asking for volunteers to sit with a wounded man. I'd hate for the girls to learn there's been killing going on around here. No child should have to find out such things." He swallowed hard. "Were you able to find out anything?"

Nell told him what they'd discovered. "And Sheriff Mast got a telegram back from the town just south of us. It was a little harder to track down because the stage was going from South Pass City to Lubbett, and it'd gone off the main trail because of a rockslide. The man who brought in Mr. Campbell was on his way north, so Pine Valley was the town closest. That brought Mr. Campbell to our doorstep."

Brand closed the last bit of distance between them. "Does it help to talk about it, or should we try to think of more pleasant things?"

Nell tipped her head, doubtful much would pull her out of the ugly memories she now had to live with. Then she lightly slapped herself on the forehead. "I know what I wanted to ask. Should I teach you to sew?"

Brand fumbled with his hat and dropped it. He became very busy picking it up, as if the hat were making a run for it.

Nell took that to mean no. She didn't wait for the words. "Samantha is old enough and Cassandra almost old enough to take over the family sewing. But usually girls that age wouldn't be in charge of it. They'd have a mother instructing and checking over their work. I suppose if you don't know how to sew at all, they will get better at it faster than you."

"My wife has been gone since Michaela was born. Pamela. She picked the name Michaela. I'd never heard of it before. Micky's seven. It's been just the four of us that whole time."

Nell heard something in his voice. Not exactly grief, maybe just fond memories? Either way, his wife had been important to him and had left him very much in confusion.

"My ma and Pamela's ma lived close. They got me through for a while when I didn't even know what to do for food for a baby. Then Pamela's ma passed, and a couple of years later my ma died. She'd been living with us, handling everything until Michaela was five. But Ma wasn't well the last years or she'd've taught the girls sewing. Sam was twelve by that time, and so much of the load settled on her shoulders. It shouldn't have, but I was running a small farm back in the Ozarks. Fighting back trees seemed to take every spare hour of every day."

"We lived on the Kansas-Missouri border," Nell said. "I've never seen the Ozarks, but I've heard tell of them."

"With everyone gone, it seemed like the time to find a new life. It took me a year to get things in order, raise the money for the supplies we'd need. In that year it never even crossed my mind that the girls needed new dresses. Then, on the wagon train, a nice lady with older sons offered Sam a pair of britches her younger son had grown out of. She said it was safer around the fire. Sam loved them. The other girls clamored for them. Two more pairs were offered by another lady with growing boys, and I learned a little sewing and made shirts out of discarded clothes of mine and castoffs from the other wagon-train folks."

He shook his head. "You saved me from being a terrible fool of a father, and I thank you, Nell. I should probably learn to sew, but I've tried a few things and have shown little talent for it. Is it too much to ask Samantha to take charge of the sewing in the family?"

He looked so worried. Like a kindhearted, loving father. Something every girl wanted in a pa.

"I have no idea. I think the girls sound really excited to learn to sew." She reached out and rested both hands on his left forearm.

The strength surprised her. She hadn't touched a man since Web had died and she'd vowed never to touch one again. She liked being in charge of her own life, and even in a territory known for equality, women still had to fight for respect. And fight harder if they were married. Nell wasn't going to do that again.

But Brand, with his kindhearted worry about his girls, didn't set her on edge like most men did.

"For now, let's not look for trouble. If they're having fun and learning, we'll just figure we're not doing any harm."

Brand looked down at her hands resting on his arm. Slowly, he raised his head until their eyes met.

And held.

He sounded reluctant when he nodded and said, "I'd best be going over to the doctor's office. I keep catching myself thinking I haven't thanked you. Not enough. Thank you very, very much."

"You have thanked me. It's been more than enough. This shop is a very quiet concern here with so few women in town and most of them fully capable of making their own dresses. My only real job is making chaps for men, who, I can promise you, never want to stay and visit, so having your daughters in to help is a delight. You're very, very welcome."

Brand smiled.

It struck Nell that he didn't smile much. And maybe

that was another thing hidden in that strange expression she'd seen when he'd spoken of his wife. A world that hadn't led to his being a happy man.

His wife, his mother-in-law, and his ma all passing away in quick succession. Well, it was time for him to face forward with three more women, who looked sturdy and likely to last his whole life. Maybe working with the girls, she could also work with him a bit and help him find happiness in the life he now lived and not look back on the sorrows of the past.

She realized she'd been holding his arm for quite some time and quickly let him go. She felt the strength and warmth from his arm in her fingertips and closed her hands to try to rid herself of that feeling.

He looked at his arm, then up at her and smiled again, wider this time. "I'll be by for the girls around four-thirty, Mrs. Armstrong."

"They'll be ready, and maybe by then they'll have earned their dime, which will be deducted from the price of the dresses. And they'll know a bit more about sewing."

Brand nodded and seemed to watch her for a few moments too long before whirling around and heading for the door. He was outside in quite a hurry.

Nell wondered why he'd sped away. She moved to watch him out her window. Maybe he'd forgotten he needed to talk to the doctor before his shift began, much as he'd needed to talk to her. She watched him rush across the street at a near run.

Men were a mystery. She was glad to have sworn off the lot of them.

She realized then that her hands where they'd rested on Brand's arm were still warm. Quite warm.

Shaking them briskly to cool them off, she settled back to cutting leather for the chaps. She was getting mighty good at the stupid things.

Unfortunately, she could make them in her sleep, or at least almost. They gave her too much time to think. She realized her plot to get the girls to make chaps wasn't going to work, or at least it wasn't enough. These girls needed to learn to sew for themselves. Girl clothes, and clothes for their pa. She'd do her best to slip in some chap making while she taught them to hem dresses.

At least now, after talking the morning through with Brand, the worst of her awful memories had been replaced with his sad story of so much loss. And the strange tingling in her overly warm hands.

13

Brand hadn't seen the gunshot victim before. Campbell, Nell had said. Ian Campbell. How were they sure of that? A letter in his pocket maybe?

"I appreciate your riding in to help, Brand." The sheriff looked weary. He sat at a table with an empty chair across from him.

"Are you watching him alone, or are you who I partner with?"

The sheriff shook his head. "Deputy Willie was here until a few minutes ago. No, you're here watching with Joshua Pruitt."

Brand's mouth almost gaped open. "Pruitt is taking a shift?"

"Yep. Surprised me too. Sounds like his daughter, Miss Becky, talked him into it. Appealed to his better nature. Didn't know he had one."

Brand had heard a few things similar to that.

"You'll have a chance to talk with a mighty prosperous man while you're here. Not sure if that'll be interesting or not. Pruitt is a hard man. Mighty proud of his ranch. Proud in a way that makes you understand why God listed it as a sin. Mighty unhappy about his daughter setting up on her own. Hard to judge which is hardest on a man's ears, the boasting or the complaining."

"Maybe I can pick up advice on how to turn a hundred-and-sixty-acre homestead into a ranch with thousands of acres and thousands of head of cattle."

"If he tells you, let me know," the sheriff said. "I'd be interested in how to do that, too."

"What about our victim here?" Brand asked. "Mr. Campbell."

"All I can say is, the doc is going to be upstairs sleeping. He's put in so many hours watching over the man, he's to the point of collapse. Even in the middle of the afternoon, if Doc's got a chance to sleep, he's taking it. He went up when I got here. But if Mr. Campbell wakes up, call the doc and do it fast. And if the man says anything to you, anything including that the sky is blue, listen to every word and pass it along to me."

Nodding, Brand said, "Anything else?"

"If you need time in the privy, take it now. No one is supposed to be alone with Campbell. Whoever wants him dead must be acting on the sly because their whole plan is to leave no witnesses. They'd have to make it look like an accident. And if there is a witness, then the witness would need to die too, and there's no way to make that look like an accident."

"But do you really suspect me or Joshua Pruitt?"

"No, I honestly don't, but just the same, no one's left alone with Campbell. I guess I was here alone until you got here, but that's probably proof I don't want him dead. So I'm the exception to the rule."

The door banged open, and Joshua strutted into the room as if he owned the doctor's office. Strange thought.

Spending a few hours with Joshua Pruitt, maybe Brand could pick up some pointers, if not how to be a cattle baron, at least how to coexist with the fierce Wyoming weather.

Sheriff Mast rose to his feet as if the effort cost him. Brand had to wonder how many hours the sheriff was sleeping at night.

"Joshua, this is Brandon Nolte. He's homesteading northeast of town. Brand, Joshua Pruitt. You know Becky Pruitt, well, this is her pa. He's a rancher even farther northeast of town." With that cursory introduction, the sheriff grabbed his hat and left.

Joshua looked hard at Brand, then looked past him. "Is that the patient over there?"

"Yep. Ian Campbell. They say he's never stirred, never woken up."

"So I heard." Joshua walked past Brand and went to the man's side. All Brand could do was imagine Joshua with a pillow, smothering the man he was supposed to guard.

To do his job diligently, Brand walked over to stand on the opposite side of the examining table from Joshua. The two of them studied the man.

"With a gunshot to the head, hard to believe the man survived." Joshua reached for the blanket covering Campbell and pulled it down. "Looks like a heart shot and a gutshot. What is keeping this man alive?"

Brand stared at the ugly wounds and wondered the same thing.

They left the man's side, and Brand settled in to listen to two solid hours of boasting and complaining.

Annoying as it was, it was mostly just boring.

A few things about Becky betraying him, though, were so outrageous, he really couldn't wait to tell Nell.

The wounded man on the bed never moved, never moaned, most certainly never had a word to say, not even about the color of the Wyoming sky.

Not nearly soon enough, Mariah and Clint arrived for the next shift. They brought their dogs and said the dogs would stay overnight. One was the sweet little puppy with the game leg, the other that old wolf-dog that seemed to be looking for someone with a throat to tear out.

Brand headed for Nell's shop to pick up the girls and found everyone there in a fine mood.

Samantha seemed a bit subdued but in a happy way. Brand couldn't quite figure out what was different.

The girls all gave Nell a goodbye hug, and instead of throwing in and making it a group hug, Sam held back, waited until her sisters were done, then gave Nell an unusually long hug, very quiet. She showed none of the chattering like the other girls did.

"You all have bonnets," Brand said, noticing them. How could he not? Like most children on the frontier, his girls had very little in the way of possessions.

As they headed for the door, Cassie said, "We talked with Mrs. Armstrong about it, Pa, and she said the dresses she made us are worth about three dollars apiece. So, at a dime a day, we'll earn our dresses in thirty days."

Sam interjected, "That's thirty working days, so a little longer than a month since we won't come in on Saturdays and Sundays."

"Yep, the dresses will be earned by then," Cassie said. "And for the bonnets, she's charging us about one dollar apiece—ten more workdays. But she said, if you approve, we can take them now and wear them because a woman needs to keep her head warm."

Brand felt that pinch again. Knowing Nell was giving his girls things they needed, but that he couldn't afford. Of course, they'd be working to earn them. That wasn't charity exactly. He looked back at her, and she smiled.

"And," Nell added, "the girls are going to help make chaps. They've got a good hand with some of the smaller details—and in only one day."

Nell gave Brand another smile that seemed to warm a cold spot inside him. "They are going to earn those dresses, Mr. Nolte. I can assure you of that. I get paid for the chaps when they're done, and I'm going to be earning that money much faster because of your girls. But I also know the girls need to learn more traditional sewing skills. So we'll work on those things along with the chaps."

She shook her head as if the chaps business was beyond her understanding.

Brand nodded. It wasn't charity, it was a loan, which was something else Brand didn't believe in: borrowing money. He'd seen people suffer when they couldn't pay back the money they owed. He didn't think Nell would foreclose on his homestead, but he was afraid he was teaching his girls a poor lesson. Yet he didn't see a way to stop it short of breaking his girls' hearts.

"Thank you, Mrs. Armstrong," Brand said. "We appreciate it."

"My pleasure. So, how did your shift go at the doctor's office?" she asked.

He smiled. "I listened to Joshua Pruitt flip back and forth between bragging about what a powerful, rich man he is and how disappointed he is in his daughter."

"The skilled, brilliant rancher who's my good friend?" Nell arched one brow.

"That's the one. The whole time he was talking, I was thinking how I couldn't wait to tell you." His smile changed to a grin. It struck him how few people he'd met since moving here last fall. It had been only him and his girls. Now he had someone he wanted to share news with. Someone who made him smile. Someone who'd rested her hand on his arm, and he'd felt the touch for hours after she let go.

Nell shrugged. "Becky handles her pa well. I've learned a lot about being an independent woman from her."

Brand began herding his girls out the door. "You might've taught her a few things, too. You seem to have the independent-woman style under your complete control."

As he reached the door, he stopped, looked back, and caught her smiling. It really was the most beautiful smile. "Thank you again. For everything."

She gave her head a quick nod. "I'm looking forward to tomorrow."

Brand had a hard time not smiling the whole way home. Of course, the girls were full of high spirits and interesting stories of their day at school, as well as what they'd learned at Nell's. But that wasn't the reason he couldn't wipe the smile off his face.

14

Nell took the night shift again.

She arrived and was greeted by both of Becky's dogs. Well, one dog was Becky's, Brutus, while the other one was Mariah's, Spike. But for now they worked as a team, and Nell was surprised how much safer she felt with them around.

Doc Preston was hovering over his patient when Nell came in. The sheriff arrived only a few paces behind her.

With the space getting crowded, Mr. Betancourt, the schoolmaster, and Peter Wainwright stood to leave now that their shift was over. Nell and the sheriff thanked them and wished them a good-night.

Nell went to Mr. Campbell's side. "Still no sign of him waking?" She noticed, out of the corner of her eye, that Peter Wainwright paused and turned back. Steven Betancourt went on out the door, but Peter was curious, and who could blame him?

"Not a sound out of him," the doc answered. "No sign of his waking up. The bullet in his chest is going to, I'm sorely afraid, leave him paralyzed. And few men hurt that badly can live for very long."

Peter remained in the doctor's office, and it didn't seem fully to be for reasons of curiosity.

"And the bullet in his gut . . ." The doc glanced at the door as if he were expecting someone. He nodded at Peter, who came closer to them.

At that moment the door opened and Parson Blodgett walked in. He looked very solemn. His eyes shifted between the three men standing there in the doctor's office. They had all been, Nell suddenly realized, expecting him.

"I've come to join in this meeting."

"What's the matter?" What meeting? Were they having a meeting?

She tried to sort out what sort of business the four men might have and realized Peter Wainwright was the mayor of Pine Valley. It was a quiet job, and no one looked to him for much. Sheriff, mayor, doctor, and pastor covered most of the critical roles in the town.

"Let me assure you," Parson Blodgett said, coming to Nell's side, where she stood close to Mr. Campbell's head, "I've prayed about this. Prayed hard. We love this town and the people we worship with, and we felt the Lord calling us to this frontier ministry. But"—Nell's gut twisted, as this didn't sound good—"Latta's father passed away three years ago. After we'd come out here. Her mother got on well enough for a time, alone on the farm. Then, when she could no longer keep up with the chores or the struggle with the cold winters, she moved to live in town near her other daughter. There are just the two girls."

Nell swallowed. She didn't want to lose Parson Blodgett, but he seemed to be building up to just that.

"But her sister's husband passed, and now the two women, each with their own household, aren't faring well."

"They could come here. We'd welcome them." Nell loved Parson Blodgett and Mrs. Blodgett and their children. They were part of what made Pine Valley such a welcoming town.

"We've prayed about it for the last six months. Longer probably, but then our prayers were just for them to find happiness in their lonely state. But now we've felt a strong leading from the Lord to go back. Mama Snyder, Latta's mother, wrote that their own parson in Savannah, Nebraska, is in failing health and can't do the job anymore. She's proposed me as his replacement—on the condition, of course, that I'm willing. She asked us if we'd consider coming back home. She doesn't have the energy to move west and start a new life. Her letter gave us the assurance that it's God's will for us. We have written to our missionary convention and told them to be seeking a new parson for Pine Valley and informed them we'll be leaving by the end of the month."

It was mid-May. Two weeks? Nell was saddened by the suddenness of it.

"Well, I will miss you all terribly." Nell gave him the best smile she could manage. "Thank you so much for telling me."

The men all appeared thoughtful, and as she looked at them, she realized something more. Three of them, excepting the parson, were on the town board of Pine Valley. They were the city council.

Losing the town's pastor was critical, but did it really involve telling the city council? There had to be something more. And that thought made her strangely nervous. Especially for how the sheriff was staring at her.

"Mrs. Armstrong," the sheriff began, "Parson Blodgett is more than just our town's faith leader, he's also our justice of the peace. I've talked with you frequently of late. I'm impressed by your knowledge of the law and your steady nerves, and we, uh . . ."

The men all looked so very official and solemn—a lawman, a parson, a shopkeeper, and a doctor. A long pause stretched as the others turned toward the sheriff as if goading him to finish his sentence.

The sheriff held his gray Stetson by the brim, gripping it tight enough he might be ruining it. He'd feel bad about that later. Finally, he squared his shoulders and said, "Well, the thing is—"

"Just out with it, Sheriff." She needed to save his hat for fear she'd end up having to make him a new one and by doing so start an avalanche of hat orders.

"The thing is, we'd like to appoint you our new justice of the peace."

Nell gasped so hard, she started coughing.

The parson spoke quickly. "When I told the city council I was leaving and tendered my resignation as justice of the peace, we debated about who to appoint in my place. Sheriff Joe suggested you, and it was soon settled that we'd offer you the job. You'd do more than just sit as judge at trials and pronounce sentences after those trials. You'd also settle disputes that don't reach the level of criminal charges. You'd do a fair bit of paperwork, accepting legal documents into the public record for deeds. Issuing sub-poenas and warrants, ruling on jury selections and such. If we have a prisoner who wants bail while he awaits trial, you'll decide if he gets it and the amount. And"—the parson clapped his hands together and beamed at her— "you'd get to perform marriage ceremonies."

Nell looked on in silence. Her eyes shifting from Doc to the sheriff, to the mayor to the parson, she made the circuit of looking into their eyes a few times while her thoughts rabbited around. "I-I . . ." Nell stopped trying to talk.

"Just say yes, Mrs. Armstrong," Peter Wainwright said. He glanced at his watch as if she were delaying him from his evening meal. "Town charter says we must appoint an interim justice. There's an election in about eighteen months. That will give you time to experience the job and decide whether to run for the office or retire from it. By then, others in town will have time to think if *they'd* like to run for the job. We'd also have ample time to decide if you're a good fit. Yet the sheriff assures us that you have the necessary legal knowledge and temperament to handle the stresses of the job."

There was something in Peter's voice that held just the tiniest whiff of derision. The man didn't think she was fit for the job. So why didn't he just say so?

Doc patted her on the arm. "It's a fine step for women's suffrage, too. Esther Morris was first, but she's already retired rather than run for the office. She was widely re-spected and believed to have done a fine job. We on the Pine Valley town board believe it brings prestige to our town. We'd be proud to support your appointment, and it's something we'd encourage with pride. You could advance the cause of women's rights and become famous for doing so, Mrs. Armstrong."

Peter Wainwright had a look on his face like he wasn't rolling his eyes through sheer willpower.

The step for women's suffrage, she liked that. Becoming famous held little appeal. She'd probably just find even more men who wanted her to make them chaps.

Which reminded her. "I've got a business to run."

"I doubt the job will require you to work every day, Mrs. Armstrong," the parson said. "I've put in some busier weeks, but usually there are very few matters to handle. Five to ten hours most weeks."

She wanted to say no, but some odd trembling in her heart told her it would be an honor to take the job. It was something she could embrace with pride for all women. And with Josette Mussel coming to speak on advancing women's rights, and possibly Esther Morris attending the speech, for Nell to greet those women as the town's justice of the peace . . . suddenly, instead of being hesitant, she was afraid she'd waited too long, giving them time to change their minds.

And Peter Wainwright's attitude pushed her that last inch to deciding to accept. "I'll do it."

The men all seemed pleased. Mostly. The sheriff looked like he was worried about her. The doctor, a strong supporter of women's suffrage, looked like he was cooking up fine speeches to celebrate. The kind parson looked anxious to get on with instructing her how to do the job. And Peter Wainwright, well, he looked the most pleased of all, but in a way that made Nell wonder what was really going on in his head. It worried her more than a little.

But then everything about this worried her. So why should Peter not be included?

"Thank you, Mrs. Armstrong." Peter jerked a satisfied nod at her, then said, "It's growing late. If you'll excuse me. I'll take over at the store and send Henry to sit with our patient."

"I need to hurry home to tell Latta the good news. Now, if we can only find a new preacher for Pine Valley, God will give us peace to support a decision we know He's leading us to." The parson whirled and rushed out after the storekeeper. Far too quick for an older man.

When he closed the door, Doc Preston said, "Now let me update you on our patient. I didn't want to speak of this in front of anyone else. It seems almost outlandish to say this, but the bullets must have missed doing any major damage or he'd've died by now." The doctor stopped and glanced at the door again. "I said that about his being paralyzed because that's what we want the townsfolk to believe, but Campbell moved his hands today and one of his feet twitched. He may not be paralyzed, though he's still at terrible risk of dying due to suppuration. But he's not running a fever and he should be by now. There are no red streaks around the wounds. The bullets couldn't have hit anything vital. So, the man has a chance. I've begun dribbling swallows of water into his mouth. One more day and I'll add broth."

"Do you want me to make it?" Nell offered.

"No, I can do that. I've got herbs and a few other things I include with a beef broth to build up his blood. All of it together should help him heal. What worries me most right now is how weak he's become with little water and almost no food. I'd like you to spoon a bit of water into him every hour."

"But no sign he's waking up?"

The doctor shook his head. "I believe he will soon, though. I hope he will. He still has dark days and a long road ahead. Likely he'll face a high fever, and if he survives that, he just might impress us all."

With that, the doctor said goodbye and left the room.

Nell's eyes slid to look straight at the sheriff. "This is your fault."

"That our patient is still ailing?"

Nell narrowed her eyes. "No, that I'm justice of the peace."

"Oh, well, you know when I first thought of it?"

"When we were looking at those corpses?"

"No, but that sure made me believe I had the right idea. It was when the doc scolded us for talking to Campbell when he woke up. You looked hard at him—the doctor, that is—and pretty much said, *We did it and we'll do it again and shut your mouth*."

Nell gasped. "I said no such thing."

The sheriff smiled. "You said it with better grace than that. But even that—saying something with nice manners to make someone back off—impressed me. That was the first time I realized our town's delicate seamstress, who grumbles about making chaps, has steel in her spine."

"I've got a bonnet to make," Nell said and sat down. The sheriff seemed so satisfied with the results of today's work that Nell decided not to ask him any of the five hundred questions she had about being the town judge.

Then Henry Wainwright came in and ended talk of any

kind. The sheriff bid them good-night. Henry opened a book she couldn't see the title of while Nell took up her sewing.

While she stitched up a new bonnet for Cassandra, she pondered the blow she was striking for all womankind. And just how much she could foul this up.

15

N ell jerked awake.

Her eyes were blurry from sleep, her head just as blurry. She saw Henry approaching Mr. Campbell's bed.

"Oh, goodness. I fell asleep."

Henry jumped as if she'd erupted from behind a door and yelled "*Boo.*" He clasped one hand to his heart. "You startled me, Mrs. Armstrong. I was just checking our patient." He turned his head to study Mr. Campbell. "I think he's breathing a bit unsteadily."

Nell rushed over and stood across the table from Henry. Then she looked at Brutus. The dog was awake, his head up and alert, staring at Ian Campbell.

Campbell tossed his head restlessly. She turned up the lantern and didn't like his color. Touching his forehead, she felt the heat wafting from his skin.

"Fever." Henry's gaze lifted from their patient to Nell. "That's a terrible sign, isn't it?"

Nell nodded, not wanting to say anything the poor

man could possibly hear. Remembering how unhappy the doctor had been the last time the patient awakened, Nell shouted, "Doc, Mr. Campbell is feverish."

A basin of clean water sat on the patient's bedside table. She found a cloth and dunked it in, then wrung it out even as she heard footsteps pounding down from Doc's apartment over his office.

Henry came around to stand beside Nell, leaving room for the doctor.

She pressed the cool cloth to Mr. Campbell's forehead, and he sighed with relief.

"Hold on to this. I'll get another one." Doc had said a fever was likely. Nell had prayed he'd somehow avoid it, but God would have needed to directly intervene. And she knew the fever would be hard to fight in Campbell's weakened condition. All they could do was try.

Henry took over holding the cloth as Nell got two more ready. The first one she handed to Henry and took the one currently in use away and tossed it into the basin. She used the second one to bathe the man's cheeks and neck.

Doc Preston arrived, took one look, and got busy with something. Nell wasn't watching, but he was rushing here and there.

"We need to get him to drink this." Doc came to his side again, straight across from Nell.

"Let Henry in there, Nell. Henry, sit him up. This concoction will help him fight the fever—if we can get him to swallow it."

Nell stepped back, armed with a newly wrung-out cloth. She let Henry into her spot and then took his. The blanket fell to the patient's waist as Henry sat him up. Nell pressed the cloth to Mr. Campbell's heart, only inches from that wicked bullet hole. It was unbelievable, a miracle honestly, that he hadn't died from his wounds.

Doc coaxed him to take a sip.

Nell stepped away to dampen her cloth again. "He's so hot that the cloth warms before it's much more than swiped across him." She reached a hand past Henry. "You need both hands to hold him up. Let me have the cloth off his forehead."

Henry passed it awkwardly to Nell. He was holding Mr. Campbell up while Doc administered the medicine.

"He's taking some of it." Doc sounded excited and hopeful.

Nell felt it might be better to not get their hopes up. She took the cloth and stayed back as the two men struggled to get Mr. Campbell to swallow.

"I'm hopeful this medicine will bring the fever down."

Mr. Campbell's eyes flickered open.

Nell gasped. "Mr. Campbell, you're awake."

She hadn't meant to shout, but she nearly had. Henry jumped and fumbled to hold on, almost letting Mr. Campbell drop back onto the table.

"Hold on there, Henry. Keep him up. I want to get more of this into him."

Nell saw several good swallows go into the poor man.

Campbell shifted his eyes from the doctor to Henry, then to her, then back to Henry again.

Nell needed to question him. "Do you remember the stagecoach holdup, Mr. Campbell?"

"Nell, not now. He's too weak."

"Yes, now. Right now. We need answers to stop the

robberies." She raised her voice and reached a hand to brace Mr. Campbell's chin until he was looking right at her. "Please, Mr. Campbell, anything you can remember might help."

Nell remembered when Mariah had been left for dead. She hadn't been able to remember anything for a long while.

"What can we do to help?" Henry leaned closer to the man. The patient's eyes darted to Henry, and Nell fought down a surge of impatience when Henry blocked the man's view of Nell.

Ready to shove Henry back, Nell heard Mr. Campbell say, "Cheroot."

Nell was very familiar with the bitter, black cigarettes. Her husband used to smoke them, and she'd seen a few men around town who'd acquired what she considered a disgusting habit.

"Cheroots," Mr. Campbell repeated, then sagged in Henry's arms.

Henry eased him down onto the bed. "He's out again."

Nell stepped back, watching their unconscious patient. "Did he mean he wanted to smoke a cheroot?"

Doc shook his head.

Henry shrugged. "Maybe he was asking for one. He's not thinking right, so you can't really believe a word he says. It's a hard business watching a man die."

"Shush." Nell went to Henry and tugged on his arm. "We're not sure how deeply an unconscious man sleeps. The doctor has asked us not to speak in ways that would demoralize the man."

Henry gave her a skeptical look, and she couldn't blame him.

"Sorry, Doc," Henry said. He went back to the table and sank into his chair.

"I'll bathe his face and neck, Doc Preston. You go get yourself a few more hours' sleep."

"No, I've slept enough."

Henry stood from the table. "I'm glad to help."

"You did help, Henry. You helped a lot," Doc said. "I'm going to get dressed for the day. The sheriff should be here in a few minutes, and then you two can leave. He and I will work together to bring down Mr. Campbell's fever."

Nell nodded and began bathing the man's face. He had none of his regular clothes on. They'd all been cut away as part of being doctored. But Nell wondered why she hadn't noticed the smell of cheroots when he'd been brought in. It was a sharp smell that she was familiar with. But maybe she hadn't noticed on account of the crisis facing them. Or maybe he'd quit the filthy habit, but now with his being so badly hurt, he craved the taste of it.

Just then, Mr. Campbell tossed his head fretfully and muttered "Cheroot" once again.

She continued washing his face with a cloth while listening for more words mumbled from the patient, clues, anything that might aid them in catching the killers who robbed the stagecoach.

16

"You're the new justice of the peace in Pine Valley?" Becky looked dazed.

Nell couldn't help but enjoy confounding her friend.

Mariah flung her arms around Nell's neck. "No more chaps!"

Nell giggled. Not a sound anyone wanted to hear coming from the town judge. But they were alone in Nell's apartment over her shop, enjoying one of the easy lunches they'd shared so often. So news of her giggling wouldn't get out, for Becky and Mariah wouldn't tell.

"I'll still run the shop. I'll work with Parson Blodgett to learn the job, but he's heading for Nebraska soon and then I'll be on my own. It's not a job to keep me busy all day, and the pay is such that I'll need my regular job to survive." Nell looked at Mariah. "I may need an assistant. If I get to pick, will you be a guard for trials?"

It was Mariah's turn to giggle. "I'm not signing on as an armed guard for you. Pick someone scarier than me to keep the peace at your trials."

"Becky's too far out of town." Nell waved away Mariah's protests since Nell had been teasing. "I think the sheriff or Willie will do it. I'm just a little overwhelmed to think I'm getting this job."

Becky poured coffee while Nell set a platter of steaming-hot scrambled eggs on the table. Mariah had made the toast, and Becky had put out the jelly and butter, plates and utensils for each of them. Their usual meal. Lately, though, Nell and Mariah ate so often at Clint's Diner, and Becky was so rarely in town—almost never during the long winter—that they hadn't gotten together for a while.

The smell of coffee, the savory scent of scrambled eggs, the warmth of toasted bread . . . it was what friendship felt like. The three of them, mostly alone in the world and certainly lonely for female friendship, had come to feel like sisters.

Mariah with her loving but gruff father and brother. Becky with her unkind, growly father. Nell with her abandoning rat of a brother. They'd needed friends and they'd found each other. Even now, with Mariah married and others becoming more important every day, their bond was uniquely special.

When Becky had arrived in town on a Friday morning and said she had an hour to spare, the meal had been quick to come together.

"You really do know a lot of laws and investigating techniques," Becky said as she divided the stack of scrambled eggs between three plates.

"I hadn't realized just how much I knew until I got thrown into the middle of this latest shooting." Nell frowned, worrying over what lay ahead. "I think justice of the peace is a big job, though. The parson has just begun to tell me all that's involved."

"You preside over trials, right? What else?"

"I'm still learning. I was surprised by all there was to it." Nell listed all she could remember.

"You issue a *subpoena*?" Becky said the word slowly, sounding it out, her brow furrowed. "What's that?"

"It's an order that's issued telling a person they have to come to court. For example, a witness to a crime might get a subpoena."

"And a warrant," Mariah said hesitantly. "I've heard of that, too. A warrant for someone's arrest. You send the sheriff out to pick them up."

"That's right. There's paperwork that needs to be filled out and that will be my job, as well. And there are several kinds of warrants." Nell talked about warrants for a bit, then bonds and how to select juries. She answered their questions and began to believe she knew most of what her new job entailed.

As they ate, the three of them discussed all that might be involved with her job. Nell could have kept busy making chaps, but instead she was planning time with the girls after school. A day of ribbons and lace.

"I'd never even seen you handle a gun before I needed a bodyguard," Mariah said before crunching into her toast.

Just because she loved ribbons didn't mean she couldn't defend herself with a side arm.

They'd talked through most of what was circling in Nell's head when the downstairs door to her shop banged open.

"Becky, get down here. We've got trouble." Nell recognized the voice of Becky's ranch foreman, Nate Paxton. "King got into it with a grizz."

Becky shot to her feet so fast that she knocked her chair over backward. She was out the door and thundering down the stairs before Nell got to her feet. Then she and Mariah were hard after Becky.

King, her black Angus bull, was a valuable animal. Becky had said at least ten times that she couldn't afford him, but she also couldn't afford to pass up the chance to buy him.

Nell got downstairs, where the front door was flung wide open. Becky threw herself onto her palomino stallion, shouting questions at Nate. They were garbled and fast.

The only thing Nell was sure of was the foreman saying, "He's gonna need hundreds of stitches and a lot of care."

Nate spurred his horse and galloped out of town. Becky saw them and jabbed a finger almost at Nell's heart. "You helped sew up Brutus. Get on horseback and come with me." Next she hit Mariah with that finger. "Clint helped—get him out to my place. And the doctor, too. We might need all of you."

Becky swung her horse around and started riding, bent low over its neck.

Nell gave Mariah a wild look. "Clint did the sewing, not me."

"The noon meal has to be about over," Mariah said. "Fetch Doc Preston, then grab a horse from the corral behind the smithy and go. My blue roan is a good one. I'll stay in town to close up the diner. Clint can run home for his horse. He'll be on the trail as fast as possible."

Nell jerked her chin in agreement and ran for the doctor's office. She burst inside, amazed that the glass in the door held. "Doc, come quick!"

Doc Preston came running.

"It's Becky's bull—he's torn up bad by a bear. She asked me to fetch you."

The sheriff stepped out of the back room. "You go on, Doc. I'll be fine here."

"Two people, remember? You need someone with you."

"I'll get Willie. You go on now. I'll be five minutes getting Willie here. He sat with Campbell overnight and he'll be exhausted, but he'll come. And it won't hurt our patient to be alone for a few minutes."

All Nell could think of was how much Becky loved that bull. She gave the men she'd spent so much time with a firm nod, then spun around to leave.

She heard the men come after her. The sheriff's boots pounding off toward Willie's house. Nell on her way to the livery. The doctor heading for the corral and small barn where he kept his horse and buggy on the edge of town.

Nell found Mariah's horse in a stall inside and had it saddled and was galloping when she saw Clint leave his diner and go running on foot for home. She didn't wait for him.

She could get to Becky's in under a half hour at this pace, and she intended to do just that. Then a rider showed up coming into town, and she recognized Brand and it hit her that the girls were coming over to sew.

He pulled up when he saw her approach. She stopped to explain what was going on.

"Becky's got trouble out at her place. Her bull was hurt bad in a run-in with a grizzly bear. She asked me to come. I won't be able to have the girls come and work today."

"I've done some animal doctoring. I'll go to the school and tell the girls where I'll be."

"Tell them I left the shop unlocked." She said it the same second she remembered it. "They can go there and wait until we get back."

He nodded. "I've got some things at home, too. I'll be out to the Idee as fast as I can." He charged his horse toward the school.

Nell galloped on.

⁓

Brand pulled his horse to a stop at the schoolhouse. He flung himself out of the saddle and rushed for the school, caught up in Nell's urgency.

Inside, he saw Mr. Betancourt standing in the front of the room, talking to his pupils. The man broke off in mid-sentence.

"I'm sorry to interrupt," Brand said, "but I need to talk to my girls for a minute."

Betancourt nodded, though the girls were moving before he could give them his permission.

Brand led them out to the front stoop of the schoolhouse, not wanting to disrupt things further. He noticed the sheriff running somewhere, and Doc Preston galloping in the direction of the Idee.

"What happened, Pa?"

He saw the fear in Samantha's eyes. She was old enough to remember Pamela dying.

"It's not serious. Well, it is, but it's Miss Pruitt's bull. He's been injured. You know I worked with Doc Gould back in the Ozarks, caring for animals. I'm going to see if I can help. Mrs. Armstrong is going, too."

Sam's eyes shifted beyond Brand. He turned quickly but didn't see what it was that drew her attention.

"Mrs. Armstrong won't be able to work with you girls today, but she said you could go to her shop and stay there until we return. I'd rather you don't walk home. Is going to the shop all right with you girls? Mrs. Roberts would be at the smithy, too. You know her and could stay with her. But the smithy has some dangers with the red-hot forge and the banging anvil. So I'd prefer you go to the shop." He left them home alone when he needed to. With Sam nearly sixteen, he trusted her to watch over them. And all three of his girls were well-behaved, and they certainly weren't babies anymore.

"Brandon . . . uh, Mr. Nolte." Mr. Betancourt drew his attention from back inside the schoolhouse.

"Brand is fine. I'm sorry about this."

"I heard just a bit of it. After school, why don't I send for Mrs. Blodgett? Three of her youngsters are in school. The oldest two, Leland and Warren, are finished, and the youngest two not yet of school years. We can see if she or her daughter, Joy, who's a good friend of Samantha's here, will stay and spend time with us."

Brand felt a wave of relief. "That would be just perfect, Mr. Betancourt. Girls, would that be all right? You could stay here at the school."

The school was used as the church on Sundays, so Mrs. Blodgett would feel very much at home here.

"We'll do that, Pa. You go on." Sam seemed to grow up right in front of his eyes.

"I'm taking both horses. I'll leave the one at home so it can graze and get to water. I'll bring it back when I come for you. I have no idea how long I'll be away."

"Go, Pa. Go help Miss Pruitt." Cassie patted him on the arm.

"Hurry, Pa. We'll be fine." Michaela's little voice sounded very sure.

"Thank you, Mr. Betancourt." Brand hurried to his horse and, leading the second one, galloped for home.

17

Nell had been to Becky's Idee Ranch many times and it wasn't too far from town. She was galloping into the yard before she'd exhausted her horse.

Commotion near the barn drew her straight there. She leapt off her horse, whipped the reins around a hitching post, and scrambled over the fence. Nell raced the quarter mile to where a huge black bull lay thrashing on the ground. What looked like every cowhand Becky had on the place were struggling to hold the bull down. His front legs were lassoed together, as were his back legs, and two cowhands held those ropes to stretch the bull out on his side. Another cowhand had a rope around the bull's neck. This cowpoke sat atop his horse, and he and his mount kept the rope taut.

It looked like King was desperate to escape, yet the bull was thrashing with less energy with every passing minute, wearing himself out. Blood flowed from the animal's wounds, and Nell was close enough to see Nate on his knees working over the poor critter.

Nell dropped to her knees beside Nate. "How can I help?"

Everyone else, including Becky, was busy holding the bull down.

"Good, I need another pair of hands."

Becky, lying across King's back, was almost nose to nose with Nate. She had her hands full trying to hold an ugly gash closed. Not easy to do with the bull tossing her back and forth.

Nell looked at Nate. "How bad is it?"

"The worst is under his belly. Some entrails are showing, but they don't look torn up. What I'm working on now is the muscle of his leg. I'm not sure if I should have worked on this first or not."

Becky grunted as King heaved his back and almost cast her off. "I've got five more men who've ridden out to check cattle. We sent one man after them. So in a little while we'll have six more hands to help wrangle this poor guy."

Nell fell silent as Nate sewed the skin shut on the bull's leg. She saw five more deep slashes. Grizzly bear claw marks. Her eyes lifted and she saw the grizz about five yards away. It was dead.

"He's going to bleed to death no matter what we do. He won't calm down, and that keeps the wounds open and flowing." Becky sounded calm. A rancher had to accept life and death. But Nell remembered well how excited Becky had been when she found this bull for sale and bought him.

King meant a lot to her.

Hoofbeats drew Nell's head around, and she saw Doc Preston riding in. Behind him, just coming into view, was Brand, who was riding fast.

"That's two more men, and Clint is coming. We'll have more hands soon."

The bull writhed so wildly, Becky tumbled backward, then jumped right back into place.

Doc came up with his doctor bag in hand.

"His belly's been slashed good," said Nate. "Work on that."

"Nell, let me in."

Nell stood and rounded the bull, then lowered all her weight onto the bull's hindquarters.

Becky, her hair gone wild, loose from its braid, gave Nell a tired smile. "Thanks for coming." Then, "Doc, thank you too. And Brand."

Brand had a cloth bag. "I worked with an animal doctor back in Arkansas." He pulled a brown bottle out of his bag, setting the bag aside. "The doctor dosed an animal, mad with pain, with laudanum. I always keep some on hand."

Becky looked up, her eyes bright, excited even. "Will that bottle be enough to quiet this monster down?"

"It might not put him to sleep, but it'll help."

A hoof thrashed and kicked the doctor, and he landed on his backside. Clint came running up.

The doctor clawed through his bag and produced another brown bottle. "I know how much a dose for a person would be, and this critter can handle both bottles at once. That'll be enough, I hope." He tossed the bottle to Brand. "Clint, can you help? Someone's gonna have to hang on to his head and twist enough that this'll go down his throat.

No, Clint," Doc snapped, taking charge. "I need you to go for a pan of water. He's got entrails exposed to the air. We can't let them dry out."

"I can wrangle this boy. Get the bottle open and ready." Becky eased off King's back. "Nell, you hold the second bottle. Men, keep him stretched out while we're off his back."

Nell had to run all the way around the cowhand holding the rope attached to the bull's back legs. She got to Brand's side and took the second bottle while Becky grabbed hold of the bull's head.

"I wish he had horns—something to grab hold of." Becky slid her arms around the bull's neck. "Ready?"

Brand dropped to his knees. "Go."

Becky twisted the bull's head so that its mouth was aimed up more than sideways. Brand thrust the bottle in deep and poured.

Nell watched, breathless, hoping the bull didn't spit out the contents of the bottle.

Brand massaged the bull's throat. "C'mon, boy. Drink it all."

He pulled his hand out of the black Angus's throat. "Give me the second bottle."

Nell slapped it into his hand and then took up the other bottle he'd tossed to the ground. Brand poured in the next laudanum dose, and Becky held on tight as he rubbed King's throat once again while crooning to the injured animal.

Everyone worked on with desperate speed. Doc was busy stitching up King's belly, with Clint close by assisting the doc. Meanwhile, Nate worked on King's leg.

Nell circled the cowpoke again and went back to holding the bull down with all her weight. She felt the poor critter heaving to be free as Doc, Clint, and Nate worked on him. Then very gradually the fight went out of King.

"It's working," Becky said. She was still holding the bull's neck, but her grip looked more like a hug now.

Brand had moved to help Nate hold the skin closed as the two of them sewed half a dozen gashes on the bull's side.

"I've got his belly closed." Doc Preston looked up from where he knelt. "What's left?"

"There are two wounds up here on his back," Nell answered, "and I'm not sure what's on the other side."

Becky released the bull. "You boys can ease up on the ropes now. I think he'll sleep for a while." She looked at Brand. "Do you have any idea how long?"

"Maybe an hour. It's hard to judge based on the amount of laudanum we gave him and his weight. This is a big animal. I was there when the animal doctor—he called himself a veterinarian—dosed a good-sized cow with a full bottle of laudanum, and she slept for a solid hour. This guy is bigger, but we gave him double the laudanum."

"Another bear attack?"

"Nope, the doctor cut a baby out of her. Stitched her back up, too. Both mama and baby lived. The vet, Doc Gould, had something he called carbolic acid that he said kept wounds from getting infected. It was so new, I saw him use it only once. On that very cow."

"I've heard of it," Doc Preston said, "but I thought it sounded outlandish, just another so-called miracle cure. But I wish I had some of it now. Even if I ordered the carbolic acid, though, this bull will be long healed or long dead before it'd get here. Still, I might look into it."

The doctor reached for the gash Nell had pointed to and got to work. Brand, Clint, and Nate were all working, as well. Soon the last of the bull's injuries were stitched up.

"I saw him before we roped and threw him," Nate said, sitting back on his knees, "and all the worst cuts are on this side. It's why we laid him out the way we did."

Becky looked over at the grizzly just as six men came tearing into the yard. She heaved a sigh of relief.

"They're too late, but they can take over on the ropes." She looked at the men surrounding her. "Thank you all. I'm hopeful we saved him, and it took each and every one of us working hard for two hours to do it." She smiled just a bit. "Do you want to hang on to a sleeping bull or butcher a grizzly?"

"I'm a good hand with a skinning knife," Roscoe Grable, Becky's bunkhouse cook, said.

"You got the shot off that killed that grizz, Miss Becky." A lean cowhand hanging on to the heel rope let go with one hand and doffed his hat. "You earned that bearskin."

"We all got so many shots into the bear that the skin isn't gonna be worth wrapping up in for all the holes."

The skinny cowpoke looked at his partner on the heel rope. "You got him, Buck?"

"So long as he's asleep."

"I'll send two men over for each rope. We'll have bear stew for supper and plenty of bear fat for candles and such." The lean cowhand started for the grizzly and called out a few orders to the approaching men, who split up, coming for the bull or the bear. "We won't waste a bit of him."

Nate quit kneeling and sat on his backside on the ground.

The doctor collapsed beside him. Brand, on his knees, shook his head. "He's got a chance, doesn't he, Doc?"

"That he does."

18

They were a while finishing everything up.

King stirred slowly, and all hands available got the bull to his feet. He was wobbly, but he stayed upright.

"I've got a stall ready for bedding down, Miss Becky." Roscoe stood at the door to the barn, holding a pitchfork. Roscoe had been foreman of the ranch before he'd had his knee stove in from a bronco. Now Nate had the job. But Roscoe was a trusted friend, and his wife, Jan, lived in the ranch house with Becky. Jan became Becky's cook and housekeeper.

"Let's get him inside, see if he'll eat any grain." Becky gave the bull a slap on the backside, though she was gentle about it.

Nell knew just how strong and tough Becky was, yet she had a soft heart she tried very hard to conceal.

They all threw in to push King into the barn. More staggering than walking, they eventually steered the bull into the stall. Buck had fresh water ready in one trough and plenty of prairie grass in another trough that they'd cut, cured, and stored in the loft overhead.

The barn smelled of hay and grain, animals and dust. Nell felt the tension ease out of her as they left the stirred-up dirt and the worst of the blood behind. She was afraid the bull would collapse immediately, but the water must have lured him because he went right in and drank it deeply.

"That'll help him build up his blood as fast as anything," Doc Preston said.

"Do you have any oats or corn?" Brand studied the bull with a professional eye, which impressed Nell.

"I do. I have a few acres of oats because the horses like a bait of it now and then. Nate, let's get some oats."

Roscoe was already getting it before Becky started talking. He brought a low-sided tin pan to the stall, opened the door, set the pan inside and filled it with oats, giving the bull a generous serving.

"That'll be enough for now," Brand said. "Wait till morning to give him more oats. He'll have a hard time resisting eating it all. He'll quit with the hay when he's had enough, but he might bloat on the oats."

Roscoe and Becky both nodded. Even Clint and the doctor nodded. Everyone seemed to be listening to Brand.

"I could use an animal doctor from time to time, Brand." Becky looked encouraged when her bull started lipping down the oats with enthusiasm. "Can I send for you if I need to? You could make a job out of it."

"I'd be glad to come, Miss Pruitt. No need to call it a job. Neighbors are to help each other when there's a need."

"Well, if you won't take money, maybe we can barter. Do you have enough chickens? I've got a new litter of piglets—have you a pig to raise?" Becky turned to Clint and the doctor. "I owe you all, and there'll be a chance to pay each of you back, I promise. And I'll for sure replace your supply of laudanum."

"We'll talk about that later." Brand tugged on the brim of his homemade slouch hat. "I think your bull will settle in for the night now. I've got to go home. I left the girls pretty stirred up when I ran out here."

"We'll watch over King. Thanks, Brand. You've got a bear roast coming, too."

Brand managed a tired grin. "Not what I had planned for supper, Miss Pruitt."

Becky gave a little laugh. "I'll run some meat over when the butchering is done."

"Maybe some idea of how to cook it, too. Leastways if there are any tricks I oughta know."

"Clint, have you ever served bear at the diner? There's gonna be a lot of good eating from that grizzly. And this warm weather will spoil it fast."

Shaking his head, Clint said, "Can't say as I have. I think I'll just postpone that honor for a while. I'll ride back with you, Brand. I left things in a state at the diner. Mariah's a decent cook, but heaven knows what's going on there."

"Can you spare us, Becky?" Nell straightened away from where she leaned on the stall and almost staggered.

Brand was right at hand and caught her upper arm to steady her.

She patted his hand. "Thank you."

"I'll head in with you all," Doc Preston said.

As they walked outside, Nell saw Brand studying the big barn.

Nell looked around, taking in the surroundings. The barn was made of cut lumber, not logs. The building had been here when Nell first arrived. She wasn't sure if there was a sawmill around here. Becky's house was of log and stone, as was the bunkhouse. She had two smaller houses where the ramrods of the ranch lived—one for Nate, the other for Buck. And she had a good-sized chicken coop and another outbuilding, a bit larger, for her hogs.

The sounds of yipping turned Nell's head as a bunch of puppies ran out of the barn door in the company of their mama, who looked more wolf than dog. Lobo was a famous critter around these parts. She and Brutus were the parents of nearly every dog in the area.

Becky really did run a first-class operation here.

"Brand, I'll be riding over with a puppy for you and your girls in a couple of weeks. I'll have Brutus back by then, and I'll bring him along to stay awhile until the puppy learns to behave. He's a fine teacher."

"I-I'm a little foggy on that. Did I ask for a dog?"

Becky laughed. "It's been a wild day. We talked about it a bit that Sunday at Clint's."

They said their goodbyes as they gathered the horses, and then the four riders from town headed home with Becky's thanks echoing in their ears.

"It was a good day." Doc Preston took the lead, Clint falling in beside him. "I hope we saved that beautiful Angus bull."

Brand ended up riding beside Nell. "You spent the afternoon draped across a bull's backside." He grinned at her.

She rolled her eyes, then started to laugh. "That I did. A lot of my days are the same as the next, but I'll never say that about today."

"The girls are chattering about sewing with you. They love visiting your shop. I should be paying you when you make them this happy."

"I enjoy having them. And they're learning fast. I'll make more money because of them, and they deserve what they earn." Nell thought this might be a good time to slip in some talk of bonnets. "In fact, they deserve more than a dime a day. For now, the girls are happy to earn the cost of a dress and they want bonnets, too. And they'll need warm clothes come fall. As long as it's not interfering with how you run your place, I'll get some good help from those girls and I appreciate it."

"They want to keep at it, and our arrangement seems to be working just fine. The girls are still getting all their chores done."

They rode in silence for a stretch, then Nell remembered her new job. "Did you hear I've been appointed to be the town's justice of the peace?"

Brand's head whipped around. "Judge Nell?"

She chuckled. "Excuse me, it's Judge *Armstrong*."

Clint and the doc looked back. Clint smiled. Doc Preston gave her a firm nod of approval.

Brand said, "I'm a pa raising young women. Looks like I've brought my girls to a territory that will do them proud."

Brand slowed his horse as they approached the turnoff to his home. "I've got to fetch the horse the girls will ride home on. Nell, would you mind coming to my place, then to town to tell my daughters about being named justice of the peace? They would be so thrilled to hear the news straight from you. It'll be all over town by the time they get to school tomorrow."

Nell called out, "Clint, I'm turning off up here. You and Doc go on to town."

Clint waved a hand, neither man looking back. Which seemed odd to Nell, though she wasn't sure why.

"Right up ahead there." Brand pointed, then he and Nell took a side trail. "I'm just around the trees. Close to town. I was glad to get this homestead. I'd hoped the girls might want to walk to school, but I'm not sure the countryside is safe."

"We're filling up in this area. You're going to be hemmed in soon enough. I reckon that's why folks pick homesteads farther out, so they have room to grow."

"I'll never be a big rancher like Becky is, or her pa. I've got one hundred and sixty acres. I think that'll keep me busy. With the girls all in school, I might be able to get work in town. I've done that a few times. Enough money to keep food on our table and—" he smiled at Nell, and she smiled back, unsure what his smile meant—"maybe I can buy some fabric for the girls."

Ah, now she knew.

"I earn enough to survive until the farm starts producing enough for us to live on with some comfort."

"The girls may earn their own fabric. That'll leave you with more cash money to build your farm."

"Samantha's almost sixteen years old."

"I was married at seventeen, and I was one of the older

girls to marry. I had one neighbor who was fourteen, another fifteen. Imagine Samantha married in a year."

Brand grabbed the reins so tight, his horse tossed its head and reared slightly. He quick relaxed his grip and patted the horse. "Well, my girls aren't going to marry so young, for heaven's sake. That's ridiculous. Seventeen is young, but fourteen?"

"She was fourteen, her husband fifteen. They were both too young. But no one could convince them it was a poor idea. That young groom and his pa built a cabin, and they lived near her folks and his. They had a lot of help. Especially when the babies started coming. The year I got married, she already had three—"

"Can we not talk about this anymore?" Brand cut her off.

Nell realized Brand had turned an alarming shade of red, and she fought down laughter. "Yes, let's change the subject. The girls are doing well, they are quick to learn, and they work hard. They'll be sewing on their own in no time."

"Thanks to you." He turned just as his house came into sight.

Nell guessed he was delighted by the distraction.

Good heavenly days, to think of Samantha married in a year. She focused on his farm, too.

It wasn't grand like the Idee with its big barn and all the outbuildings. He had the house, a modest barn, a chicken coop, a corral and that was all. But everything looked well-built. She saw a spring trickling out of stone near the house, which ran in a stream that cut across the corral, where two cows grazed.

The house had been built where it would be shielded from the north wind while also giving them plenty of morning and afternoon sun.

"You've built well here, Brand. You've got a nice start."

"Plenty more to do, but yes, it's a nice start."

19

Brand quickly saddled the second horse, and within minutes they were off toward Pine Valley.

"I wonder what the girls ended up doing?"

"Maybe they talked to Mariah and are spending time with her. We'll find them soon enough."

When they got to town, they found the girls and several Blodgett children on the grassy playground near the school.

Before they arrived at the school, the jailhouse door slammed and drew their attention. The sheriff was sprinting toward them. Nell guided her horse toward the obviously upset lawman.

He reached them, close enough to speak quietly but urgently. "Mr. Campbell is dead."

Nell grabbed her saddle horn to keep from falling off the horse. Then, after the initial shock, she swung off her horse and strode toward the doctor's office.

She went inside to see the doctor frowning at his patient. His head came up, and his eyes landed on Nell hard enough she felt it like a blow. Ignoring the doctor's frustration, Nell went to the patient, still on the table. "He's dead?" She leaned over the man, who was by all appearances quietly sleeping.

A pang passed through her. The poor man had lost the battle. It had always been a long shot that he'd live, but she'd hoped he would. They'd all hoped. Mainly because there was a chance he'd help them stop a band of murderers, but also because he was innocent. And they'd all hoped he would overcome his ghastly injuries and survive.

Cheroots. It seemed the man's last request was to smoke the slender, black Mexican cigars. What a legacy to leave behind. Nell felt a moment's twisting regret that she didn't at least attempt to grant him that request.

"He's been dead awhile now, Nell."

"What? The sheriff sounded like the news of it just hit."

"It did. The sheriff came back with Willie minutes after we left. They sat down to read, and later they played a hand or two of gin. Then the sheriff told Willie to take a nap. He'd been up and sitting with the patient all night. The sheriff went back to reading, the two of them there all afternoon. I came to town, found them all settled in, and went to check on Mr. Campbell. That's when I realized he'd died while his two bodyguards sat nearby. He must have died quietly. No pain. I guess that's one small mercy."

Nell used one finger to tug on Campbell's bottom lip, then his top. She studied his face. She lifted his hand and examined the fingers, then did the same with the other hand, reaching across his body. Staring at his hand for a long moment, she rested it at his side. She tilted his chin from side to side. At last, she lifted her eyes to the doctor's and opened her mouth, words rushing to get out.

Before she could speak, Brand came in, his eyes saddened. "He didn't make it?"

The sheriff was a pace behind him. Pulling off his hat and clutching it to his chest, the sheriff said, "Nope. He passed quietly in his sleep, painlessly. Willie and I were with him the whole time. We didn't notice when he slipped away."

"You didn't notice," Nell snapped, "because he was killed while you were going for Willie. He didn't die from his injuries. This man was murdered—the Deadeye Gang got to him."

The sheriff slapped his hat back on and charged for Nell. "What do you mean? How?"

Doc Preston spoke over the top of the sheriff. "How can you say he was murdered?"

Nell touched the man's left hand. "Blood under his fingernails. We've been over his body while we treated him. That wasn't there before. He clawed someone."

"That's it?" The doctor lifted the hand and studied the nails. "It's brown . . . it could be blood."

"He tried to fight someone off. Look at his lips. His top lip is bleeding inside his mouth. He's got blood on his teeth. Not much, but someone smothered him. Pressed a hand over his nose and mouth, or a towel or pillow, until he was dead."

The doctor began inspecting the man more closely. "There's even some mild bruising on his face where a hand pressed hard against it." Looking up with a grim expression, he said to Sheriff Mast, "Did you leave him alone with Willie?"

Nell gasped.

"No, I most certainly did not." The sheriff lifted the dead man's pillow, a flat thing with feathers that'd given up being fluffy long ago. He flipped it over, and there were bloodstains. "These stains look about the right size to be explained by a bleeding lip."

Nell couldn't help but wonder just how long the sheriff had been alone with the man. But no, he had an alibi for the time of the shooting involving both Mariah and now Campbell. Other stage robberies, Nell couldn't say the sheriff's exact whereabouts.

Shaking her head, feeling sure she could trust him and hoping her trust wasn't misplaced, she crossed her arms. She felt the scowl on her face. She was justice of the peace. She and Sheriff Mast, along with Willie, were the law in this town. And someone had just viciously violated that law.

"Who could've done it?" Nell wondered aloud. "Whoever it was had only minutes to act. I rode out of town. Mariah ran for the diner. Where was everyone? That moment of neglect had to be when our killer acted. Doc, did you leave the office before or after Sheriff Joe?"

"Are you accusing me of killing this man? Suggesting that I—"

Nell snapped a hand up in the doctor's face so her flat palm almost smacked him in the nose. "*You stop right there.*"

The doctor's jaw sagged open. Brand took a half step back. It was the sheriff's turn to cross his arms.

"I am *not* accusing you of anything," Nell said. "I'm only trying to figure out where everybody was, and when.

We need a chain of events, and I won't let you refuse in great dignity and effrontery to answer my questions. You *will* do it and you *will* set the example for every man, woman, or child I choose to question. *Is that understood?*"

The doctor seemed to have a fight on his hands getting his jaw shut.

Nell looked at the sheriff. "You should be the one asking these questions. I just jumped in and started."

The sheriff flinched as if he didn't want her glaring at him. "You're doing fine. Go on ahead."

"Now, when you left here, did you go first or the sheriff?" She looked between the two men.

They looked at each other for a long moment, then the doctor said, "I think I left first. We both took off mighty close to each other."

Brand spoke up. "I came into town to tell the girls I might be late picking them up from school. As I dismounted at the schoolhouse, I saw you, Doc, come galloping toward the trail to the Idee Ranch. Then I saw the sheriff running hard for . . . well, he must've been running to get Willie."

"Did you need to saddle your horse?" Nell asked the doctor.

"No, it was tied to the hitching post right out front of my office. I was going to call on someone later." The doctor slapped himself with the heel of his hand against his forehead. "Good grief. I never went to see Mrs. Rossi." Shaking his head, he went on, "I might have been a pace ahead of the sheriff but not much more, if Brand's remembering right."

"So, you both left at nearly the same moment. Sheriff Mast, how long were you gone getting Willie?"

"Five minutes, ten at the most. I pounded on the door of Willie's house, hard. His wife answered, and I told her to send Willie to the doctor's office. She said he'd just gotten to sleep."

The sheriff paused as if trying to force the memory. "She was upset with me. She said he was exhausted and didn't make enough money to work night and day. I-I shouted at her to send him. Then I ran back to watch over Mr. Campbell. Willie lives on the edge of town, but that's not far."

Nothing was far in Pine Valley.

"Five minutes, then, he was alone—ten at the most." Nell looked at each man, one at a time, her eyes razor-sharp. "Someone had to see it all happen. Someone had to witness it from the first moment. Nate galloping into town, yelling real loud. Mariah running to the diner. Who saw her come in? Who saw Clint run out? Who was in the diner at the time? Who was in the general store? Was anyone in the land office or the smithy or the saloon? Did Mariah throw people out and lock up, or did she stay open and cook? We need to find Mariah, see who was eating there. We'll talk to the Wainwrights, ask them who was in the store and heard the commotion. We'll see if anyone rushed out." She turned to the sheriff. "Let's split up."

Brand said quietly, "I need to let Mr. Betancourt go home."

Nodding, Nell said, "You've been working for everyone else all day. You need to see to your homestead and take care of the girls. Apologize to them for me for not having them over to work today. We'll get right back to working tomorrow."

"Thanks," said Brand. "I feel like I'm abandoning you all, but I've got to get on."

When he left, the sheriff said, "Doc, go get Jim Burk. Tell him to come for the body."

The doctor nodded, grabbed his hat, and left.

Nell said, "I'll talk to Mariah if that's all right with you, Sheriff. It's lawman's work, but I know her well."

Everyone knows everyone well around here, Nell thought. Then she questioned the truth of that. She certainly didn't know at least one person, because someone right here in town was a cold-blooded murderer.

"I'll talk to Peter and Henry at the general store." The sheriff set his hat firmly on his head. "Remember, whoever did this acted on a moment's notice. It's likely they were seen getting up and moving fast, if not actually entering the doctor's office and killing Campbell."

Nell nodded, a little bit annoyed that the sheriff was telling her how to conduct an investigation that was her idea. But since she was going to do what he ordered her to do anyway, she accepted it and headed for Mariah's house.

20

As she stepped outside, Brand caught sight of her just as he was boosting the girls up onto their horses.

He led the critters over and helped the girls dismount. "We never told the girls your big news. Do you have time to tell them, or do you have work to do?"

Nell smiled. "First of all, did your pa tell you where he was going at such a clip earlier?"

Cassie said, "He said Miss Pruitt's bull was hurt and needed doctoring."

"That's right, and your pa was the best of all of us. Four of us rode out from town. Clint from the diner, the doctor, your pa, and me. Miss Pruitt had a lot of cowhands there, too. The bull needed threads put in a whole lot of cuts, but I think he'll be all right. We did our best, and the big guy was up and eating oats when we left."

"Pa used to work with the animal doctor who served the folks in the hills and hollers of the Ozarks where we lived." Michaela beamed at him with pride.

"That's what we were doing all afternoon," said Brand, "and we were riding home when Mrs. Armstrong told me some exciting news."

As the girls stared at her expectantly, Nell realized for just a few seconds she'd forgotten about the murder. She smiled at the girls. "I was appointed to be the new justice of the peace in Pine Valley. Parson Blodgett did the job before me. A justice of the peace serves as judge at a trial. There are other legal tasks I'll be responsible for, too. I sign the deeds when folks come to the area and homestead. That's handled at the land office mostly, but the deeds need an authorized signature from the local authorities, and that's me. I can perform weddings, as well. There are other things, and we can talk about all of it later, but right now I need to get on with something else. What I do want to say is, it's a huge honor for them to ask a woman to do the job. As far as I know, a lady named Esther Morris over in South Pass City is the only other woman justice of the peace in all of America."

"So you're the second one?" Samantha's eyes grew wide. "The second one in the whole country? Mrs. Armstrong, that's such an exciting thing."

"Wyoming Territory is a land of equality, girls. In Wyoming a woman can do any job she's able to do with no law standing in her way. You've come to a very modern place to live. No other states or territories give women so much freedom. I think my new job is a step that will advance the cause of women's rights all over the country. I certainly intend to uphold the job with as much wisdom and care as any man would show."

All three girls listened with rapt attention as she spoke, then sighed.

"I've never been prouder." Brand gave a firm nod of his chin. "We've done well to homestead here in Wyoming, girls."

The girls charged at Nell and hugged her, all three of them at once. A family hug.

Brand felt something odd when he watched his girls hug Nell. It couldn't be jealousy, could it? That wouldn't make any sense.

Then Michaela reached for him and dragged him into the hug.

Smiling down at her, he forgot that foolish pang of being left out and embraced his girls. Then he stopped looking down at his littlest and raised his eyes to see he was almost nose to nose with Nell.

His heart gave a little twist when her sweet lips curved into a generous smile. For a moment, there weren't four girls but only three, and one woman.

"I'm so excited for you, Mrs. Armstrong." Michaela's high-pitched voice broke whatever spell he'd been under.

Nell looked away and beamed at the girls. "I've got to get on with part of my job now."

Brand saw Doc Preston crossing the street side by side with the undertaker. He needed to get the girls out of town before they witnessed the body being taken from the doctor's office. Though he knew all of life had hardship and loss and ugliness, he wanted to shelter his girls from as much of that as possible.

"We need to let Mrs. Armstrong go now. We've got chores waiting for us at home." He helped the girls mount up, then swung up into the saddle behind Michaela. "Congratulations, Your Honor."

Nell smiled and waved as they rode away.

He glanced back as they reached the trail that led to his place, and Nell was gone. Doing her justice-of-the-peace work.

She'd startled him earlier when she made the doctor quit talking. Nell, pretty, dainty Nell, had a spine as stiff as the Wind River Mountains.

"Girls," he said, "let's stop and look back a minute."

He turned his horse to face west, and Sam, sitting in front of Cassie on the other horse, copied him.

"What is it, Pa?" she asked.

"I just want a minute to look at those towering mountains. I'm thinking right now about Wyoming and Mrs. Armstrong being the second justice of the peace in America and how proud I am of you girls today. When I had an emergency, you were all so quick to handle the situation. I'm looking at those mountains and seeing strength everywhere I turn. A tough old bull who's going to get well. Three beautiful girls who are smart and calm and strong. Mrs. Armstrong, so willing to take on a hard job. I'm surrounded by strength. And I want to spend a little time enjoying that."

They sat together and admired the Cirque of the Towers. After a few minutes, he said, "Now let's go home."

As Brand and the girls rode out of Pine Valley, he was glad to leave it all behind. He thought of Nell and the family hug that included her and wished she was coming with them.

With her last ounce of energy, Nell dragged herself back to the sheriff's office. She didn't want to. What she did want was for this day to end.

Oh sure, she wanted to see the Deadeye Gang caught and put a stop to their murdering, getting to the bottom of all that had happened. She most definitely wanted to be safe in Pine Valley and to make the stagecoach routes safe again. And she really couldn't wait to start being a justice of the peace.

She goaded herself with all these things she wanted to keep herself trudging forward, postponing the moment her head hit the pillow.

But for all those wants, mostly, she admitted to herself, she just wanted to make bonnets and riding skirts for three little girls.

And anyway, sleep would have to wait even if she did ignore her responsibilities to the town because she hadn't eaten, she needed a bath, and she needed to scrub the bloodstains out of her dress.

And then sleep.

Instead of all that, she walked to the sheriff's office and up the two wooden steps and inside. The sheriff sat at his desk, leaning back, his hands intertwined behind his head.

He was blinking when she came in, and she was sure he'd been dozing. Now he sat forward and folded his hands on the desk in front of him. "What did you find out?"

Nell handed him a sheet of paper she'd gotten from Mariah. She'd gone to Mariah's house right after she'd been hugged by Brand. His girls too, but an adult man holding her? It'd been a long time, and she hadn't missed it. Hadn't even wanted it again. But right now she thought of a pair of strong arms and longed for that strength. Thinking about it confused her, so she focused on the case. "That's a list of names of those who were in the diner when Nate came to town. Mariah ran there very quickly. I doubt anyone had left who heard the ruckus and shouting when he came to my shop. She most certainly didn't see anyone leave."

The sheriff brought the paper in close to examine it. Curling up one corner of his mouth, he said dryly, "We can probably take Mrs. Blodgett off the list."

A small laugh escaped Nell, likely because of exhaustion. Poor Mr. Campbell.

"I don't suspect her at all," she said, "or Mrs. Betancourt, who was having dinner with her. But they are both bright, alert women, so I questioned them and added the names to the list Mariah gave me. I didn't ask them if they are the one who killed Mr. Campbell. I asked them what they saw, or if anyone left the diner quickly right about that time. Any names they gave me, I found those folks if I could and questioned them. I didn't come up with much. But I've got more people still to question."

She'd been at it for hours.

Nodding, the sheriff said, "You got more than I did. No one was in the general store right then but the Wainwrights. They were in the back room opening crates and didn't notice any of the commotion."

"I'm going home for the night, Sheriff." Then more quietly she added, "I'm sorry about Mr. Campbell. You worked so hard to protect him. What an awful end to your efforts, to all of our efforts."

Sheriff Joe nodded. "Right at first, he talked of that rifle. That Yellow Boy rifle with the carved stock. That's something."

"That is something. We'll have to question these folks, then maybe see who else was in town then. We'll ask at the land office, too. Where else?"

"We'll think of every place in town, and we'll question every person who was nearby. Go on now, Nell. You're a better sheriff than I am. I thank you for your help today. I know a lot of men not tough enough to stand up to all you've had to face."

Nell wasn't sure how she felt about being thanked for helping. It was her duty to help. It wasn't quite right that the sheriff seemed so utterly impressed with her, as if a woman knowing a few things about an investigation and working hard on a crime surprised him. It was insulting and somehow flattering at the same time.

And that was when she knew she needed to get out of there and get some sleep. "Good night, Sheriff. It'll be tomorrow soon enough. We can discuss then if we want to divide that list, or if you'd rather handle it yourself."

The sheriff rose from his desk and turned the lantern all the way down. "I'll walk you home, Judge Armstrong, on my way to get some rest. No standing guard, not anymore."

Nell stepped outside with the sheriff right behind her. The two of them were the last folks on Main Street. Even the saloon was silent and dark.

Once she was inside the house, Nell securely locked her

front and back doors, then went upstairs and locked the door to her apartment. Hopefully that'd keep all danger and threat outside. Of course, everything left undone followed her right inside. The death of Mr. Campbell especially would haunt her for a long time.

21

rand stepped into Nell's dress shop the next day and found it empty.

Considering the events in the area lately, he had to fight a momentary feeling of panic that some gang of cutthroats had attacked the new justice of the peace in her dress shop.

Then he heard a racket through the wall, a wall shared with the empty building next to Nell's.

Not so empty after all.

He stepped outside hoping to find his missing daughters, and if not, maybe to find someone who had seen them.

He found the girls and Nell with scarves over their heads, dusting and sweeping and scrubbing. Nell had them all hard at work.

As he stepped inside, they all stopped, looked at him, then smiled like he'd brought them candy and presents.

"Pa, Mrs. Armstrong is moving her justice-of-the-peace business into this building."

"Pine Valley is providing you with a real courthouse?"

Nell shook her head. "No, I'm providing myself with one. Parson Blodgett came over today and told me about all the things he had that he needed to deliver to me. I went over, and his whole front room is given over to it. He said his wife is eager to get it all out of the house."

"They have a small house. And seven children."

"Yes, they do. I could see all those things taking over my dress shop and decided something had to be done. And this building is sitting empty, so I talked with the sheriff and the mayor, and they allowed me to assume the deed for the cost of a filing fee, which was waived by the justice of the peace." She grinned. "Me. Now I'm the proud owner of two Main Street buildings."

"The city council made you buy a building?"

"I didn't ask them," said Nell. "The city doesn't have any money. And I didn't exactly buy it, because it was abandoned. No one to buy it from. But Percy at the land office signed some papers, and I made out a deed. It's mine now. This is to be the Pine Valley city office and courtroom. I told Doc Preston that the city council can hold their meetings here, though there are only three of them and right now they meet standing up for ten minutes in the general store. So, they might not want to get that organized.

"The rooms are all coated in dust and filled with debris from the last owner, who seems to have left all this trash behind when he abandoned the place. I've been cleaning all day, and when the girls got out of school, they agreed to earn today's dime by cleaning with me."

Nell smiled at the girls and warned, "It might be more

than one day. Though tomorrow's Saturday and I'll keep working on it, so we might be sewing again by Monday."

A counter divided the room, with one-quarter of the space behind the counter, where Samantha was busy swinging a mop. Michaela swept the larger front section. Cassie had a washcloth and a bucket of water. She was scrubbing one end of the counter while Nell scrubbed on the other end. A space between the counters let a person pass from the front to the back. Empty shelves spanned the wall behind the counter and were badly in need of dusting.

"What was this place?"

"Mayor Peter said it was a mercantile at one time, but the owners moved on years ago. Upstairs, there's a gable window facing my apartment, and one in my shop facing this building. I'm going to study on how I might open up those two gables and connect the building upstairs to give me a little more room. The apartment over my shop has two small rooms, and I'd love to spread out a bit."

"We can help you move the parson's things, Mrs. Armstrong." Cassie talked while she scrubbed.

Brand saw all three girls working hard and smiled.

The door behind Brand banged open, and two men, squabbling, shoved at each other as they both tried to squeeze through the doorway at the same time.

"We've got a justice of the peace who will finally do something." The taller of the two snarled and shoved at the shorter man.

"You bet she will. Judge Blodgett was always flouting the law. Never wanted to do his job."

"What is it now, gentlemen?" Nell cut through their bickering.

Brand thought *gentlemen* was a poor choice of words. "Gully's got his property line too far to the east and he's on my land. I've got the deed, and the land office agrees with me. I want him arrested."

"Macon's a liar—the land office does not agree." Gully was the tall one, who was pointing at the other man, almost breathing fire. "He's a thief and a cheat, and I want some justice." Gully waved a paper wildly in the air. "This proves my claim is right. Macon's determined to have what's mine, and I won't put up with it."

The two men stopped talking to Nell and went back to arguing with each other.

Brand was glad he was here. He didn't want Nell alone with such angry men, though so far their anger seemed to be focused on each other mostly.

Nell set aside her rag and picked up a stout stick, which must've been on the floor behind the counter. She banged away with it.

"Order. Order in this court," she demanded.

Court? Brand looked around the dingy building and didn't quite see it. But Nell kept banging until finally the men—furious, chests heaving, faces red—turned to glare at her.

She quit banging and jabbed a finger at each man in turn. "I am the justice of the peace, as you well know. You will behave yourself when you are in my presence or I will have you both arrested."

The men growled, their teeth bared, but they quit their arguing.

"I asked at the land office about your dispute," Nell began. "I told you both to let me look into it, and yet you storm in here again today arguing. You are very close to being fined for your behavior. Do you have the money to pay that fine?"

That even stopped the growling.

Cassie eased up beside Brand. "It's the third time today they've been in. They're the Stalk brothers, who homesteaded together north of town."

Brand nodded.

"The land you're arguing over is wasteland. A solid jumble of rocks and scrub trees. Neither one of you can feed a cow or grow a single cornstalk on that place."

"It's the principle of the thing," Gully said.

"I want what's mine." Macon took a step forward.

Brand braced himself to buy into a fight.

"I spoke to Mr. Kintzinger today at the land office. He said you've both been in there harassing him almost since the day you homesteaded last fall."

"That's because Kintzinger is a fool. He wrote up homesteading papers, and Judge Blodgett signed the deeds that created this mess."

Nell held up her hand, and her eyes flashed in that way Brand had seen when dealing with Doc Preston. "Do not interrupt me again, either of you."

Both men fell silent. Brand could hardly blame them.

"Percy Kintzinger said you've made nuisances of yourselves beyond rational thought. We—that is, Percy and I—have come up with a solution."

Cassie leaned close to Brand and whispered, "It won't work. They fight over everything."

Brand wondered if he should get his children out of there, but he couldn't leave Nell alone with the two men.

"The land you're arguing over is a five-foot strip of wasteland. Percy and I were able to solve your dispute because no one lives on either side of you. So, we're adding five feet to the east of your property, Macon, and five feet to the west of your property, Gully. Percy has the paperwork in order. Go get it, bring it here, and I'll sign over the provisional deed."

Both stood with their mouths agape.

Finally, Gully said, "B-but the land to the west of my property is no good. It's a tumbling pile of rocks. I don't want that land."

Nell jammed her hands on her hips. "Then why do you want the tumbling pile of rocks that is between your property and Macon's?"

Gully, subdued, answered, "It's the principle of the thing."

"The truth is, you both now own a bigger piece of land than you're legally allowed under the Homestead Act. Besides, much of the land near the mountains is wasteland. There's no way to prevent a few acres of it from being part of your claims. You may leave now."

The two men hesitated. Finally, together they turned and left the building. Brand watched them through the window and saw their scrapping pick up again as they crossed the street and disappeared into the land office.

Nell tossed the stick onto the floor behind the counter.

"Keep that stick close," Cassie said, "until Parson Blodgett gets here with his gavel."

Nell rolled her eyes. "The parson told me there wasn't much to this job. He didn't mention the Stalk brothers." Then a smile crept over her face, and she started laughing. The girls joined in.

"Thank you for all your help today, girls," Nell said.

"I can help, too." Brand felt left out. "I have some carpentry skills. I can open up this wall and put a door in. I'd have to see what's upstairs. I don't want to promise to do that work until I'm sure what all's involved."

Nell beamed at him. "That would be wonderful. And it's a paying job. I heard you've been hired for work like that around town. I'll have to hire someone, so it might as well be you."

"Sounds great. Show me what you want upstairs."

"We're almost done cleaning down here," Cassie said. "We can be finished by the time you show Pa the upstairs."

"Thank you, girls. Thank you so much." Nell started for the back. She led the way into a back room that looked clean already.

"I hauled things out of here all morning, then got this back room and the one across the hall tidied up. The front is the last of it down here, but we haven't worked upstairs yet."

A stairway stood at the back of the small room, built along the outside wall that formed the back of the building. Brand followed Nell upstairs. What they found there stopped him in his tracks. The whole room was filled with rubbish. Broken furniture and piles of scrap cloth. Wooden boxes and scattered heaps of unidentifiable trash.

Brand shook his head. "I can see what you mean about their leaving junk here. This will take awhile to clean up."

Nell shrugged one shoulder. "I'm planning to just toss things out the upstairs window. It'll drop into the alley, and later I'll drag it away to be burned."

"Let me go through some of this." Brand pointed to a

pile. "That looks like an old shelf with a broken board. I might be able to fix it. You could maybe use it as a bookcase."

Nell studied the refuse with her hands on her hips. "I think you're right. I saw a disaster and ignored the potential." Nell took a step closer to another pile of things, picked up something by the corner, and shook it. "This is a dress. Filthy, but I think it could be altered to fit Samantha. I need to be careful what I throw away. And yes, I'd appreciate it if you could salvage things from up here."

A large spider scrambled out of the stack of clothes, and Nell squeaked and stumbled backward right into Brand, who caught her before she fell.

Brand chuckled and set Nell back on her feet. "Are you scared of bugs, Judge Armstrong?"

She had staggered backward into him. Now she turned and gave him a sheepish smile. "No, I'm not afraid of bugs. I was just startled." Nell tilted her nose slightly in the air and sniffed. "I"—she touched herself lightly with her fingertips on her chest—"a duly sworn justice of the peace, do not scare easily."

"I've seen you in action the last few days, including just today downstairs, and that is the absolute truth."

She smirked at him. His eyes seemed to lock on that charming smirk. His hands came up to support her by holding her upper arms.

It flickered through his mind that he'd never really spent much time alone with Nell. Just the time riding home from the bull surgery, both of them filthy, bloody, and exhausted. But that wasn't a fair test. There had been that family hug. Right now, though . . .

"It's the absolute truth that you're brave and kind and smart . . ."

Now Nell was studying his lips, but he knew he wasn't smirking.

"And you're generous to my girls. And . . . the most beautiful woman I've ever seen."

He kissed her, tempted beyond words to see what her smirk tasted like.

She kissed him back, her arms wrapping around his neck. His surrounded her waist.

Footsteps pounded on the stairs. "Pa, why did Mrs. Armstrong scream?"

Brand dropped her like a hot coal, turned, and ran smack into the sloped ceiling that angled down beside the gabled window. He staggered back but took a few more steps than necessary to pretend he'd been looking out the window.

Samantha entered the room while Brand kept doing his best to look absolutely transfixed by the fascinating scene out the window—of another gabled roof and some shingles.

"It was a spider," Nell explained. "Silly of me to make a fuss." Her voice drew a glance from Brand. She was picking up a pile of . . . of something. "I'm not scared of spiders, but the way it jumped out startled a scream out of me." Then Nell paused and looked at Sam with an exaggerated scowl. "No, a squeak. Surely I didn't *scream* over a silly old spider."

Sam giggled. "Call it whatever you wish. From downstairs it sounded like a scream."

"I-I think I can figure out a way to connect these two

upstairs rooms." Brand kept his eyes on the window, except for that one quick glance over his shoulder at Nell, who somehow looked for all the world like a woman who was completely calm. A woman who hadn't just been kissed.

A woman who felt nothing of what Brand felt.

It helped clear his head, at least a little. He focused on what lay before him and that it wouldn't be too hard to connect the two buildings. The gables would be large enough if he took out the windows, frames and all.

"Sam, come and look out here," Brand said.

His daughter went to his side. "Samantha, Pa, you promised."

He rested his arm across her shoulders. "Keep reminding me. I'll do it, but I might slip up once in a while. Now"—he pointed to the front of the stores—"see how the roof is peaked but the front of the building is squared off?"

"Yes, I didn't even think of that, but from the front the buildings look like they have flat roofs."

"That's called a façade. It makes the buildings look fancier than they are. A common enough way to build a business along the main street of town. But if we opened up this gable, and that one across to Mrs. Armstrong's room, we could build a walkway, enclosed, up here. It would be such a short walk, it'd be like stepping from one room to another."

Brand was all the way calmed down by the time he finished answering Samantha's questions.

Nell had moved to the other side of Samantha to listen, out of reach of the lummox she probably regretted hiring now. Nell Armstrong, suffragist who made no secret of her wish to have no man in her life.

He was lucky she hadn't slapped him. Although from his extremely vivid memory of that kiss, there'd been no protest from those pink lips. No, he still felt her arms sliding around his neck. In fact—

"Pa, are you listening?"

His head snapped around to look Nell in the eyes. Then his gaze slid down to his exasperated daughter. "Um . . . I-I'm sorry, I was thinking about . . . about, well, uh . . . the buildings." He cleared his throat because he needed a few seconds before he could say things that made sense. "No, I didn't hear you because I was so busy thinking about building the walkway. What did you say?"

"I said *let's go*. We're gonna be late for supper as it is."

"I've got a stew on, and the chores are done except we'll need to put up the horses and grain them. But we can be washed up and eating a few minutes after we get home."

Samantha nodded, said goodbye to Nell, and hurried for the stairs, vanishing from between Brand and Nell. Their little safety barrier was gone.

Nell caught his eye again for one long second before turning away, as if it was all she could do to force herself to stride away toward the stairs, then down without a backward glance.

He followed more slowly. The girls were ready to go and stepping out the door by the time he'd reached the bottom of the steps.

"Pa," Cassie said as she climbed onto the broad back of their gray mustang, "we should have Mrs. Armstrong out for supper. It's not fair she's worked so hard all day, and now we leave her to a lonely meal."

"I'm used to it, Cassandra. And I'm tired. I'll be glad for a quiet night." Nell thanked the girls again as she was always so mindful to do.

Brand feared he wasn't as kind to his girls as she was.

Samantha clambered up behind Cassie.

Resolving to do better, Brand said, "We have our usual chores tomorrow, but with the girls home to help, it'll go fast. We'll come in tomorrow to help clean out the new town courthouse, and maybe I can get a start on the downstairs door at least. I've got the tools I need to do the work, and I'll cut the boards carefully and use them to make a door. I will need lumber to connect the two gables. I'll have to find out how to order that. I'll do it tomorrow."

"That's not necessary." Nell took a quick glance at him that reminded him he'd had her in his arms not that long ago.

Her protest was drowned out by the girls' cheers of excitement.

"There . . . you've got your answer," he said. "We'll be in, and maybe I can bring that pot of stew if there's any left." Brand plopped Michaela up onto their chestnut draft horse. They were a funny-looking pair of horses because the draft horse was huge and dark, the mustang small and gray. "By suppertime tomorrow, you'll be dreaming of a quiet meal alone."

Samantha reached across from her horse to where Brand had swung up behind Michaela and gave her pa a teasing swat on the arm. Cassie giggled. Michaela leaned back so her head rested right on Brand's heart.

"I'd appreciate the help very much. You can ask Mariah about hinges and nails and whatever else is needed to work on the building. She'd know more about sawn boards than I do, too. I'll see you all tomorrow."

Brand took one good long look at her, and her gaze met his for too long. Her fingers crept up to touch her lips. He thought she was remembering being kissed. He sure knew he was remembering that she'd kissed him back.

Then Samantha steered her horse toward home, and Brand's horse followed, impatient for the rider to give it some guidance. The horse must've decided that if Brand wasn't going to take charge, it would put itself in charge.

Which left Brand with nothing to do, since the horse was doing just fine on its own. Brand's mind went straight back to catching Nell when she'd fallen.

And how he'd held her too close for too long. And now he was left with a restless, overly warm feeling and no idea what to do with it.

Well, being an honest man, he admitted to himself that he had some idea.

He kicked his horse to catch up with Samantha and Cassie, and they all took to chattering about their day cleaning. Brand paid rapt attention to keep his mind from wandering to where he knew it wanted to go.

22

Nell worked until after midnight because she was afraid to close her eyes and think about kissing Brandon Nolte.

She had the downstairs completely clean. She'd burned the midnight oil sorting out a lot of serviceable clothing. Everything she could save she'd hauled downstairs. There were women's and children's clothes, some suitable for Brand's girls, but there were things for little boys too, and those could go to the Blodgett family. There were also several pieces of furniture that must have been cast aside when they broke.

That'd keep Brand busy for a while. The moment his name came to mind, she threw herself even more frantically into work.

She clearly had no business deciding anyone's guilt or innocence, even though a jury would do most of that. But Nell had to sentence them, and she could torment herself thinking of locking up someone innocent.

She'd found a repairable chair and a table she could sit

behind downstairs. Oh, there were treasures here. Filthy, dust-coated treasures for sure, but treasures nonetheless.

She'd worked until she was about to drop and finally believed she could get to sleep. And after a bath, she did.

Then she dreamed and dreamed and dreamed until the dream turned into something closer, something more familiar, and she roused to the sound of someone climbing her stairs.

"Nell, are you all right?"

The blur of sleep was swept away as she heard Brand's voice. A very worried voice.

Throwing off her blanket, she rushed for the door to block him from coming in. "I'm—"

The door swung open on her first word before she could reach it. Brand rushed in and caught her around the waist. "Is everything okay?"

The feel of his strong arms around her muddled her mind enough that she couldn't answer. She rested her hands on his shoulders to balance herself.

His eyes were wide, searching the room before coming back to settle on her. "We went to the other building and saw how much work you'd done. Do you know what time it is? Is everything okay?"

"Everything is fine. I suppose I just worked too late last night."

"Oh, thank God. I've been praying like mad since we found your door unlocked downstairs."

"I left the door unlocked?"

"Yes, to the dress shop and the other building. I was afraid something terrible had happened to you. I set the girls to working—if they can find any work left to do. They headed upstairs with buckets and brooms."

Which meant he was alone here with her. A man she should not be alone with ever, let alone while wearing her nightgown.

"Go on now. I'll be right along as soon as I—"

A kiss quieted her right down.

Once again it went on far too long. And she wanted it to go on longer. At last he lifted his head. "I've been thinking of you, of nothing but you since we kissed yesterday."

She stepped out of his arms. It was harder than she'd expected because her arms were wrapped around his neck. She had no memory of grabbing ahold of him like that.

He reached for her and brushed the hair back from her face with gentle hands. She realized the braid she'd worn to bed was all loose.

"Your hair is soft and beautiful. I want to touch it again, often." Then he smiled. "You go get ready for the day. I'm going next door to try to get ahold of myself by tearing down a wall."

He spun around as if forcing himself to move and was almost running when he went out the door. He clicked it shut. His feet thundered on the stairs, and Nell staggered as she headed for her bedroom. She had some work to do to make herself presentable for the day. Touching her lips, they felt swollen and tender.

She hesitated, wanting to think about what he'd woken up inside her. Then she decided thinking could wait. She rushed through her dressing, wearing an old riding skirt and shirtwaist. The one similar outfit she had was dirty from yesterday.

Taking as little time as possible, she went to join the Nolte family at work.

"Nell, the place looks wonderful. We came to work, but it looks like you're mostly done."

Nell glanced up from where she knelt over a washtub full of soapy water. She'd washed and rinsed and emptied and refilled it again many times.

"Mariah! Hello! Clint, both of you come on in. The place is almost ready to use. And we've found some old clothes I think the girls can wear and maybe a few things for the Blodgett family, too." Nell pointed to a rope she'd hung across the side of the room, clothes hanging from it.

Clint came in behind Mariah, carrying a basket. He looked at Brand, who stood by the shared wall between Nell's shop and the courthouse.

Brand said, "We were going to open this wall to connect a doorway to Nell's shop, but Nell's got second thoughts. If she doesn't stay on as justice of the peace, she might regret joining the buildings. We're discussing it. She wants the upstairs connected, too. Maybe we should do that first."

"I've got the hinges you asked for." Mariah held them up.

"And I brought fried chicken, so we have a meal." Clint set the basket on the front counter. Their puppy, Spike, and Brutus had come along.

Spike came to Nell's side and sniffed her wash water, then lapped at it.

Nell caught him. "No, Spike. Soapy water isn't good for you."

A thump from upstairs drew Mariah's attention. "Are the girls here working?"

Spike heard the noise and ran toward it, Brutus on his heels.

"They're doing fine work up there, scrubbing and sweeping and dusting. We've got all the junk hauled down. What can be saved is in the back room on the left. What we're burning is out back, ready for when I can build a fire. There is a nice pile of clothes the former owner abandoned. They'll need some mending, but that can wait."

"You'll be able to start working by Monday." Mariah took the dress from Nell and hung it while Nell picked up another one.

"I've already started working. The Stalk brothers were in three times yesterday. I've also signed three provisional deeds to new homesteaders. And I've had two lawsuits filed—both of them foolish, in my opinion. There was a fistfight at the saloon last night. Sheriff Joe was in to tell me he's got two men locked up and doesn't like keeping them over the weekend because he has to feed them and stay close by, sleeping at the jailhouse. I guess we're having a trial this afternoon."

"All that already?" Mariah said.

"Yes, and then there's the case concerning Mr. Campbell's death. Working as justice of the peace is a bigger job than Parson Blodgett made it out to be. Maybe folks were too afraid of him to come in with their complaints?"

"Could be. Anything else?"

"No," Nell replied, "except that Mr. Kintzinger has brought in a printing press from Laramie. He's starting a newspaper in Pine Valley, only he's been slow about getting the first issue out."

"Percival is starting a paper?" Clint was setting out the food, which was much more than just fried chicken.

"That's great." Brand came in from the back room with a tub of clean rinse water. "This town is getting to be a real city. A newspaper and a courthouse. I picked a good place to settle."

"Seems like plenty has been going on here. Percy was already here last fall when I was shot. Why didn't he start a newspaper then? Strange he's just now decided to write up the news."

"Maybe your troubles influenced him to get the press this spring and start a newspaper. I guess having a woman justice of the peace is big enough news he thinks the bigger newspapers will pick up his story and reprint it. Stories about Esther Morris from out of South Pass City reached as far as New York. Now he wants to do a story about me declaring the triumph of equality in Wyoming." Nell grinned. "I'll be in the first issue of the *Pine Valley Mirror*. He said it's going to be one page—the newspaper, not the story about me. Just one sheet, front and back, to start with. I offered to write up court news and even perhaps write a column for him."

"So, you'll be on the front and back of the newspaper?" Mariah straightened the clothes hanging on the line. "And you're writing half of it? *You* should have started a newspaper."

Clint said from behind the counter, "You're doing everything else, why not that?"

"I'll wait and see how many copies the poor man sells

before I let it go to my head." Nell chuckled as she plunged a child's dress into the clean water and rinsed it. Satisfied the dress was clean and the soap gone, she wrung it out good. "I'm hoping the man can think of someone besides me to write about."

"You should put in an ad for chaps."

Nell feigned throwing the dripping dress at Mariah, who didn't yelp or run. Nell figured her threat wasn't overly frightening.

"Clint could put in an ad for the diner."

Brand went to call the girls down to eat.

"You know, that's not a bad idea." Clint set out a bowl of potato salad and a platter of biscuits. "I could plan out a week's worth of menus and put it in the paper so folks would know when I'm serving their favorites. Some might come in who otherwise wouldn't, and that would more than pay for the ad."

"The parson stopped in when he saw us working here, then went home to gather the things he's storing. He's bringing them over right away. I worked so late last night that I slept until midmorning. But the downstairs is ready." Nell didn't mention that Brand had woken her up and kissed her—in her nightgown.

Mariah came to take the dress while Nell got to her feet, her knees creaky after an hour of scrubbing filthy but mostly unstained, unfaded clothes.

"I'll need to do a bit of mending on a few of these things, but the parson can take most of the smaller boys' clothes home with him. He's bringing Mrs. Blodgett and the children over to help carry everything. Now I won't send them home empty-handed."

Mariah hung the dress over the rope, then went to the picnic Clint was setting out and put the food on a shelf behind the counter.

"Why did you do that?" Nell asked.

"We didn't make enough for the whole Blodgett family. Bless their hearts, but they eat like a locust swarm."

The parson appeared at the door carrying a wooden crate. Behind him, four of his boys held a heavy table. His daughter carried an infant and a large book. Mrs. Blodgett stood behind them with an armload of papers and holding the hand of a little boy.

They came in, and Parson Blodgett set his box down, asked Nell where to put everything, then out of his box he drew a gavel made of highly varnished dark wood.

When they were all inside and Nell had her hands dry, Parson Blodgett said to Nell, "It is my great honor to hand this gavel to you. I have every confidence that you, Judge Armstrong, will tend to the duties of your office with wisdom and honesty."

He bowed slightly, then extended the gavel to her. "Her Honor, Judge Eleanor Armstrong, first female justice of the peace in Pine Valley, Wyoming. You are now part of history, Judge Armstrong."

Nell couldn't be so solemn. She smiled as she took the gavel. Then she went to the table the judge had brought in and hammered it. "Case dismissed."

Mrs. Blodgett started laughing. Clint and Mariah joined in. Nell's grin went to a full laugh as Parson Blodgett added his. Their children were soon snickering. Brand laughed out loud. His girls came down to see what the fuss was all about just as Mrs. Blodgett uncovered the bundle she'd carried over. It was a basketful of ham sandwiches and a small container of cookies. Parson Blodgett pulled out a big jar of iced tea from his box and plenty of glasses.

They'd brought lunch as well as the tools needed for her job as justice of the peace. Mariah gave Nell a sheepish grin, then got her chicken back on the countertop.

She was right, the Blodgetts did eat like a swarm of locusts. But so did the rest of them.

The nicest locust swarm in the land.

23

Nell had a gavel.

A gavel and a black robe she'd made for herself.

It was Monday morning. She'd released the men who'd been in the fistfight at the saloon on Saturday. She'd already signed off on one provisional deed, and the Stalk brothers had already been in once. Gully and Macon had their adjusted deeds. Now Macon was accusing Gully of teaching Macon's horse to kick.

Nell sat behind a table in her robe, held the gavel up in front of her face, and couldn't stop smiling. She was a judge. And by golly she was going to rule this town with a firm hand.

She had the green clothbound docket showing the history of the town's cases. Parson Blodgett, with Mayor Wainwright, the sheriff, and Doc Preston at his side, had come over and ceremonially handed over the docket with great pomp. Each man had shaken her hand and wished her the best.

Her first actions were far less than fierce and firm. She'd

signed the provisional deed for a nice couple who came over from the land office after filing a homestead. It was hard to be fierce when a hopeful young couple, the wife clearly expecting a child soon, was glowing with excitement to set down roots.

Nell was so happy for them that she resolved to arrange a house raising and meals and introduce Doc Preston to them. And maybe she'd make the woman a dress. Hers was uncomfortably tight. Nell would make it into a personal *Welcome to Pine Valley* gift.

After the couple left, the woman clinging to the young man's arm, the two of them chattering and planning, Nell brought down her gavel on the wide oak table for the empty office to hear, then set the gavel aside.

In came the Stalk brothers. They'd gotten to the land office after Percy had closed on Friday. Nell knew he was in there, but he'd probably hidden under his desk until the brothers went away.

Next came James Burk. He was angry at the land office because they didn't show proper respect for the dead. Apparently, folks tended to speak with some volume and excitement when they signed up for a homestead.

"They should speak more quietly so near my mortuary. I have a sign clearly posted. What is the world coming to if people don't speak quietly next door?"

Nell thought of Mrs. Mussel coming to speak in Pine Valley. She thought of Wyoming Territory voting for women to have the right to vote. She thought of herself right now, sitting behind an impressive oak table with her very own gavel. She thought the world was coming to something much better.

"I'll speak to Mr. Kintzinger," she said. "He can remind his customers to speak more respectfully so near the dead." Nell looked at the rather peevish man. A black frock coat. A somewhat tall top hat. He was dressed nicely, but it was all rather old and careworn.

Being an undertaker probably didn't pay well, especially considering the last few corpses he'd had to see to were taken away by family, with two exceptions. No one came for the gambler or one of the men wearing Western garb. And no one paid Mr. Burk for his hastily knocked together coffins for strangers. But known or not, coffins had to be built, holes dug. Mr. Burk handled all of that.

"You haven't heard from anyone concerning Mr. Campbell?"

"No, but the sheriff is trying to track him down. If family wants to come for his body, they're welcome to, otherwise we'll just plant him in our own boot hill."

Mr. Burk's eyes narrowed, and he planted his hand flat on Nell's table. "The town should pay me something for tending to the bodies of strangers. If they don't, I'm not standing the cost of any more pine boxes."

"I can't blame you for that, Jim. But it's not really the city's responsibility, either. No one paid Doc for sitting with Mr. Campbell for a whole week. That poor man had been thoroughly robbed. However, I think you're right. You've stood the cost of the pine boxes and you've done it graciously, contributing your time because you like to see people buried with decency. Still, that shouldn't be at your cost. I'll bring it up at the next town council meeting. Maybe something should be done for the doctor, too."

Jim straightened to his full height, and Nell had to wonder if he'd made this same complaint to Parson Blodgett
a number of times. Jim's expression turned grudgingly
pleased. To describe it as cheerful would take more opti-
mism than Nell had. "That's mighty good of you, Mrs.
Armstrong. Uh, I mean Judge Armstrong. Or maybe Your
Honor? Should I call you that?"

Nell fought a smile because she liked the sound of it so
much. "Any of those names are fine. I'll answer to all of
them. Thank you for coming to me with a very reasonable request."

He left without his usual dour expression. Nell had
heard he charged one dollar for his services, pine box,
and the hole dug and backfilled. He used scrap boards
for the coffins, which he'd stolen from a collapsed house a
mile south of town. She decided she'd donate to the town
treasury for undertaker services for which there was no
family. Because the only other choice she could see was
to drop strangers into a shallow hole she dug herself. Not
having to do that was well worth one dollar.

She'd hung a sign she'd hand-drawn in the window of
her courthouse:

Pine Valley Town Council's Office
and
Pine Valley Courthouse

She saw no one coming, so on a little hook she'd screwed
into the bottom of the main sign, she hung a second one:

Go next door if you need service.

Signs in place, she hung her robe on a nail behind her tidy judge's desk, with the green book centered on it. Then she went back to her shop to work on a dress for the newest homesteader. She'd eyeballed the young woman enough to not need measurements. The woman was a bit taller than Becky, a bit shorter than Mariah, and quite round in the belly. She had her friends' measurements on hand, so she'd use them.

Nell spent her first morning as Judge Armstrong, Your Honor, making a dress for the new homesteader. In the afternoon, when the girls arrived after school, she could keep them busy with the clothes she'd salvaged, washed, and ironed. She'd need to make some alterations, as the dresses seemed to be cut along slightly larger lines than the girls, but that wouldn't be hard and the girls could help. She'd teach them how to make the clothes fit.

While they worked, she'd tell them more about the cause of suffrage and about the doors opening wide to women. And that included them.

No chaps today. But the girls were coming along nicely with their sewing skills, and it had only been a couple of weeks. Nell would feel comfortable leaving the girls here to work if she was called next door to her justice-of-the-peace duties.

Brand rode into town later than usual. Not late to pick up the girls, just later than usual because, since the girls had started working with Nell, he'd been coming in to watch the unfortunate Mr. Campbell. But now, with the tragic end to sentry duty, he waited as best he could for two hours after school let out, then rode into town. He didn't quite make two hours, of course, because he just couldn't quite stay away that long.

He kept thinking of Nell and how she'd fit in his arms.

As he rode in from the east, behind the row of Main Street businesses, Henry Wainwright waved him down. The man was standing behind Nell's shop, almost like he'd been watching for Brand.

Maybe he wanted Brand to do a day's work. The money was always welcome. It'd been a good week for advancing the financial stability of the Nolte family.

A pig arrived from Becky, along with a crew to build a pen. She'd also sent a month's worth of corn for feed plus a bear roast along with cooking directions. And the bottle of laudanum with a note that her bull was recovering nicely.

Now maybe he could add a day's wages.

Dismounting, Brand said, "Hello, Henry. Did you need something?" Brand hoped so.

"Yes, I need something. You seemed to be pretty tied up with Mrs. Armstrong."

"T-tied up? What?" Brand's mind went wild. Had someone seen him kissing her? But that was impossible, wasn't it?

"Your girls are in there every day. You come calling and speak to her frequently."

Brand nodded, silent, afraid of what might come out of his mouth.

"Well, I want this nonsense stopped. This town doesn't need a woman justice of the peace. It's outrageous. It's a disgrace."

189

Brand's pounding heart slowed, then sped up again as his temper ignited. And he was an even-tempered man. "Isn't your brother the mayor of Pine Valley?"

"Yes, yes, of course he is. But he got hog-tied into going along with the sheriff and the doc and Parson Blodgett. He's only got one vote, and when he saw the way the wind was blowing, he went along. But both of us are sick about it. No decent woman would have any part of it."

"Nell is a decent woman, Henry. I won't stand by and hear you say otherwise."

Henry waved his hands almost violently. "I'm not saying she's not decent. Don't get all het up about it. I'm saying she *is* decent and so she's going to hear things no woman should be exposed to. This job can't help but make a good woman coarse and unladylike."

It flickered through Brand's head all he'd seen and heard. Nell backing the doctor off when he took offense at her questions. Nell had examined those dead bodies. Nell had helped with surgery on Ian Campbell. For heaven's sake, she'd helped with surgery on an Angus bull.

"The West is a rough place. I doubt that anyone, whether man, woman, or child, can get through life without seeing some terrible things. I don't really like what she may be exposed to, but Mariah Roberts was shot during a stagecoach robbery. Becky Pruitt had to shoot a grizzly that tore up her bull. It's said that Parson Blodgett discussed all his cases with his wife and considered her counsel as excellent. It's kind of you to worry about Nell, but she can handle this. I have confidence in her ability to remain refined and ladylike throughout her work as a judge."

Brand thought he sounded pretty good and even-keeled there when what he really wanted was to plant a fist in Henry's face. Nell had talent and strength and the knowledge this town needed to do the job. And she couldn't be coarse if her life depended on it.

"I'm not the only one who feels this way. Being a woman, she's weak, her intelligence not up to the task. She'll make Pine Valley a laughingstock, and knowing we have an incompetent woman doing the job only a man is fit to do might attract crime to our town. In the end, Nell might even be in danger because she took this job. You mark my words, Brand, she won't be in the job long. If we can't get her to do the right thing and resign, then we'll vote her out and be glad to do it."

With his jaw clamped so tight he was afraid his teeth might be grinding down to powder, Brand had to take a few breaths before he could speak. "If there's a vote, then my vote will be for Nell. Give her a chance before you go around stirring up trouble."

"I figured there was something going on with you two. I reckon a man sniffing around a woman's skirts can't be expected to be honest about much." Henry spun around and marched toward the back door of the general store. He moved fast, and it was a good thing, because Brand grabbed at him and missed.

Then Henry was inside, and Brand caught a glimpse, or thought he did, of Peter standing by an open window.

Did that mean Peter agreed with Henry? Did Henry speak for both Wainwright brothers? Brand's respect for the men faded. It was a shame too, because he'd liked the Wainwrights. He hated being at odds with them.

Shaking his head, fighting down his temper, Brand caught up his horses and led them around to the front of the dress shop, where he tied them up. Through a window he saw all three of his girls, sitting neatly attired in their perfect ladylike dresses, fabric in their hands, needles tightly gripped, hard at work at whatever task Nell had set before them.

And then there was Nell, sitting beside them, all four of them in a row working at her table, matching expressions of concentration on their faces.

He wanted to shout about what Henry had just said. He was furious and he wanted to tell Nell everything. He even wondered if he should warn her. Henry's words could be taken as a threat. But Henry was a good, hardworking man. He wouldn't *threaten* anyone. But he could be warning Nell.

Or hoping Brand would.

But Brand couldn't do that. Why would he say something that would only upset her? Worse yet, say it in front of his girls.

He'd gone to considerable lengths to protect his girls from the ugly talk of the Deadeye Gang, the wounded man, and the dead bodies.

"In the end, Nell might even be in danger because she took this job."

He should tell her. But he'd just scare her, and over nothing but the empty words of a disgruntled man.

Brand shoved aside his anger at Henry and walked up the steps to enter the shop.

Nell saw the girls perk up and that told her Brand was coming.

He opened the door as she stood to gather the girls' new things.

"I found clothes the girls can use among the abandoned things in that building. Girls, help me carry this."

Nell had packaged three piles, wrapped them all in one of the sturdier dresses, and tied it tight with string. "I hope you'll be able to tote this home on horseback."

She was very deliberately avoiding looking at him. Then she thought that might be noticeable, so she looked at him, and he seemed to be very deliberately not looking at her.

Internally shaking away all her confused feelings at the sight of him, the memory of his kissing her, she gave each girl her bundle.

"What's this?" he asked.

That made her look at him, and this time their eyes met.

"I-I just said. These are some of the clothes from the building next door. They'll fit the girls." She thought he looked upset. Was this a trampling on male pride again? Then she looked closer and saw something else, something more. He was upset. In fact, his expression reminded her of Web when he'd come home in a temper. She'd never seen much sign of a bad temper in Brand before. But maybe all men lost their temper from time to time.

Joshua Pruitt was known to be mean, though Becky never spoke of her pa hitting her. It was impossible to imagine Clint slapping Mariah, or for that matter, Parson Blodgett getting after his wife. But who knew about such things? She suspected no one had ever dreamed that the honorable Sheriff Web Armstrong slapped his wife.

Right now, what she saw in Brand frightened her.

"Thanks for the help today, girls."

They all walked out of the shop, bundles in hand. Brand stood there as they passed him, watching her. Finally, he shook his head, almost like he'd been asleep and was waking up.

"You be careful, Nell." He said it quietly and used her first name, like he had a right to such familiarity. And maybe he did. "Be mighty careful. There's . . . there's . . . well, there might be trouble ahead."

Then, because he'd already stood there for too long, he whirled around, stalked outside, and mounted up behind Michaela.

Nell couldn't move for a few seconds, so instead she stood there and watched the Nolte family ride away.

Feeling nervous after Brand's strange warning, she hurried to the door, slipped inside, and locked it. She no longer felt comfortable in her shop alone, so she went to the lantern and turned it down, then ran upstairs to lock her apartment door, as well.

She lay awake a long time trying to figure out just what kind of trouble Brand was talking about.

24

Brand let it chew on him, worrying about what Henry had said about Nell.

The next Monday, he went to ride home with his girls, picked them up from Nell's. Stayed inside just long enough to say thank you while the girls filed out, then he left.

Nell surely didn't try to keep him longer, so he was thinking she was in agreement that they needed to stay away from each other.

His girls were dressed properly now, though the clothes from the courthouse weren't as nice as the new ones. Nell and the girls had done a stellar job of repairing them, so the girls now had three dresses apiece. They'd set aside the dresses Nell had made to be their Sunday best for church.

On Tuesday, Samantha had her sixteenth birthday and declared she was done wearing britches at home, preferring to wear a dress all the time. She had a cup of coffee with Brand in the mornings, too.

"But you've tasted it before and said it was nasty," Brand reminded her.

"I have more grown-up tastes than I used to, Pa. I like a little milk in it, but I've decided I like it."

Brand looked at his two other girls, sitting at the breakfast table, all ready to head for school. "Do you girls want coffee, too?"

Cassie's lip curled. "Ugh. No."

Michaela giggled. "I'd as soon chew ashes from the fireplace. It's a strange business, drinking something so bitter."

Samantha finished her coffee and rose from the table. "I'll go saddle the horses. Michaela and Cassie, you clean up the kitchen. Pa, you've got time to gather the eggs and feed the chickens."

Samantha grinned at Brand, sassy, giving orders as if she were in charge. She liked it, though, and he liked watching her run things because she was good at it. And besides, they all did things this way every day.

Samantha walked outside. Cassie rose from the table and picked up her plate. Michaela jumped in to help. Brand watched the girls, so proud of them he could hardly stand it. Then he grabbed his hat and opened the door just as the screaming began.

A vicious growl accompanied Samantha's cries of fear. His rifle was over the door. He grabbed it and ran.

He reached the barn door, which was closed. Sam must've gone in the side door, but that wasn't usual. He tore it open to see a wolf drag Samantha to the ground. He lifted the rifle, hating to shoot so close to Sam, but there was no time. He fired. The yelp told him he'd made a hit, but the wolf wasn't down. Brand sprinted and dove at the wolf, still growling and biting Sam. He slammed into it, carrying the monster to the ground. The wolf snarled, and its teeth snapped just inches from Brand's throat. Another impact took the weight of the wolf away.

He barely registered his daughter's blood-soaked face as he wheeled and grabbed at the attacking beast. He rolled the wolf off Samantha and wrapped his arms around it from behind. He lay on his back on the floor, trying his best to choke the life out of the animal.

He felt a blow to the wolf, then another. Voices shouting, screaming got through the ugly snarling. The wolf yelped and fought Brand's grip, but he would hang on while there was life in his body.

Finally, a crack of gunfire stopped the wolf's fight. It dropped dead on top of Brand.

Heaving to catch his breath, Brand blinked to focus on his barn. Samantha stood, bleeding terribly, but on her feet. Cassie stood next to her with Brand's still-smoking rifle in her hands. Michaela wielded a bloodstained knife. A glance at the wolf told him one daughter had fought with the blade, another with the rifle. One with her bare hands to save him.

He wanted to hug them all, but there was no time.

"Sam, we've got to get you to the doc."

Cassie dropped the rifle and sprinted for the horses. "In the corral. I'll get them."

"I'm coming." Brand wanted to gather Samantha into his arms, but for now he had to get her to help. He dashed outside to see Cassie holding both horses by their halters, leading them in.

"Don't spook them, Pa."

"I know they were inside last night." Brand stayed back.

His wild surge of fear and the turmoil he still felt from the fight might indeed spook the horses.

Cassie got them inside, and Brand rushed for the first saddle. Michaela held the halters as Cassie saddled her horse.

"We all go. Now! Michaela, ride with Cassie."

Brand gathered Sam up and swung up on his horse with her in his arms. They were galloping before they got out of the yard.

Brand looked down at Sam. "You've been bit. How bad is it?"

Samantha wept in his arms, her hands on the wounds on her face. She shook her head and didn't speak.

They were in town in record time. "Girls, tie up the horses and then come inside with me."

His boots hit the ground with his daughter in his arms. Only then did he realize Samantha had fainted. He couldn't bear to imagine it was something worse.

He crashed through the door. "Doc, help!"

Doc Preston tore out of his back room. "What happened? Come this way." He rushed into his examining room, Brand close on his heels.

"Wolf attack. I don't know how bad it is."

"Down here." Doc pointed at the table.

Cassie and Michaela ran into the room.

Doc looked at them. "Cassie, get Mrs. Armstrong. She's the best nurse, and I need the best."

Cassie did as she was told.

Michaela, her face streaked with tears, blood on her hands, wept as she stood by Samantha.

"Are you hurt, too?" Doc asked Michaela.

Brand saw that her hands were crimson. He'd barely glanced at her as he wrung out a wet cloth and swiped the blood away from Samantha's neck.

"No. It's the wolf's blood, not mine. How can I help?"

"Wash up." Doc Preston pointed to an empty basin. "Then refill it with clean water from the hot water wells on my stove and bring it here."

Brand thought of how the wolf went for his jugular. It would've done that to Samantha too, if given a little more time.

"No severed artery here," the doctor announced. "Bad bites on one arm. Her face, her scalp. You're bleeding too, Brand."

He hadn't noticed it and didn't feel it.

Nell and Cassie came charging in. Nell seemed to take everything in with one second's attention and said, "Cassie, we need more hot water—keep it coming. Toss the dirty water out in the street, then bring fresh. Michaela, on the shelf over there"—she jabbed a finger—"are clean rags. Get them." Her eyes flew to Brand for a split second. "Let me in there. Doc, did you order that carbolic acid? Wolf bites are filthy."

"I did. Brand, it's in the glass-fronted shelf. It's marked."

Brand realized that for all his running, his desperation, his standing ready to help, he'd frozen and done little. Getting a direct order helped him move.

Nell took his place.

"Look for more bites," Doc said. "I see no arteries bleeding, but she got torn up pretty bad. We'll be stitching on her awhile."

Brand returned with the carbolic acid, desperate for

more orders. Desperate to help. But no one said a word, so he turned his attention to his girls. The ones not lying stretched out on a table.

Nell snapped at Brand, "Before you do another thing, check your own bites. Staunch the bleeding. If you can't, tell us. Doc has more basins, so get clean water for yourself. You can wait until we've helped Samantha."

Michaela set a stack of rags on a table by Nell's left hand.

Cassie said, "I'll check him over."

The young'un was so calm, Nell worried about her. It wasn't natural. Unless the child was just excellent in an emergency. Right now, Nell needed the help, so she'd worry about the unnerving calm later.

Cassie set a pan of steaming water by Doc's side and took a basin away. Then she brought one to Nell. By then Doc needed clean rags, and by the time Cassie took half of Nell's stack to him, Doc needed more clean water. The little girl was rushing around, doing exactly what was needed. Michaela was doing the same.

Cassie turned her attention to her pa whenever she had a free second.

Nell pressed a warm cloth to the nasty bite that had ripped up the right side of Samantha's face. This one was going to scar, and it made Nell sick to think of it. Samantha's eyes flickered open. "Pa?"

"She's waking up." Nell reached for the laudanum.

"Just half a spoonful." Doc barely looked away from where he worked on a bite on Samantha's shoulder. It would scar too, as would the ones on her head and three on her back. But clothing and hair would cover those.

Brand was at Samantha's side before Nell could pour out the dose.

"I'm here, Sam. I'm here. You're going to be fine. Let Mrs. Armstrong give you some medicine." He eased back, holding his daughter's gaze but getting out of the way.

Nell felt the love coming from him in waves. His fear and worry and compassion for his badly injured child.

Sliding an arm under Samantha's shoulders, Nell eased her up enough to get the bitter medicine into her. The doctor stopped working to let his patient take the painkiller. She shuddered but swallowed it.

"Here, drink some water." Nell set the spoon aside and picked up a tin cup of water. "Wash the bad taste away."

A few sips later, Sam's lids began to close. Her muscles relaxed, and Nell laid her down flat.

"Give it another minute until she falls fully to sleep." The doctor looked at Brand. "I'll check your wrist while we wait."

"No, Sam comes first. I—"

The doctor quieted him with a look and soon had his wrist bathed and bandaged. "You need stitches, but it can wait. You're going to be fine. Both of you are going to be fine."

While Doc worked on Brand, Nell focused on Samantha. "You should take the stitches here, Doc." Nell didn't say where. She didn't want the girls to hear it. They'd see it, but later. When the wound was closed. It would be bad enough then.

"I saw the stitches you made with Campbell, Nell.

You've a fine hand with them. They'll heal up better with your touch."

Nodding, she hated that it would be her hand on the sewing up of this sweet young lady, but also knew the doctor was right. She had a finer hand than he did. She drew a deep breath and set to work.

Nell lost track of time as she took over the right side of Samantha's body while Doc did the left.

Washing the wounds, dusting them with the carbolic powder, she focused on repairing them. She refused to think of the scars and pain. She was deeply grateful that Samantha was sleeping through it all.

Cassie said, "There's a nasty bite on your shoulder, Pa. Some claw marks, too. Not too serious, I hope."

The doctor looked over at Brand and his eyes narrowed. "I didn't even notice that other bite."

"Neither did I." Brand, his voice unsteady, said, "A wolf in our barn. I sent Samantha out by herself."

Nell heard his voice break. She could imagine how a father would blame himself. She would like to comfort him, hold him, but there was no time for that now. Stitching up Samantha while she was in a faint was far too important.

Doc snipped at Sam's hair. He had to clip it short to get his threads in without any hair getting in the way. Nell fought down the terrible regret for what they were doing to Sam. The scars, the shorn hair. The kind of thing that made a girl feel ugly for a long time. Yes, her hair was already short, but this was different. This was dreadful.

"Sit down, Pa." Cassie, still in charge, still eerily calm. Michaela, running, fetching, helping any way she could.

Nell, busy with her stitching, said loud enough to pene-
trate all the fear, "Brand, you have some of the finest young
women I've ever known. Girls, your help . . . well, you're
all heroes. I'm so proud of you."

She never missed taking a stitch, but she thought she
saw the girls move a bit more steadily. Their shoulders
square. Their eyes more determined. Cassie might have
eased her ruthless calm slightly.

Brand even sat down without protest. Maybe because
he wanted to make things easier for Cassie, who couldn't
reach the wound on his shoulder. Maybe because his knees
were giving out.

Nell could sympathize.

An hour stretched to two until finally Samantha was all
stitched up and bandaged. She was still sleeping.

Doc turned to Brand. "We're finished here."

Brand stood from his chair to come to Samantha's side.

Nell said, "Girls, come with me. I've got clean clothes
for you at my shop. Those shirtwaists and riding skirts
I was making are finished. We'll bring clothes over for
Samantha, too."

Nell heard Brand say quietly to Doc Preston, "I need
to talk to the sheriff."

Not wanting the girls to hear what he said, she went
on out when she wanted to ask him what was going on.
What business of the sheriff's was it when a wolf attacked
someone?

Instead, she left the doctor's office, determined to care
for the two girls as best she could, then get back to help
care for the third one and their father.

25

W hat is it, Brand?" The sheriff had come fast. Sheriff Joe had been on edge for a long time. Brand was sorry he wasn't going to help ease anyone's worries. "Did the doctor tell you about the wolf attack at my place?"

Doc Preston was back at Samantha's side. She remained stubbornly unconscious. Brand wanted to shake her awake, while at the same time he knew every moment of the coming pain was best to let pass. And the thought of doing a single thing to cause her pain nearly ripped his heart in two.

"It was a wolf attack, yes, but someone set it up."

Sheriff Joe straightened, his eyes sharpened.

Doc, bending over Samantha, turned to Brand. "What? What do you mean 'someone set it up'?"

"I saw it myself, plain as day. The barn's big front doors were latched. Sam always unlatched them when she went to saddle the horses."

"Always?" The sheriff strode toward Sam, looked at her

and turned back, his face grim. "She had the chore of saddling up?"

"Yes, and it was planned. The horses had been let out into the corral. I always leave them in the stalls overnight when we're riding out to school or church first thing in the morning. It's easier that way to get them ready."

"You mighta forgot one night. Sam might've gone in through the side door for once. As upset as you are, a worried pa might be jumping at shadows."

"I wish I was." Brand shook his head, his jaw a hard line. He sank into a chair, bite marks on his wrist and shoulder hurting, claw marks on his face on fire. "I wish by all that's holy I was."

Brand sank his face into his hands, thinking it all through again, just as he had a hundred times already. He rammed his fingers deep into his hair and lifted his head to glare at the sheriff. "The side door was locked too, from the outside. I ran for the front door and saw from a distance it was locked. I heard Sam screaming from behind it. I went straight for the smaller door, and it was latched same as the big one. We leave them locked overnight. She had to've unlocked one of them to get inside. She couldn't have relatched them. Someone waited until she went in, whichever door she picked, and then locked up behind her. They had the horses outside so the wolf wouldn't attack them. Sheriff, they locked her in with a vicious wolf."

The sheriff and Doc sat there frozen, as if their minds were too busy to find extra time to make their bodies work.

Quietly, the sheriff said, "Why?"

Brand shoved himself to his feet. "That's what I want to know. *Why?*" He moved to Sam's side.

Shaking his head, the sheriff said, "There's only one outfit around here mean enough to do something like that. And devious enough to go to such lengths to try to blame this on an animal rather than just firing a gun. Brand, did you somehow get crosswise of the Deadeye Gang? Are they sending you an ugly warning that your family is in danger?"

Brand ran his hand lightly over Samantha's hair, studying her ashen face, the awful stitches. There was a nasty row of stitches in the exact shape of a bite on one shoulder, as if the wolf had picked her up with his teeth. There were plenty of other, smaller bites on her arms and legs."

"This isn't how wolves act, is it? He was trapped in there or he'd've run off."

The sheriff came up and stood at the foot of the bed, looking down at Samantha with solemn worry. "What reason could there be to do something so horrifying?"

Brand looked up from Samantha to these two men he respected. Men who'd been out here a lot longer than he had. "We can't stay out there anymore, can we?"

"You have to, Brand. It's the only home you've got."

He thought of all he'd need to do. Go ahead of the girls into every situation. Go armed at all times. Every day scout his property carefully before any of them stepped outside.

Then he thought of a solution that might just work.

"Doc, are you done seeing to Samantha for a while?"

"Yep, I'm just checking bandages."

"Could you go and get Nell and send her over here?"

"You want the judge?"

Brand realized what he'd done. He thought of her often

as Nell, he'd even called her that a few times when they were alone, but using her first name wasn't right or proper, and both men had noticed it.

"Yes, please. I want the judge."

Doc gave his chin a firm nod. "Stay by my patient." With that, he left the room.

"What do you want with Judge Armstrong?" The sheriff's eyes narrowed, almost as if he feared Brand might do Nell harm.

It flickered through Brand's head that someone might indeed do Nell harm. Henry Wainwright came to mind. But she would be safe from that kind of hostility with Brand.

Nell came in at a near run. She set something she clutched in her arms aside and hurried to look at Sam.

Brand wasn't sure what Doc had said to her, but it'd got her moving.

"Doc stayed with the girls," she said. "They've changed into clean clothes. I was on the sidewalk, heading with them for lunch at Clint's. Doc took them along and will see they get a hot meal."

Brand turned to the sheriff. "Can you leave us alone for a minute, Joe?"

Sheriff didn't seem to like it, but he stepped outside nonetheless.

The words that were trying to escape from Brand's throat seemed to clog as he looked at Nell. He regretted what he was about to say, but that regret wouldn't stop him.

"Nell, will you marry me?"

Nell's eyes went wide. Her jaw dropped. She seemed

to have words that she couldn't get past her throat just as Brand had a minute ago. He decided to explain himself fast before she got her refusal in.

"That wolf attack this morning"—he glanced at his precious Sam, still unconscious, so terribly harmed—"it was no accident."

"What?" Now she could speak.

Brand explained the same concerns he'd shared with the sheriff.

"Someone put that wolf there. He was locked inside, possibly overnight. Possibly hungry. Very much a cornered and trapped wild animal, it attacked the first thing it saw. Samantha."

"I didn't know all that happened." She stepped close to him and rested both hands on his forearm just above where the doctor had bandaged him.

"I'm afraid for my daughters, Nell. I'm afraid to have them out at the homestead. That wolf attack was meant for me. The Deadeye Gang must think I know something about them. Maybe they think I saw something in town that day Campbell was attacked. I need someone to take over for me if something happens, and the girls love you."

Brand didn't say he loved her, but it struck him suddenly that he did. Or at least he was powerfully drawn to her. He respected her. He cared for her. What was love if not that?

"I want you to marry me. I think . . . no, I *know* I can't let the girls stay out at the homestead anymore. Or if they're out there, they need to stay in the house all the time." He turned away from her, and her touch. He shoved ten fingers deep into his hair. "I-I can't abandon my home-stead. I need to live out there. But the girls, if we move fast to connect the upstairs of your shop to the upstairs of the courthouse, they'd fit in there with you. I can't risk—"

"Brand, stop talking," she said, cutting him off. "Just stop. Calm down."

And that was when Brand decided he did love her. She was going to say something wise and sensible. She was a woman to count on, to share the load with. He'd needed the kind of help Nell could give him for a long time now.

He turned back to see what she'd say. "I'll calm down. You're right. I'm in a flat-out panic to think someone tried to kill me, and his deadly trap ended up hurting Sam." He stepped closer to her. "But I care about you, Nell. I never thought I'd marry again. Pamela paid with her life for being a mama, and I've been giving my life to being a pa. I've never seen room for another woman. Until I met you."

Brand reached out and took both her hands in his. He considered dropping to one knee but instead looked deeply into her beautiful blue eyes. He remembered kissing her and knew he wanted to do it again, next time with the full rights of a husband.

"I'd like to join my life with yours. I want to marry you. Please say you want to marry me. For the girls, if not for me. I think it might save my girls' lives."

He realized then that he hadn't given her a chance to talk at all. Watching her eyes, he tried to gather what might be going through her head.

26

Nell thought of ten things to say, each of them beginning and ending with *No*.

But those eyes of his. Dear Lord God in heaven, Brand thought marrying her might be the difference between life and death for his girls.

Had a man ever bestowed such an honor on a woman? A man who loved his daughters as much as Brandon Nolte loved his?

And he kissed like a dream. In fact, she'd had a few dreams about that.

"I could take the girls to live with me while you live on your homestead," she finally answered.

"I'm not giving up my girls." He went from truly beseeching her to looking furious. But for his girls' sake. "Do you think I'd abandon them?"

She walked up to him as close as she could get, which wasn't far because they were already standing very close to each other. In fact, she leaned so close, their noses almost touched. "I will tell you one thing loud and clear, Brand.

You don't respond to my perfectly generous offer with anger. I won't stand for it. And if you ever lay a hand on me in anger, I will make you sorry you were ever born. I will never tolerate that in a marriage. Never again."

"I would never do such a thing. No decent man would." Then his mouth clamped shut as he realized what she'd just admitted to.

He reached up and took both her shoulders in a firm but not painful grip. Now his nose did touch hers. His voice wasn't a shout or a yell. It was low and serious. "You have my solemn vow that I will never do such a thing. I'll get a stout piece of oak and let you hide it somewhere to whack me to pieces if I ever do. And you'll never need it."

Silence stretched on for a moment. He drew back far enough to look her in the eyes. "Is that promise enough for you to say yes?"

"I'm not sure it's wise. We haven't spent time enough together to make such a rash decision." Then she brought her hands up to rest them flat against his chest. "But yes. For the girls and for your promise and"—her voice dropped to a near whisper—"for how I feel when you kiss me. Yes, Brand. I'll marry you."

"Yay!"

Nell's head whipped around. Brand was a second ahead of her. He dropped her arms like they were white-hot and rushed to Samantha's side. Her eyes were open and alert. Nell went to her other side, and the two of them, doting parents it seemed, smiled down at the young lady. Not a little girl anymore. Her hair would grow back. Her scars would heal and mostly vanish, it was to be hoped. Yet for a while she was going to need a lot of support and encouragement and care. A mother's care.

"Did you hear me propose?" Brand asked with a sheepish grin. "I wanted you to wake up something fierce, Sam. But I can't imagine what you must've thought about my proposing right in front of you while you were still sleeping from the laudanum. That don't seem like something a pa oughta do."

Samantha smiled in a way that made the sunlight look dim. "Cassie and Michaela and I have been hoping you two would hurry up and get married. We need a ma, and we all love Mrs. Armstrong."

"You can call me Ma from now on if you want to." Nell took one of Samantha's hands. Brand took the other.

"I'd like that, Ma." Samantha beamed but then flinched. The stitches must have pulled on her skin. She reached for her cheek, which was covered with a bandage that wrapped most of the side of her face and all of her head. "What happened to me? Why am I . . . the wolf? Pa, what happened?"

Nell held on to her hand and noticed Brand did the same.

"Yes, there was a wolf," Nell said. "You have bites that needed stitching up and bandaging. I've brought you a riding skirt and shirtwaist, the ones we've been working on. When you're ready, we'll get you up and dressed. It may take some time to heal, but you're going to be fine. The upset of it all made you faint. When you roused, Doc and I gave you medicine to make you sleep so it all hurt less. But now you're awake. How much of your pa's ham-handed proposal did you hear?" She smiled as Samantha left off trying to touch her wounds.

"Ham-handed?" Brand said indignantly, but she saw the glint of humor in his eyes. "Why, that was the most romantic proposal a woman ever fetched out of a man. It's got to be some kind of world record for romance."

Samantha giggled. "I only heard the very end. I heard Mrs. . . . I mean, Ma say she liked how it felt when you kissed her. When did you kiss Ma, Pa? We've been praying and wondering what we could do to bring you two around, but it sounds like you didn't need our help at all."

Then she clasped both of their hands tight. "I heard her say that about kissing, then say, 'Yes, Brand, I'll marry you.'" Samantha sighed at the romance of it, and Nell hid a wince at how unromantic some of it had been.

"I think your pa should go get Parson Blodgett and the girls, and maybe Mariah and Clint, if they can come. While he's busy with that, I'll help you get changed. We'll get married right here, right now. How does that sound?"

Nell surely hoped they could keep Samantha busy and distracted until she was cleaned up and feeling stronger, because Nell was sorely afraid the girl would have a painful recovery for a time.

Which led Nell to the next thought. Had someone really tried to kill Brand? If so, who? The Deadeye Gang came to mind instantly. Did Brand know something but not realize it? The gang was known for not leaving witnesses alive. What had Brand seen on the day Mr. Campbell was attacked? He needed to be questioned about that.

Nell decided to speak out loud her next thought. "I'd like Becky at my wedding too, Brand. Could you send the sheriff after her?"

She didn't want Brand riding out alone. She looked Brand in the eye and hoped he got the message to just do as he was told and not ask awkward questions in front of Samantha. "And have him bring Nate in, please. I'd like all my friends here."

Nate wasn't exactly her friend, but he was the best tracker in the area. Someone needed to ride out to the Nolte homestead and check around. She paused as another thought came to her. "Is your house by any chance near the property line of your homestead claim?"

"It is. I built it right up against the edge to be as close to town as possible."

She nodded. "And is the line right over your boundary claimed by anyone else?"

Brand hesitated and gave her an odd look, then shook his head no. Almost like a man who had life-and-death matters to fret over and didn't appreciate being distracted from them.

Well, too bad. A woman getting married needed to think ahead. And she was tired of thinking of things, so she hoped this was the limit. "Good then. Before we get married, I think I'll go file a homestead claim on property right next to yours. We can add a room onto your house that straddles the line and prove up on both claims. I can claim a homestead as a single woman rather than as a married woman whose husband already has one. It's a strange quirk in the law, and one that needs fixing."

Which was yet another thought worth thinking, but nothing she could fix right here and now, so she'd worry over that later.

"Uh, well, that's good thinking. I'll double the size of

my property with one 'I do.' You realize that once we're married, your homestead immediately becomes mine."

Nell saw Brand look down at Samantha and it dawned on her he was taking an amused, rather sassy position with her to keep things light. Behind the amusement, Nell knew the man who stood before her was likely ready to panic. She strung out the lighthearted talk for Samantha's sake and for Brand's, too. He needed to remain calm, to think of something besides his badly injured daughter and the danger stalking them. Yes, there was plenty to worry about, but the biggest thing to remember was that God had protected Samantha. She was going to heal and be all right. And they *were* going to put a stop to the monstrous Deadeye Gang.

"I'm a justice of the peace. I might just write an article from my lofty position of authority demanding that law be changed. A woman's property should remain her own after marriage."

Gently, Brand rested his hand on the large bandage on Samantha's head. He leaned down close to her. "I believe that by the time my girls are grown, the law should be very favorable and fair to women. But right now, it suits me to gain my new wife's holdings." He looked up at Nell with a smirk that cost him a lot. "How much money do you charge for making those chaps anyway? I get that too, right?"

Nell couldn't quite keep a giggle from escaping. "I charge every penny the market will bear, Mr. Nolte, let me promise you that. And I keep raising my prices hoping to discourage all the chap-loving cowboys in the area to no avail. I make them wait weeks, sometimes months, for their stupid chaps, and yet they all agree to whatever I demand."

She rolled her eyes, then looked down at Samantha. "I'll teach you everything I know about being a ruthless businesswoman in a place full of cowboys."

Samantha grinned, then flinched a bit.

Nell looked at Brand. "Go on now and find the sheriff, tell him to fetch Becky and Nate so we can get on with this wedding. The noon rush should be over by the time Becky gets here. Before you come back, talk to your daughters, to Clint and Mariah, and warn the parson there's going to be a wedding. Then run to the land office and pick out the correct homestead and tell Percy what land I'm going to speak for. When you get back, I'll go become a homesteader. We'll have six months to build, what, a ten-by-sixteen building on my land? Which can be a bedroom with me sleeping over the border to my property."

She was very sorry she'd brought up bedrooms and sleeping.

Brand's cheeks pinked up in a way that fascinated her and told her his mind was a bit distracted by talk of bedrooms, too. "I'll go now. I won't be long."

He dashed outside. As he left with his list of things to do, Nell felt a twinge of regret that nowhere on the list was what she'd actually call love. Praying she wasn't making a terrible mistake, she watched Brand hurry away until she was distracted by a faint voice.

"I hurt, Ma."

Nell turned back to Samantha. Her daughter. She had three daughters she could fully, eagerly love.

And Brand seemed all right. Three new loves and an

all-right man. God wasn't whispering in her ear to *stop, run, no, no, no.* He was going to have to do that, and do more than whisper, to stop her. And it didn't look like that was coming.

Which gave her heart a nice peace.

Looking down at Samantha, yes, her wounds were awful. But right now, the pain was what she could hardly bear to see. Nell wanted to cry, but that wasn't what Samantha needed. She steadied her feelings and flooded the room with prayer and her words with hope. "The wounds you got from that dreadful wolf are nasty things, but you *will* heal. You will be all better soon. Most stitches come out within a week, so those will be gone." She gave her head a jaunty little tilt toward the armload she'd brought back with her. "And I have clean clothes, including a new bonnet for you. The doctor had to snip your hair in a few places, which you won't like."

Samantha frowned and reached up for her hair. She felt the bandage wrapped all around her head and covering a good part of her face. "It must be so ugly."

Nell remained firm and no-nonsense. "The bonnet will cover the bandage and the snipped places, and your hair will soon grow back. This time we'll grow it out as long as you want. I know how to put hair up, and I think you're old enough to wear your hair in a bun."

Samantha's eyes lit up.

Nell raced through her mind for every mirror she could remember in town, determined to hide them all. She had one in her shop and one in her apartment. Those would go before Samantha got near them. "Let's get you dressed, young lady. This dress you're wearing is badly damaged and stained, but I am a talented seamstress. We can save it."

It wasn't the pretty blue one Nell had made. It was one of the dresses found in the upstairs of the courthouse. Nell was grateful for that.

She eased Samantha forward, then very slowly swung her legs around until she was sitting on the edge of the examining table. Nell watched closely and gave Samantha plenty of time to steady herself. Then, with aching gentleness, they got busy changing Samantha for the wedding.

Nell had probably better put something new on, too.

27

Brand found his girls eating with Doc Preston. The morning had slipped away enough that they were having dinner. He made his wedding announcement, and the girls shrieked until everyone in the diner—and it was crowded today—heard the news.

Judge Armstrong was getting married.

He darted into the kitchen to tell Clint he was invited to the wedding as soon as Becky and Nate could get to town. Brand gave a quick rundown of the morning's madness.

Next, Brand ran to the blacksmith shop to invite Mariah and fill her in on what was going on. She was shutting the forge down before Brand had finished the story.

"I'll go sit with Nell. She shouldn't be alone. No one should ever be alone around this town." She said the last part with a lot of bitterness.

Brand knew she was right, and that included Mariah, who'd been working on fine metalwork, so Willie wasn't around. She probably shouldn't be in the smithy alone. He waited until Mariah locked up and watched as she walked toward the doctor's office.

It jiggled something in his head to see her go, but he couldn't think of why watching someone cross Main Street to the doctor's office could be buried in his head. Once she stepped inside, he went to talk to Percy in the land office. Not only did he get things in order for Nell to come and homestead, but Percy got really excited about writing a story about the local Judge Armstrong soon becoming Judge Nolte and being a homesteader as well as a businesswoman.

Brand didn't tell Percy she was also a fairly competent doctor and a decent lawman and she had some veterinary skills to boot. There wasn't much he'd seen so far that the woman couldn't do.

He caught the sheriff up on what was going on, and afterward the sheriff rode out for Becky and Nate.

Next, he talked to Parson Blodgett, whose whole family wanted to come to the wedding. They were packing up their house and planning to leave within the week, but they quickly set that aside to attend the wedding.

Brand didn't think he could manage a cake or flowers or a ring. If someone expected a fancy wedding, they were doomed to be disappointed.

When he came out of the Blodgett house, he saw his girls walking with Doc back to his office. It seemed things were shaping up for his wedding day.

As he walked up the steps to the doctor's office, following in his girls' tracks, Nell came rushing out.

"Time to homestead?" he asked her.

She glanced behind her, then drew him along a few paces

from the office. "Samantha is all cleaned up and wearing a bonnet. She looks much better, but the doctor is going to keep her lying down, sipping water, resting until the wedding."

"Thanks for the help, Nell."

She rested her hand on his arm. "I'm going to hide the two mirrors I have. I want her to have some healing time before she sees the stitches. She'll heal in time, but seeing that bite on her face right now, when she's in so much pain, would be hard for her. Do you have a mirror at your house?"

Brand thought through what they'd carried west with them. He didn't think he'd brought along a mirror. "No, but a body can see their reflection in a washbasin or a window after sunset."

"We'll just have to do our best and not make a big deal out of it." Nell patted his arm, then headed toward her shop.

Brand fell into step beside her. "You're not going anywhere alone."

Nell didn't even bother to argue. "I'll talk with the sheriff later, but I'm going to consult with the U.S. Marshals Service and the cavalry at Fort Bridger. We have pure lawlessness in the countryside around us, which has to stop. We need help, and I'm going to demand we get it."

They entered her shop, and she rushed upstairs and was back down a few moments later with a handheld mirror clutched in one hand and wearing a clean dress, her hair neatly combed. She went into the room at the back of the shop and came out with another mirror. "Let's put these in the courthouse and then head out."

The rest of their errands went without a hitch, and they were back in the doctor's office in quick time. Nell was now the proud owner, or perhaps *claimant* was a better word, of her very own homestead.

They'd entered the doctor's office to see Samantha sitting at the small table Doc had there. The clop of hooves drew Nell's eyes out the window, and she saw Becky and Nate riding up. She wanted to go out, talk things over with them, but she didn't want to do a thing to scare the girls. Her investigating would have to wait. For now, these were her wedding guests. Sheriff Mast rode up behind them, and all three dismounted and entered the office. Clint appeared from the front door of his diner. The noon rush must be over.

It was only minutes later when a portion of the Blodgett clan came, with Percy Kintzinger joining the party, though whether as a guest or a reporter, Nell couldn't say.

Nell sure hoped no one needed a doctor because the office was plumb full.

Parson Blodgett went to stand beside Samantha, where she sat in a chair, wearing her new outfit and bonnet.

Cassie stood at Nell's left, Michaela on Brand's right, holding his hand, each wearing a tidy riding skirt, shirtwaist, and bonnet. It was a fine-looking wedding party.

"Dearly beloved . . ." the parson began.

It crossed Brand's mind right then that he was marrying a woman who could have performed the wedding herself.

It crossed Nell's mind that she'd worked for years to be independent. She'd left behind her husband's grave. She'd come west with her brother, but when he wanted to go on farther, she'd let him do so without her. She'd become a businesswoman who put aside what she loved to do—make dresses—and instead did what bored her, yet it was what the market demanded. And whether she liked making chaps or not, she'd succeeded. She took great satisfaction in that.

And now, after coping with so much for so long and doing it well, she was marrying again when she'd firmly decided not to. What's more, she was doing it mostly to get Brand's children for herself.

Sighing quietly, resigned to her fate, she heard the parson ask for anyone there who objected to the marriage to "speak now or forever hold your peace." Nell knew for a fact that no one was going to speak up.

She accepted that.

Far too late, she asked God if this was His idea.

About that same time, she heard Parson Blodgett ask her for some really serious promises before God and man: "for better or for worse, rich or poor, in sickness and in health, till death do us part."

Since someone had tried to kill Brand just this morning, and he'd proposed in large part to have someone legally in place to raise his children, well, *till death do them part* might not be that far off.

Before she could give God a chance to speak to her, she heard that fatal question and, unwilling to start complaining in front of the girls, replied, "I do."

It was Brand's turn, and she knew he had no doubts.

And why would he? She was one of very few women in the area—very few single women at least. And a financially well-off woman at that.

She knew how to braid hair and sew dresses. She had room in her upstairs apartment for the girls.

She was a great catch.

As she mulled over just what she'd gotten herself into, it occurred to her that no reasonable man—and she most certainly hoped Brand qualified as one—could fuss about a mother making dresses for her daughters. If he did insist on paying her, she had plenty of money, now his, to pay her. At which point she'd put the money in with the family's funds.

Then he could use those funds to buy more dresses.

However he handled it, she finally got to make pretty dresses for three young women. That was the best reason to get married she'd thought of so far.

"I now pronounce you man and wife." Parson Blodgett gave Nell an odd look, almost like he knew there was a riot going on inside her head when she should have been paying strict attention.

She really should have listened. Maybe he'd handed out some good advice.

Then he arched his rather bushy brows and said, "You may kiss the bride."

Almost like he knew they'd already kissed on a few memorable occasions. And Nell wasn't opposed to doing it again.

Brand kissed her, but it was quick and not very romantic, as it most certainly should have been in this instance. Then he bent down and kissed Samantha on her forehead just to the side of the bandages. Michaela and Cassie squealed and hugged Nell, then whirled to hug their pa, then they all gathered into a knot, including a very gently hugged Samantha.

Cassie said, "Our first family hug with Judge Armstrong as our ma."

Nell's rather doubtful heart warmed and enjoyed every second of it. She decided, serious doubts notwithstanding, she'd done the right thing after all.

The family hug eased off, and Becky pulled Nell into her arms, Mariah right beside her. Nell saw Nate shaking Brand's hand. Clint was next, who clapped Brand's shoulder and offered a handshake of his own.

Mrs. Blodgett pushed through the crowd and embraced Nell.

That was when Nell realized others seemed to be arriving to celebrate with them. Percy was taking notes, smiling to beat all. The Blodgett children were milling around.

The oldest son, Leland, was talking to Samantha. "Yep, I'm going to stay out here on Pa's homestead. It's a good life. I like Wyoming. And I'm old enough now to not go along when my family leaves." The Blodgetts' second oldest son, Warren, and Leland hadn't been in school all year. All the children had worked hard to run the Blodgett homestead while their pa did his parson and justice-of-the-peace work.

Nell felt a pang of sadness for Mrs. Blodgett, who'd be moving away from her children. But it was the way of the world in recent years for the children to leave home and wander far. In this case it was the Blodgett parents wandering.

Leland hunkered down in front of Samantha. He murmured something, and the badly injured young lady, whose shoulders were slumped, straightened and a genuine smile bloomed on her poor face.

Nell wanted to give the boy a hug for taking a moment to encourage poor Samantha.

More townsfolk strolled over and joined the celebration.

Henry Wainwright patted Nell on the back. He moved on to Brand with his congratulations. Nell wasn't sure just why he'd come. Surely he was needed at the general store. Henry gave Samantha a worried look and went to her, speaking quietly.

Then Nell saw Mr. Betancourt, whose presence meant school was out. Behind him trailed a few more Blodgett children.

Honestly this was no time for a party. Nell had a lot to do, and the day was wearing down. Speaking briskly, she said, "Thank you all for coming to our wedding. We need to get on with getting Samantha settled in. We'll see you all on Sunday, if not before."

Most everyone got the message.

The crowd thinned.

Finally, it was time to go. Becky and Nate remained, both talking with the sheriff.

"Let me walk you all home," Clint said.

He and Brand helped Samantha to stand, and without asking, Brand picked her up with aching gentleness. The two of them were bandaged, both exhausted, their lives forever changed today.

Nell hurried ahead of him to get the door. They needed

to get Samantha lying down and resting. Probably Brand, too. But first, Nate needed to ride out to Brand's place and look around. And Nell wanted to go along with him.

She held her younger daughters' hands, leading a short parade to her shop with plans to abandon her family as soon as possible.

Brand, a pace behind, said, "I'd hoped to spend some time working on the two gables, connecting the buildings. And I'll need to build bedsteads and bring in enough prairie grass to fill a mattress tick."

"Tomorrow is soon enough for that," Nell said. "Samantha will sleep on the bed. That's the most comfortable. The girls can sleep with her, if we're sure Samantha won't be harmed."

Becky came up beside Nell with a squirming puppy in her arms. "The puppies are ready to be weaned," Becky said firmly. "Brutus is done seeing to Spike's training at Mariah and Clint's place. My wedding present to you, to the whole Nolte family, is this puppy." She turned to look Brand in the eye. "No wolf will ever take you by surprise again."

The girls abandoned Nell to fuss over the little black dog, who licked their faces and paddled his feet with desperate excitement. He whined and yipped, and Nell hoped Brutus got him trained fast, because her already overcrowded house had just added a new dweller. A noisy one.

"I think," Becky said delicately, clearly fighting her natural urge to take charge, "you should stay out at Brand's house tonight. I've got three good reasons, the most obvious one being there isn't room in your house."

"I've got two bedrooms. Not much bigger."

Becky rolled her eyes as Nell thought it all through. Two bedrooms, one of them set up for three girls, no doubt. Brand could sleep in his own bed. She'd take the floor in the front room next to the fireplace. Her friend was right.

"Also, once I separate Spike and Brutus, it's going to be hard to keep Spike at Mariah's house. His pa is too close. He'll be able to track him right to Nell's shop, if he slips away. You'll end up with Spike living with you, besides this pup"—Becky lifted the little dog a few inches—"and Brutus."

"You said three reasons. What's the third?" Nell faced Becky, the girls looking only at the puppy. Samantha was even staring at it and smiling. The puppy brought out smiles that Nell was worried would be hard to come by.

"Third is, I want the girls out there while Nate and I look around. And I want Samantha close by if we have any questions about how that wolf got in the barn."

"No, Becky," Brand said. "I don't want the girls to have any more worries loaded down on them."

Becky looked at him with nothing but kindness and sympathy. And Becky wasn't overloaded with either of those. Sounding compassionate, she said, "I know that and understand it, Brand, but this time you may not be able to get what you want."

"Pa, what does she mean about how the wolf got in?" Samantha asked, resting her head on Brand's strong shoulder.

More quietly, Becky added, "We've got to do whatever it takes to end this, Brand. And nothing we talk about at your place is going to give her more nightmares than she'll already have." She reached out to Samantha and laid her hand on the young woman's face, the unbitten side.

"Suppose you're right." Brand looked between Samantha and Becky, then turned to Nell. "Let's go on home. Nell, you go with Clint and Mariah and pack a few things to bring home. Take the girls along. Becky and Nate, can you get our horses ready?"

"Sheriff Mast put them up at the smithy," Clint said. "Their saddles and bridles are all there."

"I'm going to hang on to my Sam."

Becky with the puppy walked with Nate toward the smithy.

Nell saw Henry Wainwright standing in the doorway of the general store, watching them.

Doc Preston was locking the front door to the doctor's office.

Percy Kintzinger watched from the land office, still taking notes.

She saw Jim Burk sitting on a bench outside the mortuary.

It seemed everyone in town was either watching or had come to their wedding or had heard about it. And among that crowd was at least one man who knew how that wolf had gotten into Brand's barn. A man who wanted Brand Nolte or perhaps his daughter dead.

Nell went along with Clint, Mariah, and the girls. When they stepped inside the shop, Nell said, "Can you stay with Brand, Clint?"

She watched Brand sit on the steps outside her place, still holding Samantha.

"Let me check upstairs first." He rushed up the steps in the back of Nell's shop and was down again a minute later.

He went outside as Nell, Mariah, and the girls went up. Nell had a satchel handy and packed a nightgown and rack of pins, her hairbrush, a few underpinnings, and a single, clean dress. She'd get more things tomorrow if they decided staying out at Brand's place was wise.

"Mrs. Armstrong?"

Michaela's little voice drew her attention. Nell said, "You can call me Ma if you want."

Michaela's cheeks turned pink with pleasure. "I do want that, Ma. My own ma. Samantha and Cassie said my mother died birthing me. I've never in my life called anyone ma. Thank you. Can I ask you something?"

Cassie took a firm grip on the satchel, ready to bear this burden. "What is it, Michaela?"

Michaela exchanged a long look with Cassie. "What really happened to Sam? Miss Becky said something about that wolf being put in the barn by someone, like to hurt her. Why would anyone do that?"

Cassie added, "I could tell Pa didn't want Miss Becky asking that question, and I could tell Miss Becky thought it needed asking, and right in front of us."

Nell wanted to protect the girls from this ugliness just as much as Brand did, but it wasn't going to be possible. Not if they needed the girls to be cautious for their own safety.

"You're right that your pa and I didn't want you to hear of such a thing. And you're right that Becky thinks she's got the right of it, and maybe she does. We'll ask your pa to talk about it on the ride home. I won't answer your questions here and now, not without your pa's knowledge.

But when you ask him the question you just asked me, I'll take your part and encourage him to tell you what's going on. I'm sadly afraid it's past time for you all to know."

Michaela held her gaze, then finally gave her chin a firm nod of agreement.

Cassie headed for the stairs. Over her shoulder, she said, "If Pa won't talk, and you won't tell us, and I can't get it out of Miss Becky, I'm going straight to the sheriff. It ain't safe for us to be so ignorant."

Cassie was absolutely right, but sadly the sheriff wouldn't know any more than anyone else. But they'd figure it all out soon enough, Nell was sure of that.

28

It was a parade going home. Brand didn't feel one moment of danger, not right here and now. But the parade would march on, and he'd be alone with his family soon.

In a land of wild wolves and vicious men who didn't care who they killed.

Sam rode on his lap, facing forward. He could have put her on the horse with Cassie the usual way. Sam seemed steady enough. But he wasn't quite ready to let go of her yet.

Nell rode beside him to his right. Cassie and Michaela were on his left. Clint and Mariah brought up the rear, while Becky and Nate, along with the sheriff, led the way, with Becky holding the puppy. Brutus trotted along beside his mistress, seemingly unconcerned that he kept being loaned out. Loyal as always. Almost like he understood and took his responsibility to keep others safe very seriously. The dog, more than anything, gave Brand a feeling of safety.

"Pa, I asked Mrs., uh . . ." Michaela glanced at Nell and smiled. "I mean, I asked *Ma* what all that talk was of someone putting that wolf in the barn and why we need the puppy and Brutus for protection. I asked her what's going on."

"You need to tell us, Pa." Cassie gave him a very grown-up look. Serious and mature. A tough young woman who was wise beyond her years. "She wouldn't, but we need to know. It's the only way we can be careful enough to stay safe."

Sam . . . Samantha, hugged the arm he had wrapped around her waist. "It's got something to do with that gang that's roving the hills of Wyoming, doesn't it?"

Brand should know better than to believe his girls could be completely sheltered from such terrible crimes.

With a deep sigh, he said, "I wish none of you had to ever know a moment's fear or pain. What I'll tell you is a fearsome thing, but there's no sheltering you from it. Not if there are men who mean us harm."

There was a pause as he tried to figure out where to begin. Yet there was no right place, so he plunged in. Hating it when he had to tell them about no witnesses being left alive.

He felt Samantha clutch his arm. "And you think they were after you, Pa?"

"That's all that makes sense. But I haven't seen a thing. Somehow, some member of that gang thinks I did."

"And you've been helping guard a wounded man?" Cassie's smooth brow furrowed. "That man ended up dead on the day you rode out to help with Miss Becky's bull?"

Nell dropped back a few paces, then guided her horse so Cassie and Michaela were between them. Guarded on both sides. She said, "We wonder if whoever killed Mr. Campbell thinks your pa saw something that day. He was in town talking to you girls, explaining he might be late to pick you up because he was coming out to help with the injured bull. He wanted to let you know both of us might be gone. The time you all spent talking outside the school was the only time Mr. Campbell was alone. If the killer slipped into the doctor's office and noticed your pa outside, he might have decided something had to be done. Just on the chance your pa saw something."

They rode along in silence for a while. Becky, ahead of them, turned in her saddle to say, "I wonder if they got the idea for the wolf from that grizzly attacking my bull. They would've had more than they could handle trying to catch a grizz and shove him into your barn. But a wolf, while it's a mighty dangerous critter, isn't so large and a bit less hard to corral and tie up tight enough he can be moved around and controlled. At least somewhat."

Nell looked across the girls at Brand. "Samantha's asleep," she said. "We need to get her settled into bed."

"My house is, uh, it's got . . ." Brand cleared his throat and went on. "The girls sleep in a loft, and they climb a ladder to get up there. I don't want to try and get Samantha up there tonight."

"Then she'll sleep in the downstairs bedroom, and we can make up a pallet on the floor, if that suits you."

"Maybe, um . . . that is, if you want, you can share the bed with Sam."

Nell shook her head, then smiled. "That's not necessary, but thank you. Let's give Samantha a chance at a very comfortable night's sleep. Maybe by tomorrow night, she'll feel up to climbing the ladder. And maybe it's time to add on that room, as soon as possible, so we can begin claiming my homestead. That way, the girls can spread out a bit. But my place is beside you, Brand. If you're on the floor, then I'll be beside you."

Brand nodded silently. Because, at least for the moment, he was beyond words as he thought of her taking her place beside him.

The house came into sight, and he looked at it with new eyes. It was a well-built structure, but small. To reach Nell's holding they'd need to add on enough that it wouldn't be small anymore. Looking at his home, he saw he'd left the barn doors thrown wide. The house door stood agape.

"We sure enough were in a headlong run for the doctor this morning. I didn't do a single thing to lock up behind myself."

Nate and Becky rode straight for the barn and hitched their horses well away from it.

Nell quietly said, "It shows a man whose priorities are exactly as they ought to be. You're a good pa, Brand. A good man."

Nate stood at the barn door and said over his shoulder, "Get your girls settled. Stay well away from the barn for a time."

"I'll be here if you need anything." Sheriff Mast stood near the barn but didn't go inside.

Becky said, "I'll get the dogs settled along with the girls."

She turned, puppy in hand, as Brand dismounted holding

Sam. It nearly closed his throat to have his big girl in his arms like this, sleeping like a youngster. The day had taken it out of her, and that was that.

He strode inside and straight back to his bedroom. It shared the back half of the house with the kitchen. The front was a room with a fireplace that shared a wall with the kitchen. A small table and four chairs stood before the fire. He was short a chair, and that was just for his own family, let alone for any visitors.

Becky came in with the puppy, Brutus at her heels. Nell and the girls entered next, then Clint and Mariah. As he entered his bedroom with his daughter, Brand glanced sideways and saw that the house was mighty full.

"Shut the door, Clint." Becky waited until it was closed, then set the pup on the floor next to its pa.

Brand came out of the bedroom after laying Samantha down to see his girls drop to the floor with quiet squeals of pleasure. They'd been fighting for their sister's life just hours ago out in the barn. Cassie with a gun. Michaela with a knife. Fighting for his life, too. Now they cooed over a puppy.

The dog was for safety, as a guard dog and a warning of danger, but right now the dog was about healing rattled nerves and pushing back the nightmares that might lie ahead. He sincerely hoped Samantha would wake up soon and get a turn petting the puppy.

Brand raised his eyes, and they met Becky's. He said, "Thank you."

She gave a firm nod of her chin, then sat right on the floor with the girls and started talking about what a puppy needed to be happy. Brutus came up to Cassie and slipped his nose under her arm until she had him hugged around the neck. He licked her cheek, and she giggled.

Brutus had a reputation as a mean dog—tough and dangerous when he had to be. Right now, when he had to be, he was a big old softie.

Brand went back to Samantha's room and sat on the edge of her bed, watching her sleep.

She was alive. She was going to survive this. His precious firstborn. Brand knew, as a man who'd lost his wife, that life was precious, and since Samantha was alive, everything else could be handled.

Nell came in carrying a chair and sat in it to keep vigil with Brand.

He looked away from Samantha and reached out a hand for Nell, and she took it. They sat together.

From behind them came an occasional yip. A giggle now and then. Brand wasn't sure what all his life had come to today.

A deadly threat from a killer. A new wife. A house that was going to grow but that right now was filled to bursting with good people. Friends.

Nell had brought friends into his life.

A sizzle from the kitchen reached his ears.

"Clint's making supper."

Brand didn't bother to ask what was on the menu. He knew it'd be delicious and no doubt made from the same things Brand would have cooked with but tasting like it could be served in heaven.

He looked at Nell and said what was on his heart. "Our family is better for having you in it."

Nell leaned forward and kissed him. A warm, sweet

kiss. The kiss of a woman who was going to help him handle this life. He'd done a poor job of handling it alone. Yep, they were better now.

They both turned back to watch Samantha sleep. Brand watched her chest rise and fall. How could a man know such peace and such terror at the same moment?

29

The sheriff rode back to Pine Valley with Clint and Mariah.

Becky and Nate had talked over the tracks they'd found, and listening to them helped Nell see it more clearly. It sounded like a nightmare. She hugged Michaela and Cassie tight as they talked it all through again.

Becky promised to come back tomorrow with a crew to add on to the house, then after supper they headed for the Idee Ranch.

They'd all eaten a meal that surprised Nell. Chicken stew over biscuits. Clint made it delicious, of course, but it was simple. And that wasn't like him. He was being kind by letting them eat and enjoy the basic but tasty meal without having to find the energy to impress anyone.

The girls had climbed the ladder to their loft.

And Samantha slept on.

"I'm going to sit up with her, Nell," Brand said. "I'll bring out some blankets to spread them in front of the fireplace for you."

"Thank you. I'll take a shift, if you can bear to leave her side. It'll help us both get through tomorrow if we've had a few hours' sleep."

They stood in front of the flickering fire. Nell thought the girls overhead were asleep, but she didn't for one moment trust that they had privacy. That day would come, but not tonight.

Brand nodded, fetched a few blankets, spread one on the floor with a flick of his wrists and left a second for her to cover up with. Then he drew her into a hug.

They held each other for a long stretch of minutes. Finally, he pulled away, just a few inches, and said, "We'll be passing each other in the night tonight, Mrs. Nolte, but our time will come."

He kissed her, and she returned the kiss in full measure. When it ended, he turned and left the room.

The next day, Becky showed up with half her cowhands. Mariah arrived, riding with the sheriff as escort, in a wagon loaded with nails and such iron as she thought might be needed to build a house.

She brought a haunch of beef Clint had started before first light and enough bread to make them all a few sandwiches apiece.

Nell really had the world's best friends.

"How's Samantha this morning?" Mariah headed out of the house with Nell after getting the roast on to keep tenderizing until the noon meal.

"She woke up a few times in the night. Brand sat with her half the night, then I took over."

Mariah made a sympathetic little hum. "Not the wedding night of a woman's dreams, huh?"

Nell smiled. "We are both so relieved Samantha is going to be all right, we were glad to take turns sitting with her. The girls didn't go to school today, so we can't talk much about this." Nell glanced behind her to make sure they were alone. "At least not talk about how much I'd like to get my hands around the neck of whoever turned that wolf loose in the barn."

Mariah nodded silently. They heard axes chopping in the woods near the house. Nate was consulting with Brand about the location and size of the new room they'd be adding.

Becky came up to them, Brutus at her heel. The puppy scrambled along behind its pa. "We buried that wolf first thing this morning," she began. "Nate wanted another look at it in the full sunlight. It'd been hurt. And it looked to be skin and bones. Someone trapped that wolf in what looked like a leg trap. Then kept it and starved it. The poor critter was half mad from pain and hunger. I've no use for wolves preying on my cattle, but whoever did that . . ." Words seemed to fail Becky then. She shook her head. "We've always known the Deadeye Gang were a brutal bunch, but they're getting worse. They must be scared that they'll be found out and figure they'll face a noose. There's not much that'll stop them from taking desperate risks to silence any witnesses of their evil deeds."

Mariah said to Nell, "Well, Your Honor, what are we going to do about this?"

"To start, I'll be sending some wires today. I want cavalry officers here. U.S. Marshals too. The Deadeye Gang must be stopped. I want escorts with all the stages. Meanwhile, I'd like to wrap all three girls, as well as Brand, in cotton wool with a ring of soldiers around them."

"You gonna be inside that ring, Judge Nolte?"

"I just might—"

"Ma, come quick!" Cassie's frantic voice spun them all around to face the house. "Samantha's awake. She wants to see you and Pa right away."

Brand came running from the back of the house. Nell caught up with him a pace from the door. She stopped to let him go in first.

He rushed inside, and she was right behind him. They reached the bedroom to see Samantha sitting up, her feet swung over the edge of the bed.

Brand stopped beside her and dropped to sit down, his arms supporting her. "What is it, Sam?"

She looked wobbly. Nell poured her a glass of water and held it to her lips. She took a few sips, then gave her head a tiny shake. Nell didn't push, though the girl had lost a lot of blood and would need lots of water and good, solid food to regain her strength.

With Brand at her side, Nell dropped to her knees in front of their eldest daughter and clasped both her hands. "Are you hurting? Do you need to see the doctor?"

Samantha shook her head, then winced in pain and tugged on Nell's hand to be let go.

But Nell held on to her. "Don't touch your stitches. Give them a few days to heal first. I can give you more laudanum if the pain is too much to bear."

"Maybe later," Samantha said, "but I want my head clear for a few minutes. I need to tell you all something."

Nell nodded. Brand leaned close. Cassie and Michaela came up to stand by Nell.

"What is it?" Brand held her just a bit tighter.

"I know who put that wolf in the barn." Samantha's blue eyes widened with fear and determination. "That means I know who killed that man in Doc Preston's office."

Nell followed her thinking. "You saw someone run toward the doctor's office that day. You just remembered?"

Nodding, Samantha said, "I was hurting so bad last night when we rode home. I heard you talking about the gang and Mr. Campbell's murder and all that had gone on around here." She glanced sideways at Brand, looking disgruntled. "You should have told us what was going on, Pa. We're a tough bunch of frontierswomen, and we should know the truth of our life out here."

"You're right, Samantha. I've learned my lesson about keeping things from you. I need all the thinking power I can get from the whole family. Who was it?" When he spoke the last sentence, Brand's voice sounded as cold as death.

"The man I saw, not run, but walk briskly from his store, across the street toward the doctor's office, was Henry Wainwright."

Nell sat down on her heels. Stunned. Shocked honestly.

"I watched him walk across the street. I looked at him, and he looked back. He knows I saw him."

"He's gone from town often enough making supply runs," Nell said. "The sheriff was going to question the men around town to see if anyone paid attention to any cowhands who'd ridden off and been gone a few days too long. Did the sheriff question Henry and Peter?" Nell climbed unsteadily to her feet. She needed her gun.

Brand shook his head.

"I know he questioned them about anyone leaving their store around that time. We didn't doubt them when they said the store had been empty of customers. And they were an alibi for each other."

"I'm riding to town to talk to the sheriff," said Brand. "I'll go with him to arrest the man who almost killed my daughter. And make sure the sheriff knows it was an attack on Sam."

He'd tortured the wolf, that was what Becky had said. Then he intentionally set out to kill an innocent child.

"That injured bull gave Henry the chance to finish one witness, but it set him up with another to deal with. He must've remembered the bull getting mauled by the bear and got an idea of trapping a wolf, arranging another wild animal attack, this time on an eyewitness. He must've hunted down that wolf immediately because he held it a few days. And how could Peter not know about this?"

Mayor Peter Wainwright. Nell could hear the man encouraging her to take the job of justice of the peace. "Did he appoint me to be a judge because he thought I'd be gullible and never suspect what was going on right in my own town?"

Brand frowned. "Doesn't matter why he did it. I say yes, he's in on this. Though the two of them aren't gone from town together ever. They boast about the lengths they go to in keeping the general store open. Henry rides out to pick up supplies regularly. That would cover his absences. So, Peter must not do the actual robbing and killing. He stays in town to man the store. No doubt Peter knew that Henry was gone for a few minutes when Mr. Campbell was killed. And he lied about them both being in the store the whole time."

Brand hesitated, then added, "Henry said he wasn't happy with a female justice of the peace, and he said Peter agreed with him but went along because he was outnumbered by the other two council members." He turned and took the few steps needed to leave the room. "I'm going to stop this."

Nell went after him. "I'm coming with you. We'll have to arrest Henry. The sheriff will need me to issue a warrant for his arrest and a subpoena to compel Peter to testify at a trial. And we'll need to have a trial and do it fast before the Deadeye Gang gets word of it and tries a jailbreak. We need to—"

"Pa! Ma!"

Brand skidded to a halt. Nell plowed right into him. They turned to see what Samantha wanted.

With a shaky voice, Samantha asked, "Do you think you should leave us here alone?"

Brand froze. His eyes flew to meet Nell's gaze.

"You stay here with the girls, Brand. I'll get Nate to ride to town with me so it's safe."

"Nate's not enough protection. And I want to get my hands on—"

The outside door crashed open, and they both spun around. Once again they were moving in a rhythm.

Sheriff Joe Mast stepped inside. "Is everything all right in here? Mariah said you came running in. That Sam needed help."

Brand looked down at Nell. "He's enough protection."

Nell would rather take Becky, and she just might, but she'd settle for obeying her new husband, as he was looking right at her.

"I want you to come in and talk to Samantha, Sheriff. She's got a tale to tell, and I'd like you to hear it straight from her rather than me filling things in on the ride to town."

Sheriff Joe's eyes narrowed as if he knew something serious had happened. He tugged his hat off his head. "Let's go talk with her then."

It was good they hadn't rushed off. Nell thought of more questions to ask. Sheriff Joe let Samantha tell the story in her own words. Afterward he asked questions to draw out more details. Included were questions about the wolf attack and a review of all Nate had found yesterday.

"I'm going to question Nate again right now," the sheriff said. "Nell, you come along to town with me. Half will come with us, and half will stay here. I don't want anyone alone until we get that rattlesnake arrested . . . and I might just toss his brother in with him."

"You can arrest the mayor?" Brand asked.

"You just better believe I can. Making a false statement, providing an alibi to a murderer is aiding and abetting murder. That makes him almost as guilty as the killer. That's bad enough, but now add in that Mayor Wainwright has sworn an oath to protect the people of this town and uphold its laws. He might avoid a noose, but he's going to jail right along with his brother."

The sheriff turned to face Brand. "I'd like to have you along, but I think Samantha needs you here more than

I need you at my side. I know a father wants some vengeance when his child's been attacked. I understand that."

Brand went to Samantha's side. "I want vengeance a bit too much for the good of my soul, Joe. I don't trust myself. Staying here is for the best." He took Samantha's hand and sat in the chair at her bedside. Then he looked up from his daughter to Nell. "Be very careful. We need you back out here, Mrs. Nolte."

Nell watched him and thought of Web, her late husband, his arrogance and unkindness, and his belief that he was so important that nothing would go right without his being in charge. What she felt right then toward Brand seemed the true opposite of that. A strange warmth, an ache in her chest . . . she wondered if she might be falling in love with her husband.

She stepped to Brand's side and kissed him on the forehead. "I'm going to be very careful, I promise. I'm not planning to get involved in the actual arrest."

"No, you most certainly are not." The sheriff jammed his Stetson down hard on his head. "For heaven's sake, you're not part of this arrest at all. But there will be a trial, most likely yet today, so I'll need a judge handy."

"Do you need me to come to the trial, Sheriff?" Samantha asked. She was holding tight to her pa's hand, her eyes wide.

"I hope that won't be necessary, Samantha. Can you face Henry if you have to?"

"I'll come if'n you need me, sir. I'd tell the truth and say it right to the man's face that I saw him . . . and I know he saw me."

"I believe you, and the rest of the town and the jury

we gather will believe what you tell them. Thank you for helping us, Miss Samantha." Sheriff Joe tipped his hat to her and walked out.

Seconds later, Nell heard him shout Nate's name.

Bending down to kiss Samantha's cheek, Nell said, "You're a brave girl, Samantha. I'm proud that I can claim to be your ma."

Nell hurried out of the room before she broke down and started crying in front of her courageous, wounded daughter.

30

The general store was locked up tight. The Wainwright brothers' horses were gone.

"How did they know we were on to them?" Frustrated, Nell clenched her fists at her sides.

"Henry was at the doctor's office for your wedding, wasn't he?" Sheriff Joe asked.

"I-I think so. It was an unexpected crowd. I think, um . . . yes." She looked at Joe. "He was there."

"Can you trail them, Nate?" The sheriff fumed as he paced back and forth in front of the store.

"I won't stop till we find them, Sheriff," Nate answered. "And see 'em arrested."

Nell swung up onto her horse. "We've got to get back out to Brand's place. They may have cut and run. Most likely because Henry was afraid Samantha would remember and he'd be exposed. They might still think they've got a chance at silencing their only witness. We have to guard Samantha night and day."

"I'm going to search the general store and the Wainwrights' house." The sheriff had stopped his pacing. "We might find solid evidence of those two being part of the Deadeye Gang, and we might learn the names of other gang members. I don't want to make Samantha testify, but I will if it means holding on to these outlaws. If we find the right evidence, we won't need her to. We might clean this whole rat's nest out here and now. Nell, you put out that wire to the U.S. Marshal in the area. Owen Riley will come running and bring any friends he can round up. The Deadeye Gang is their top priority and has been for a while now."

Nate tugged his Stetson low on his forehead. "We can't wait for the U.S. Marshal to get here, though. We have to pick up a trail right now. Sheriff, you and Deputy Willie need to be with me. We should form a posse in case the Wainwrights are riding out to meet their gang. We could be up against a dangerous bunch."

Clint stepped out of the diner, and Nell realized that meant the lunch rush was over and it was already midafternoon. He'd planned to come out to help with the building.

"Clint can ride home with me," Nell said. "Becky, you're a good tracker, so you can decide what you want to do, but I'm going home. My family is safest when we're all together."

"I'll go with Nate." Brutus trotted along at her side. The dog would be a big help with tracking, especially with the puppy back at the homestead.

Clint approached the group, and they quickly caught him up on the Wainwright brothers and Samantha being a witness.

"I'll fetch my horse from the smithy," said Clint, "and we'll ride out to Brand's place together."

Minutes later, as they reached the edge of town, Parson Blodgett, his wife, and their son Leland caught up to them on their way to help build onto the cabin and offer pastoral support to the wounded and newly married. Quite the full day planned.

"Can we set a faster pace?" Nell asked. "I want to see what I can do to help Samantha and keep the other girls calm and busy. It's a frightening time."

The Blodgetts spurred their horses and kept up well until soon they'd reached the Nolte homestead. Apparently hearing the pounding of hooves, Brand walked out onto the porch of the cabin with a rifle in his hands. But when he saw Nell, his shoulders went from taut to relaxed. Yet he couldn't quite manage a smile.

"No trial?" he asked her as they dismounted.

Nell shook her head and told him of the unfolding search and how they needed to stay on guard. "I can sit with Samantha now if you'd like to help with the building."

Brand nodded, then stepped back into the house and grabbed his hat.

"I'll put your horse up, Nell," Parson Blodgett offered. "In fact, I'll see to all of them."

Clint handed over the reins and thanked the parson.

"I'll see how the building's coming along." Mrs. Blodgett walked toward four men shoveling dirt. "I know how to swing an ax."

"I'd like to go in and say hello to Samantha," Leland said. "Then I'll be out to help build."

"Thanks, Leland," Brand said. "She'll appreciate it. She and the girls are in the bedroom, but she's sitting up and dressed. Nell, she wondered if you'd help her do something with her hair. She said it looks a fright."

Nell felt her brows slam down. She dragged Brand away from the door and whispered, "Looks a fright? How did she see it? There isn't a mirror in the house."

"She looked at her reflection in a basin of water when I was changing the bandage. I never thought to—"

"I'll see if company can cheer her up, Mr. Nolte." Leland entered the house and went straight to the bedroom. Not hard to do in a house with three rooms.

"No, Leland. You can't—" Samantha's voice went silent.

Nell almost charged for the back of the house but then halted before she took a single step because she heard voices. All three girls. Leland talked then, quietly, but his voice was deep, and whatever he said stopped Samantha from her fussing.

Nell had her hand sunk into Brand's arm, but she relaxed as she listened to the foursome talk. Her eyes swung to Brand's. He was listening too as he met her gaze.

"Maybe it's all right." He looked at the bedroom with a worried frown, as if he could see through the walls. "Now, tell me why you're back. Why isn't there a trial?"

Nell told him quick.

"There'd be no sense in harming Samantha now, would there? She's told her story, and the secret is out. The Wainwrights would never be allowed back in town, whatever happens with a trial."

Nell shook her head. "It should be over, but the way that gang operates, their willingness to kill to keep their secrets . . . that's not normal. Any rational gang would move out of the area and take their thieving and killing somewhere else, which makes me sick to think of it. I hope this means we're safe, but I won't sleep easy as long as a single member of that gang is on the loose."

Cassie and Michaela came outside.

Cassie looked suspiciously at her pa. "What is going on? What aren't you telling now?"

Nell's eyes burned. She remembered how they'd finally told the girls all that was going on, after yesterday. And it'd helped them solve the crime, though solved didn't mean safe if Henry Wainwright was at large.

And now here they were, back at keeping things from them. Nell had no idea how to be a mother. And she'd certainly been thrown into the deep part of this parenting river.

Brand sighed, then rested one hand on Nell's shoulder. "All right, girls. You're right. It's just that this gang is so ruthless. I just wish you didn't have to know such people existed in this world." He ran his bandaged hand over Cassie's short, dark curls. "I'll go through it with both you and Samantha. Nell just told me what she learned in town. No sense talking it over more than once." Then his brow furrowed. "Where are Samantha and Leland?"

Cassie said, "They're right behind us." She looked back, then frowned. "Sam was standing up. I know he offered her his arm to steady her. They were coming . . ."

Brand pushed past his daughters, who whirled around to follow him. Nell was right on their heels.

They reached the bedroom doorway to find Leland holding Samantha in his arms while she wept.

"What's going on here?" Brand demanded.

"Mr. Nolte, please, she's just a little overwhelmed. It's been a hard couple of days. Nothing improper has happened."

Except, to Nell's way of thinking, a young man and a young woman, hugging each other, alone, in a bedroom, was exactly what the word *improper* was invented for.

"She's crying because . . ."

Samantha's head came up. She rested her hand over Leland's mouth and said, through a watery smile, "Let me tell them."

Leland smiled from behind her fingers, then nodded.

The touch, his expression, it was all very intimate. Nell's stomach sank as she figured out what was coming.

"Leland has asked if he could court me."

"What?" Brand sounded stunned.

Nell, just inside the bedroom door, sagged back against the frame.

"I'm staying here in Pine Valley when my folks go back to Nebraska. They've proved up on their homestead and have a nice start with it. I don't have much in the way of cash money, but the homestead doesn't have much in the way of value, so they don't plan to charge me for it." Leland smiled like it was a family joke. "They're signing the place over to me, leaving the livestock and a garden all planted. They'll be well set up back in Nebraska, so they don't have to take much with them. Samantha and I can live there after we get married."

"Married?" Brand seemed to be capable of just one word at a time.

"You're too young to get married." Nell found a few more.

"I'm sixteen, Ma. Leland is old enough to want to settle down, and so am I. We've been talking a bit after school. He's old enough to homestead."

"You've been talking after school?" Brand's voice was too high-pitched. "And you didn't tell me?"

Samantha shrugged, then glanced at Leland and smiled. "He said he was planning to homestead before his folks decided to move east. He hasn't talked to his folks about taking a wife yet, but he said he'd already"—Samantha looked up at him with shining eyes—"gotten his hopes up about me."

Leland nodded.

"No, absolutely not."

Leland and Samantha didn't even look at Brand.

"We'll want Pa to perform the ceremony." Leland rested a gentle hand on Samantha's face, the unbitten side. "And he's leaving in a few weeks."

One, if Nell remembered right. One week. She felt a little dizzy and continued to rely on the doorframe for support.

"And I'll have my stitches out by then." Samantha blushed faintly. "But I'll still look a fright. My hair's all hacked off. The bite marks will show. I may have scars, Leland." Her voice turned very soft, her eyes wide and vulnerable. "I'd un-understand if you w-wanted to wait and see how I heal up."

It was Leland's turn to touch Samantha's lips with his fingers to stop her words. "You're the prettiest thing I've ever seen."

Nell felt Michaela crowd up against her leg and take her

hand. She glanced down, and Michaela looked worried and sad. Losing her sister.

"And if you have scars from these wounds, then I'll see them as badges of courage. I'll have a wife who won a fight with a hungry wolf."

That wrung a little smile out of Samantha. "My pa and sisters helped. They won the fight."

"Then I'll have a wife with a family who'd fight off a hungry wolf to save her. That's a family I'd love to marry into. I'm not marrying you because of your looks, Samantha. I'm marrying you because you're a decent and smart and kind woman. I wanted to take my time about courting you, but yesterday at your folks' wedding, when I saw you all pale and so badly hurt, it was all I could do to not just scoop you up and take you away with me. I don't want to wait one day longer than I have to for you to join your life with mine."

Nell felt Brand flinch with every word. As if each of Leland's sweet compliments hit him like a red-hot poker. Because it was working like a charm. Samantha was glowing.

"Let's step on outside." Nell straightened her knees and took charge because she wasn't sure if Brand was capable of it. She caught his arm and dragged him away. He never quit watching the young couple. And they came along without any urging, though they seemed oblivious to Brand's upset. They only had eyes for each other.

They'd yet to tell the girls about the continued danger to Samantha. Now Leland would need to know. It wasn't safe for Samantha to be at the Blodgett homestead. Heaven forbid if the Blodgetts moved away, and Leland left her alone for even minutes. No, she needed to be right here, surrounded day and night by a family on guard.

Nell, with Brand's arm in one hand, Michaela clinging to her skirts, said to Cassie, "Bring a chair outside. Samantha needs to sit down. I'm going to call Parson and Mrs. Blodgett over." She looked hard at Leland. "Is that all right with you?"

Leland gave her a quick glance. "Good idea, Judge Nolte."

Judge Nolte. Nell should have had Cassie get a chair for her, too. She felt dizzy again.

And the Blodgetts needed to understand what was going on, as well.

Brand was right—better to tell it just once.

31

Nate swung down off his horse, a black stallion that was one of Becky's favorites.

He crouched low on the stony, hard ground, studying a trail Becky couldn't see. "Both of them, the brothers, riding together and heading east."

"There's not much east of here but South Pass City," Becky offered. "But they're well south of the road that leads to town."

Silent, Nate nodded. Becky, Sheriff Joe, Deputy Willie, and two men who'd joined up with a crew from Joshua Pruitt's place all stayed on horseback while Nate did his thinking.

"They sure seem to be riding hard straight out of the area." Sheriff Joe's horse, restless from the tension, stepped around. The sheriff controlled the animal with great skill.

"I think we should keep following," said Nate, "until we're sure they haven't circled back. But they seem to be riding out of the territory."

Sheriff Joe nodded. "We know there are other men in

the Deadeye Gang. They're not turning aside to find them. Unless, of course, they live a distance away, and the Wainwrights are riding out to tell them what's going on."

Nate pointed at the ground. "If I'm reading these tracks right, they're angling up to join the road. They're far enough from Pine Valley, they don't have to worry about running into a familiar face. Anyone coming back to town wouldn't have gotten word about the trouble back home. They could doff their hats and keep riding."

Nate looked over his shoulder at Becky. If he was asking her advice, she likely couldn't give it. She couldn't even see what he was looking at on that rocky ground.

"Once we rejoin the main road, they'll be riding flat-out. I can probably pick out their tracks, but in the meantime, we've already ridden two hours away from Pine Valley. They could be drawing us away so their cohorts can attack Brand's place."

"No, too many people there. Including a few of my toughest cowhands. The Wainwrights are cowards. They'd never face so many people head-on."

"True, but for how long? Folks won't stay out there forever, so when will everyone go home for the evening?"

"Especially," Becky interjected, "if we keep on riding away from town."

"So, we'll keep at this until we reach the main road," Nate said. "I'll see if I can pick up these two sets of hooves. If I'm sure we're on the right track, I say we keep after them. But I suspect that trail has hooves and wagon wheels churning up the ground. If I can't be sure whether those riders went on or turned back, we'll have to give up and head back to town."

The sheriff said, "I might ride on into South Pass City, talk to the lawmen there. See if two riders matching the Wainwrights came through town."

"They'll have been careful not to show themselves." Nate seemed to know more than just tracking. He seemed to be inside the outlaws' heads.

Becky admired his skill immensely and wondered if he'd ever spent time as a lawman. She had a hard time not just letting him take complete charge. And she was the boss. She never let any man take charge. She'd learned that lesson the hard way from having her father direct most every step she took from the time she was born to the day she moved off the ranch, with his angry threats not to come crawling back when she failed following her down the road.

Finally, Nate stood and led his horse forward, his eyes narrowed and keen as he walked, focused strictly on the ground. It was slowgoing when they could probably guess where these evil men would go.

Evil men. Henry and Peter Wainwright. Becky mentally shook her head to get her thoughts to roll around into some kind of order.

She knew the Wainwrights. She *liked* them. She did *business* with them. They'd treated her fairly.

Nate looked back over his shoulder. His eyes shifted from the sheriff to Willie to Becky but stayed on her. His horse kept walking while he studied them.

"Not everyone knew this because he kept it quiet, but Brand told me he had to stand and listen to Henry go on a tear because Nell was named justice of the peace."

Becky was indignant on her friend's behalf, but she kept quiet. It was clear Nate had more to say.

"Sheriff, when did this plan come about to appoint Nell to the judgeship? Whose idea was it?"

"Let me think a minute. I know I was all for it. I suppose I brought up the idea, but it could have been Doc Preston." The sheriff, his horse walking along, followed Nate, who'd gone back to searching for tracks. "When the parson came to me to say he was moving, we talked about it together. We were amazed how good Nell handled a lot of the investigation. How well she knew the law. Doc was impressed with her steady nerves while they were doctoring Campbell."

There was an extended silence, then the sheriff nodded and went on. "The two of us talked about how skilled she was, and just then Parson Blodgett came by the doctor's office. We called him in. Asked him what he thought about Nell as his replacement. He was all for it. Then the three of us went to see what Peter thought. The mayor needs to vote. Doc and I are the city council. Parson Blodgett was the current justice of the peace."

Becky said, "So the three of you had it all settled, and you were in agreement when you went to talk to Peter? Seems he didn't have much hope of stopping you, so he went along."

"Honestly, I think he agreed with us." The sheriff followed when Nate veered off the trail and headed slightly north in the direction of the road to South Pass City. "Henry was there in the store when we talked. He said something about the female mind being weak. Peter waved him off and said he approved of the choice and that he'd go with us to ask Nell if she'd take the job."

Becky's voice was cold when she said, "If Peter shared

Henry's low opinion of the female mind, he might've agreed to go along with the choice hoping there'd be no strong judge in Pine Valley."

Nate guided his horse to where the trail he followed intersected with the road to South Pass City. He stopped and dismounted, then crouched beside the trail. "It's either that or he just knew he was beat by two votes and saw no sense in making a fuss. But if Henry was that opposed to Nell, there's a good chance Peter was getting a few discouraging words muttered into his ear."

"What do you say, boy?" Nate rested a strong hand on Brutus's neck. His fingers sank into the shaggy black fur. Brutus wasn't really a tracking dog, but if he knew who he was after, he could find a trail. But this time, the dog just looked up the road, then down it. He had no idea what Nate was asking for.

Finally, Nate rose to his feet. "I'm almost sure this trail goes on headed east, but I can't swear it on my honor. Especially if they went on, then turned around. The trail is too churned up. I just can't be sure." He turned to look at his saddle partners. His gaze locked with Becky's, and she saw the same worry in his eyes she knew was in hers. And the sheriff's.

"Let's go back." Becky waited to see if anyone would argue with her. "There are too many stretches on this trail where someone could set up an ambush. If we ride on, we'll need a bigger group. Let's leave it to the U.S. Marshals or the cavalry."

Nate nodded and swung up onto his horse. "Let's take the road back. No sense wandering down that same trail we came here on."

Becky set out for home at a steady trot when she wanted to gallop. She felt pushed and tense and unhappy that they'd let a murderer and the man who covered up his crimes get away.

"I'm wiring Fort Bridger when we get back. And I'll contact the folks in South Pass City to be on the lookout." The sheriff caught up to Becky on his sturdy horse and passed her. "In the meantime, we'll post a watch at the Nolte place. It's not the same as with Campbell in the doctor's office. Lots of folks live with Samantha."

"Women and children," Nate muttered as he caught up to Becky and passed her. "But that won't stop them. These outlaws show no mercy nor decency."

By the time Nate quit talking, they were all galloping.

"Y
ou have to talk to her." Brand had waited until the house settled for the night before he lured Nell outside.

Okay, fine. He badgered her out with a combination of begging, insisting, and gentle yet relentless force to get her far enough away from the house that the girls couldn't overhear him.

"You mean-talk her out of getting married?" Nell tilted her head and studied him as if she'd found something odd under the table. Something that required the application of a few broom whacks.

"She can't be getting married. That's just ridiculous."

"Many girls her age marry. I think you're just not ready to let your little girl grow up. I suspect most fathers feel that way. But I happen to agree that they should wait. Samantha's so hurt, and she's vulnerable right now. I'd like her to heal up, be stronger, and make this decision when she's not twisted up inside worrying about scars.

And when Leland's not bent on rescuing her. They should take more time."

Then Nell spoke what was really in her heart. "And . . . I just got her as a daughter. I don't want to lose her so soon." They walked along the front skeleton of their room that was coming along. It was going to be a nice-sized room thanks to the stretch needed to reach the border of Nell's homestead property.

Brand froze. As if begging was all he had planned, and now that she was cooperating, he was out of ideas on how to proceed. "So, what do we do?"

Nell ran her hand up the chimney to feel the masonry that held the stones together. Becky, without consulting either of them, had decided they needed their own fire-place, and that was up and drying. They'd yet to put a roof up, and no door had been cut between the cabin and this addition. No sense knocking a hole in the wall that would open to an unfinished room that'd let wind and maybe rain in.

"I think you have to talk to her."

"Me? I'm a failure at everything about being a father. I didn't know wearing britches to town would embarrass her. I didn't listen when she tried to tell me. You're already smarter about the girls than I ever have been."

"That's true."

"Hey. You don't have to agree so fast."

Nell's lips quirked.

"Are you laughing at me?" Brand fumed. "This is no laughing matter. My daughter cannot get married to a boy she's known only a few weeks."

"It does seem rather sudden."

"Leland said his brother Warren is staying with him. Neither of them is twenty-one, but today they went in and filed on homesteads anyway. Neither of them has a document stating when they were born. They both see themselves as adult men who do the work of adult men." Brand shook his head trying to make his thoughts orderly. "That's all beside the point. My daughter is too young to get married and . . . and . . ." His voice faded with each word. "I'm not ready to let her grow up and leave me."

Nell patted his arm, and he felt it as pity because he was going to lose his child. "To be honest, Brand—"

"Don't be honest. Think of something else."

She quit patting. "She *is* old enough. And Leland is a fine, honorable young man. She's a decent cook, you've let her run the household, so she understands laundry and sweeping and caring for the livestock. She can't make or mend clothes, but I can help her with that."

"The Blodgetts want to see them married. If there's to be a wedding, Parson Blodgett wants to preside over it, and Mrs. Blodgett wants to be there to witness her son taking a wife."

The puppy had followed them out of the house, and suddenly he yipped and tore off into the dark.

"Come back, little guy." Brand had stepped forward to go after the pup when something whizzed by his head so close that he felt the heat of it. He heard the crack of gunfire a second before he felt that heat. If he hadn't made that move for the dog, he'd be dead.

Nell's hand grabbed his wrist.

"In the house. Now. Fast." She dragged him two steps before he shook off the stunned realization that someone was shooting at them. He took charge of rushing for the house as bullets whipped past them. Brand felt one burn his arm, but it wasn't bad enough to slow him down. He was soon ahead, towing Nell along. They rushed into the house, and Brand swung the door shut with a bang just as a line of bullets exploded against the door. He had a heavy wooden plank nearby that he latched into place, barring the door.

Brand pulled down his rifle from where it hung above the door. He thrust it at Nell, then saw she'd pulled a six-shooter out of a pocket and was rushing to the back door. She dropped the heavy brace across that door.

"Girls!" Brand shouted. "Wake up! Get dressed fast. Someone's coming. Someone bad."

He checked that the shutters were locked as more bullets struck the door. He quick turned down the lantern. Two guns were firing, he figured from the sound of it, though he couldn't be sure. Two at least, and the shots came from the front of his property.

He heard the girls overhead, moving fast, dressing. Samantha in the downstairs bedroom was moving, too.

"I'll see if she needs help." Nell hurried toward Samantha's bedroom.

Brand heard a terrible yelp from outside. The puppy. Silence followed the yelp, and it tore him up inside not to go help that little dog.

Nell hit him in the back with her full weight and slammed him forward into the door. "Don't you even think of opening that door. Listen. The puppy is alive. He's running off, saving himself, and there was no gunshot to go with that yelp."

Brand heard it then. Whining, growing more distant.

"They probably kicked him or something to make him yelp. Hoping I'd come out."

"Remember they did that. Kicked a puppy. Remember the kind of men they are if you get a clean shot at 'em."

"You think there's two of them?" Brand had a wife with more Western skills than a lot of women. Maybe more than a lot of men. Maybe more than him.

"Two men, I think. Both shooting rifles. One sounds like a Winchester. I'm not sure of the other. They probably have pistols, too."

"Henry and Peter?"

Nell tilted her head, listening, then shook it. "I can't identify the men by the sound of their guns, but that's a real good guess. The Wainwrights seem like civilized men, yet one of those civilized men smothered a helpless man to death and unleashed a wolf to kill our daughter."

The girls came flying down the ladder from the loft. Samantha moved more slowly than her sisters, but she was dressed and ready for whatever lay ahead.

"Pa, you're bleeding." Cassie rushed to look at Brand's arm. It was his left arm. His right still had a bandage from the wolf attack.

"I got hit, but it's just a scratch. My arm works okay—we can bind it up later."

Nell studied the bleeding with a furrowed brow, as if *she'd* make the decision on when to bind it up. She must have agreed it wasn't serious because she found Brand's six-shooter, checked it with astounding speed and skill to see if it was loaded, then handed it to Cassie.

"Samantha, I'd give it to you since you're the oldest. But the recoil on even a small gun might cause you trouble."

Brand watched the two of them and saw understanding between them. Nell had considered her feelings, and he felt a moment of failure because he'd've never given any of his girls a gun, let alone worried about how they felt about it.

Nell added, "It probably wouldn't harm you, but tonight we'll let Cassie handle this."

Michaela darted into the kitchen and came back armed with the family butcher knife. She had a shorter knife in the other hand and gave Samantha the larger one.

Brand, looking at his salty daughters, was struck by the thought that he should never have brought them out here to such a dangerous land.

The Ozarks had their own danger, though. Truth was, all of life carried risk.

More bullets struck the door, the walls. Not a barrage, but a steady stream of them. How tightly was this house built?

"They're coming closer." Nell looked at the girls. "They probably can't get through log walls. But be ready."

Brand looked at his daughters, loaded for bear. "Girls, if there was a place I could take you so you wouldn't need to face evil, we'd go there. But I know now that trying to protect you from danger kept us from identifying Henry Wainwright earlier, because Samantha didn't realize that what she'd seen was important. I'm not going to keep the truth hidden from you anymore. We'll face what life brings us together."

A bullet struck the shutters of the front window. Then more bullets rained against the shutters. The Wainwrights were closer and picking off weak spots in the house. The shutters held, but for how long?

A splinter cracked on the shutter to the right of the front door. The shard flew into the room and missed Cassie by mere inches.

"Let's get up in the loft. They're aiming low. If they get through, we'll be in a good position to fight." Brand looked at Nell, unsure, and she nodded and headed for the ladder, hustling Samantha in front of her. Samantha went up slowly, but she made it. Michaela was next.

Cassie handed Nell her gun. "I'll take it back once I'm up."

"I'll be right behind you."

Cassie nodded, then scrambled up the ladder. Nell was up two steps when one of the boards covering the window shattered. Nell reached high and gave Cassie her gun and Nell's so she had two hands to climb fast.

Then Nell was up. Brand waited until she was on her belly facing the front of the house, and then he was up those rungs quick as a squirrel.

The five of them lay side by side, watching the bullets shred the one window. Once an opening was created, they focused on that spot.

"Don't shoot," Nell said quietly. "Don't any of you shoot until you see someone to shoot at. They'll figure out where to aim if we fire a single time."

"Everyone, get back from the edge. I will too with only the tip of my rifle ready to fire. Once they get inside, we'll have just one chance to shoot before they find us." Brand propped himself on his elbows, belly flat against the loft floor. He aimed at the busted-up shutter, expecting a gun barrel to come through any minute. Maybe a face.

He heard his girls backing away. He prayed with all his

heart for them to survive this. He wanted almost as much for his girls not to have to kill someone to save their own lives. It would be a hard and ugly thing to carry on their souls.

The girls stayed quiet as they scooted back. Steady. Yes, life was dangerous, but he had raised himself some tough women.

Nell had pulled back, but only a little. He found he liked having her close and ready.

Whispering, he said, "Let's let both of them come through." He hoped it'd be just a matter of seconds because that was about as long as it would take for these men to scan the room, find the loft, and decide to fire some bullets just in case.

A gun butt slammed into the shutter and broke it open, wide enough for a man to poke his head in. He didn't look up as he slipped through. Brand waited, aiming. He knew Nell was doing the same. Knew Cassie, Samantha, and Michaela were ready.

Peter Wainwright stepped into the house, then moved to the side as Henry leapt in, his gun waving side to side.

"They're gone." Peter lowered his gun in disgust.

"We saw them go in here." Henry kept his rifle at the ready. "They're here alright." Henry raised his eyes to the loft.

Brand shot him. Henry's bullet went straight into the fireplace, ricocheted off the stone hearth, and hit Peter in the belly.

Pete's gun fired wildly as he fell, striking the ceiling just inches in front of Nell. The shooting went on until the rifle clicked. It was empty.

Henry, bleeding bad from his right shoulder, clawed at his six-gun as he stumbled for the blasted-out window. He got the gun, lifted it toward the loft.

Brand leveled his gun.

Brutus bounded through the window. Both Brand and Nell took their fingers off the triggers. They didn't dare risk shooting Brutus.

Henry took one terrified look at the snarling dog and threw himself out the window.

Brutus's growl was enough to tear at a man's flesh without any teeth involved.

Then a shout rang out from outside. "Brutus. No . . ."

"Becky," Nell whispered just loud enough to be heard.

Brand felt himself almost deflate, he was so relieved.

"Put down the gun, Henry. Now." The sheriff. Then two shots. From a pistol. But away from the house, not Henry's gun.

The shooting stopped.

At last, utter silence.

Brand eased forward and eyed Peter lying on the floor, motionless. He needed to climb down there and see what was going on, but he was so shaky he was afraid to move too soon.

A few seconds later, they heard a voice roar, "Brand! Nell! Are you there?" Nate Paxton.

Then Becky Pruitt shouted, "Are you all right?"

Brand almost melted into a heap.

The sheriff was next. "Brand, Nell! Girls! Answer us!"

Cassie, cool in a crisis, was the one who found her voice first. "We're fine. Peter Wainwright is dead, I think. Henry ran off."

"I got him." The sheriff sounded as grim as death. "He's not dead, but he's bad off. I'm coming in. Don't shoot." The sheriff peeked through the busted window.

"We're up here, Joe." Brand laid his gun down. "Everyone, put your weapons down. We don't want a gun going off by accident."

"I never even pulled the trigger." Cassie sounded disappointed and eerily calm.

Brand remembered how she'd acted that morning when Sam was hurt while his hands were shaking.

Brand turned to climb down the ladder.

The sheriff was inside by the time he got down, lifting the door latch. Becky and Nate rushed in, still armed, and looked at the man on the floor. Willie was just a pace behind them.

Peter lay still, staring up at the rafters, round-eyed. Not a breath coming from him.

Nell was down the ladder next. The sheriff met her eyes and said, "If Henry lives, you may preside over your first trial, and sentence one of the leaders of the Deadeye Gang to hanging."

33

I can't be objective, Sheriff."

"Sure you can, Your Honor." Sheriff Joe seemed to use that most weighty of titles when he wanted her to stand strong, or maybe it was better to say when he wanted her to do as she was told. "This man committed a crime right in front of your eyes. How can you be more objective than that?"

Nell was pretty sure that made her a witness, not the judge. And shooting the suspect made her . . . well, she wasn't quite sure what. But she didn't think the law would allow her to preside over a crime in which she was the victim. She'd argue with Joe about it later, if Henry lived.

She stepped outside to see Henry lying on his back in the dirt just under their shattered window. His gun hand twitched as if he still wanted to kill.

He had three bullet wounds. One low on his belly. One high that looked dead-center, just an inch or two from the man's heart. And one in his shoulder, courtesy of Brand.

He should be dead, but instead he lay there, his eyes

open and narrowed, watching her with hate. Nell knelt beside him, found a knife in a scabbard inside his shirt. That might've deflected the bullet some. She took the knife and cut strips off his shirt to make bandages.

Michaela came up beside her in the darkness. "Is he dangerous, Ma?"

"No, he's helpless with these wounds."

Henry growled, and his hand twitched again. But he made no move beyond that. "I'm going to cut his shirt up to make bandages, staunch the bleeding before Sheriff Mast takes him to the doc."

"That's mighty nice of you to doctor him, Ma. I'm supposin' it's what Jesus would want you to do, but it don't exactly sit right."

Nell smiled at the solemn-looking girl, regretting she had to see such ugliness. "You don't see me cutting strips off my skirt or your pa's shirt, do you? Now, *that* wouldn't be right."

Through the window, Nell saw Brand help Samantha down the ladder, then guide her to a chair to rest herself.

"Michaela, come on in here, please."

"Go on," Nell said. "I'm almost done here."

As Michaela went inside, Nell saw Brand carefully disarm Cassie and direct her into a different chair. "Just sit a few minutes, girls," he said. "Sheriff Joe and Deputy Willie will soon load these outlaws onto their horses, and then we'll get right back to bed."

Brand wasn't even going to tie a bandage around his own wounded arm, and Nell had her hands full currently. "Becky, Brand's been shot. Girls, do you have any bandages in the house, or should I cut up more of Henry's shirt?"

Cassie rushed into the kitchen.

Nell tightened the final bandage on Henry's shoulder. The sheriff came close and put shackles on Henry's hands and feet. Nell didn't think it was necessary, but she appreciated it nonetheless.

She walked over to the sheriff and started doing the work of an eyewitness. "Henry is the one who shot Pete," she began. "Both men came in through that window after they shot the shutter to bits. We had climbed into the loft hoping we could get them both inside before there need be any shooting. Henry hadn't seen us overhead, but he looked to be getting ready to fire a few stray shots. That was when Brand shot him in the shoulder. Henry's gun fired. A bullet hit the fireplace, and then it ricocheted into Pete's gut. Pete shot wild until his gun was empty, then he dropped. Henry couldn't aim his rifle—his right arm was useless—but he was drawing his pistol with his left hand when Brutus came leaping through the window."

Nell let out a long sigh. "So, the combination of the shot-up shoulder, the attacking dog, and his brother being out of the fight made Henry jump out the same window he'd come in. That's where you found him, Sheriff. I assume those are your bullets lodged in him?"

"They are for a fact, Your Honor." He looked a little pale. It took a much more hardened lawman than Joe Mast not to be upset when he shot a man.

Becky didn't spend long on Brand's shoulder. Nell noticed she was considerably gentler with Brand than Nell had been with Henry.

She tied the bandage off and turned to look at Pete's body. "Who'd've ever thought it would be the Wainwrights to blame. But that's the truth, isn't it? All of this points to the Deadeye Gang."

Brand nodded. "If Henry killed Mr. Campbell, it had to be to silence him."

Nell suddenly straightened. "When I was bandaging Henry, I smelled cheroots. But I've never known Henry to smoke." She looked at the sheriff. "We thought Mr. Campbell was asking for a smoke, remember? Turns out he wasn't. He saw Henry bending over him and recognized him. Henry must smoke when he's doing his robbing and killing. We didn't understand Campbell, but Henry did. He knew from that moment on he'd have to kill Campbell."

The sheriff pointed to a rifle on the floor. It had an elaborately carved stock "And that's a Yellow Boy. I've never seen either of these men with that gun before. Of course, I've never seen either of them armed. I'll bet Henry saves that rifle for his outlaw work." A whine sounded at the door, and they all turned to see the puppy come in, nudged along by Brutus. The little guy was limping. Nell turned her attention to the little puppy. She caught him close and ran her hands over his legs and back and ribs. The puppy didn't seem to be injured gravely. But Nell knew some wounds inside could be dangerous and not show. Well, they'd take very good care of him until they were sure he was all right.

"Thank you for this dog, Becky," Nell said. "He saved our lives. He heard or smelled the Wainwrights when Brand and I were outside talking after the girls went to bed. He reacted to them in time to warn us there was danger approaching." Nell pressed her cheek against the puppy's warm fur, then handed him to Brand. "Have the girls tell him thank you, too."

Brand, a bandage on each arm now, but not seriously hurt, took the dog to the girls. As they petted him and fussed over him, something eased in Nell's heart. The girls were going to be all right.

Even Cassie, with her tight control during all the ruckus, smiled and petted the little pup.

"We need to name him," Brand said. "We've been calling him 'the puppy,' but this boy has earned a name today. Any ideas?"

"Um," Cassie said, "Killer?"

"Not gonna name him Killer." Samantha shook her head. "I'd as soon name the poor thing Fluffy."

Cassie giggled. "Maybe Killer is a little much."

"How about Guard Dog?" Michaela offered, scratching the little guy between the ears.

A stretch of silence ensued as the sheriff hoisted Peter Wainwright by his hands. Willie grabbed the man's feet, and the two lawmen carried him outside.

"I like Guard Dog, but it's not quite right for a name." Nell stared at the pathetically fawned-over dog.

"We could call him Brutus Junior," Brand suggested. "He's going to grow up to be tough as his pa."

Brutus wandered over to the fuss being made over his son and earned a scratch or two for himself.

"How about," Samantha said quietly, "we name him Hero?"

All three girls smiled at once. Nell was sure she had the same expression.

Brand looked at the three girls, then at Nell. "We've got

a name. He's our Hero, just like you girls and your ma are all heroes."

"And you, Pa." Samantha leaned close and kissed him. "And Becky for giving us Hero, and Nate for coming with her to our rescue. And the sheriff and Willie. It's a day for heroes, and naming him that will honor this day."

Hero rolled onto his back with his paws in the air to get his belly rubbed. There were plenty willing to help him out.

Nell took in all their smiles. The sheriff must've seen them too because there was a gleam in his eye that hadn't been there when he first came in. Behind him, Willie stood a little straighter as the two of them hauled Peter away.

Becky had found a bucket and rags and made short work of mopping blood off the floor.

"I'll get the horses, and we'll ride for home," Nate said, heading for the door.

Becky dumped out the water and brought the bucket and mop back in the house in time for Nell to hug her tight.

"We can stay if you want," Becky whispered.

Nell pulled back, and the two of them studied Brand, his girls, and Hero and Brutus. "I think we're going to be all right. Thank you so much for the tracking today and for coming out here to help us. Yep, heroes all around."

Becky smiled, gave her another hug, then said, "I'm leaving Brutus for a few more days, but I think Hero is going to be settled in fine now. I'm proud to have found him such a good home."

Becky added quietly, "I think you've found a good home too, Nell. I'm happy for you. I'll be over in the morning with a building crew. We'll have a room up on your home-stead attached to this cabin by nightfall."

Becky went out just as Nate came leading the horses.

They galloped away, leaving the Nolte family alone with their enemies in custody or dead, their cabin's peace re-stored, and their dogs Hero and Brutus close by to make the night secure.

Nell saw the calm turn to exhaustion for the girls. She helped urge them to bed.

"I think I'll sleep in the loft tonight," Samantha said, weary but determined. "I don't want to be in that room alone. Having my sisters close will be a comfort, and I've proved I can get up there. I'm going to sleep well."

The younger girls scampered up the ladder, Samantha following more slowly. The dogs settled down in front of the fireplace. Nell hoped there would be no need to hide in the loft again because she didn't think Brutus or Hero were climbers.

Brand took Nell's hand and led her into the bedroom. "Get ready for bed in here. I'll change in the kitchen."

Assuming every word they spoke could be heard, he said no more.

Nell found a nightgown in the satchel she'd brought from home. She'd hung two dresses on nails in Samantha's room and kept everything else packed away. She changed after Brand left.

Once he'd pulled on his nightshirt, he rigged a blanket to cover the busted-up shutter. It wouldn't stop bullets, but the night was cool, and the blanket might slow down the breeze. He sincerely hoped they were done with bullets for a while. Hopefully forever. But he knew there were still gang members out and about. At this point, no one in this family had seen any of them, so no witnesses to protect here anymore.

He headed for the bedroom. Knocked softly and heard Nell's quiet, "Come in."

She was wearing a pretty nightgown. It was light blue, though the darkness washed out most of the color. But she had a lantern burning, which cast enough light that he could tell it was blue.

He could also tell she was blushing . . . and he was sorely afraid he was, too.

Brand looked away from her, not easy to do. He got very busy climbing into bed and covering himself up.

Nell lay down beside him. He felt every shift of her body as she pulled the covers up very gently, almost as if she hoped he wouldn't notice her there.

They didn't dare talk. Any words more interesting than *I heard it's going to be warm tomorrow* would perk the girls' ears right up. Even through a closed door, every sound could be heard in the little cabin.

But he wasn't going to pretend he hadn't noticed his flesh-and-blood wife lying right beside him. He'd been married before. So had Nell. There were no innocents in this bed tonight.

He rolled onto his side and slid an arm under her neck and turned her to face him. She didn't resist. But then she knew the girls were at hand, so she'd probably avoid shouting at him to get away from her if she could.

"Good night, Nell." Brand kissed her. The sweetness of

it helped him to push back the terror of the night. "We'll all ride into town tomorrow morning, together. Sam may not feel up to school just yet. If she chooses, she can spend the day with you, if that's all right."

"Shouldn't we stay here and help with the building work?"

"You may be needed as judge. And the sheriff will want to question us more thoroughly, so I'll ride with you and the girls and make sure you all get to town safely. We'll talk things through with the sheriff, then come home. I think the girls could use a day away from here."

"Going to town would be fine. I think the girls need a day or two off school, too."

Both of them spoke just above a breath, not even a whisper. That way maybe the girls couldn't overhear them.

"We'll let the girls decide if they feel settled enough for school." Nell seemed closer than before. She'd turned down the lantern, but Brand felt her nearness.

"It's been a hectic few days. A day or two of respite might be called for. I can set them up with their sewing, and they can work at that if I'm needed for court."

Brand drew her close, and she wrapped her arms around him. It was a wonder how precious a woman could feel. He'd never expected to hold one after Pamela died. He hadn't wanted to. But now he thought his heart had healed enough that he could want someone else to make a life with.

They held each other. He felt her shiver and knew it was her thinking about those foul Wainwright brothers and the danger they'd all faced.

Her shivering eased just as his began, and she held him

through that. Then the long day and all the fear and fighting wore through them, and Brand felt Nell's muscles relax and her heartbeat slow. He rolled onto his back and pulled her to rest against him, her head on his shoulder. Her breathing became even as she fell asleep. He doubted he'd find much rest tonight, but he could hold her and keep vigil over his family.

Tomorrow he'd definitely see to it, alongside Becky's work crew, that before another day passed, they'd finish adding a new room just a bit farther from where the girls slept.

34

Henry Wainwright hadn't survived the night.

No trial. No conflict to settle for Judge Nell. She and all three girls got to work. The girls now had plenty of clothes, thanks to what Nell had found in the new courthouse, but Samantha would be needing a wedding dress. And she needed to learn how to sew for a man. If they ran out of lessons, there were always chaps.

Nell saw Parson Blodgett walk into the jailhouse. "Girls, I'm going to see what the parson and Sheriff Mast are meeting about. Your pa said he'd come to town about the time school would be out, so it won't be much longer until we head home."

The girls nodded and got back to their sewing. Nell could see they were all learning fast. Her excuse that Samantha couldn't sew wasn't going to hold up for long.

As she stepped outside, the Blodgett children arrived. School had been dismissed, and their ma was out working on the Noltes' cabin. Because she'd given them a few lessons before, and Samantha was a good leader, the Blodgetts, Leland included, went to work on chaps.

Parson Blodgett was sitting in a chair in front of Sheriff Joe's desk. He looked over his shoulder when she came in, and both men stood.

"Sit down, Nell." The sheriff gestured to a chair beside the parson. "Rolly here thinks we need some kind of legal action concerning the events of last night. But he thinks it'd be wrong to have you preside over this trial."

Parson Blodgett said quickly, "I'm sure you're up to it, Nell, but you're a witness. Moreover, you're a victim who was aiming to shoot both men, if necessary, which makes you a defendant in the crime. Even with self-defense, you need to have the law clear you—which, here and now, the sheriff and I decided you're cleared. Still, it just isn't right for you to preside."

Nell heaved a sigh of relief. "I agree with you."

"So, if it's all right with you, Nell, I'll get Doc, and he and I can swear the parson in as the judge temporarily for this one case."

"The mayor is dead," Parson Blodgett said. "Doc and Joe are all that's left of the city council. Although I'm not an official council member, I was always consulted on matters. But now we can consult you. And Doc and Joe need to appoint a new mayor. He's suggested Clint, and that sounds agreeable to me. We haven't mentioned any of this to Clint yet."

Nell said, "Doesn't Clint live outside of town? I know he's a businessman in town, but I'm not sure if he can be mayor."

Besides, Nell thought, Mariah would be a better choice.

She'd lived in this town far longer. Yet they already had a female justice of the peace. Maybe there was only so much progress to be hoped for at one time . . . even in an equality-minded territory like Wyoming.

"I got Henry to town alive last night," the sheriff said. "I tried to question him while Doc tended him, but he just glared at me. Never seen more hate in a man. I want the names of the other men in his gang."

"What legal proceedings do we need?" Nell asked. "I mean, the criminals are dead. If you think we need to somehow, um—" she hesitated, then shrugged—"make sure the record shows that Henry killed Pete, it might be wise to have that in order. Can we hold the trial today?"

"It's a little bit late in the day. Let's wait and do it to-morrow. It's only a routine thing. No need to rush over it."

"With Peter and Henry dead, and Key Larson last fall, who I now suspect Henry killed, we've taken a big bite out of their gang. We may have to live with that small victory. We may have gotten enough of them that their evil ways will stop."

Nodding, Nell said, "Let me know when it's time to testify, Parson. Brand and I witnessed them shoot their way into our house. We saw Henry's bullet ricochet and kill Pete. If you need Samantha to testify, she's willing to do so. She seems almost eager to speak of what she saw, and that'd for sure tie Henry to Mr. Campbell's murder. We'll be heading home once Brand comes to town to fetch us, but we'll ride right back here if you need us."

Nell stood, reached into her pocket, and pulled out a twenty-dollar gold piece. "This is a donation to the city, which I want to make anonymously. It's to pay Jim Burk for all the men he's had to bury lately. Tell him the city will pay him a dollar for every coffin, laying out the body, and digging the hole. Go back to the two unclaimed bodies from that robbery with Campbell. Do *not* tell him where the money came from. And heaven help us if twenty dollars isn't enough. We've had enough dead strangers in the last few months to last us a lifetime."

The sheriff took the coin, studied it, then his eyes lifted to Nell. "Those chaps you make and sell must earn you mighty decent money, Judge Nolte."

Nell nodded. "No matter how much I charge for them, and how long I tell folks they have to wait to get them, everyone agrees to it." Shaking her head, she realized she was trading money earned through hard work she didn't enjoy for the digging of graves for strangers, some of whom might be criminals.

Life was one strange turn after another.

35

Brand swung the door closed between his old cabin and the new room. He'd just toured the finished room with Becky, Nate, and Latta Blodgett.

Becky and her crew, along with Mrs. Blodgett, had also knocked together a bedstead with a mattress. The room was otherwise empty.

"It's a big room," Brand said.

Mrs. Blodgett nodded. "My son Warren is building the smallest cabin legal for a homestead. His whole house is smaller than this room. But we had to reach Nell's property line."

"The bedstead straddles the line," said Becky. "By my way of reckoning, you have to sleep on the left side, and Nell on the right, for each of you to legally be staying on your own property and fulfill the requirements to prove up on your homestead."

Nate led the women out of the cabin. "It needs more work, a floor and more furniture, but you've got a good-sized house now."

"Thank you. I appreciate all your hard work." Brand waved to Becky and Nate as they rode away. Her crew of six cowpokes had already headed back to the Idee.

He glanced back at the house and saw they'd even fixed the broken shutter. Mounting up, he decided to ride to town with Mrs. Blodgett. Riding with Latta helped Brand to come to grips with her sincere wish to see Samantha and Leland married before she and Parson Blodgett left Wyoming. It was coming on to mid-June, and they planned to be gone by the end of the month.

Samantha had to wait a week before her stitches came out. Latta intended to witness a wedding a few days after that.

They approached Nell's shop, where they saw Leland and Nell through the front window, probably making chaps. No doubt she was giving him a dime a day, too. After dismounting and tying up the horses, Brand held the door for Latta, and they stepped into a very somber room.

Doc Preston, Sheriff Mast, and Clint were all there with Brand's family. Not a smile to be seen among them, though the girls, Nell, Leland, and the rest of the Blodgett children kept busy with their stitching.

Nell had all the younger Blodgetts working—well, not quite. The baby and the toddler weren't making chaps. Not yet anyway.

"It's time to head home, children." Latta waved her youngsters, three of them taller than her now, out the door.

Once they left, with the parson, doctor, and sheriff going too, Clint paused before following them out. He said to Brand, "There's some question if it's legal exactly, but it appears I'm the new mayor of Pine Valley. Didn't see that coming." He then left, closing the door with a firm click.

Nell said, "I don't think Clint can legally be the mayor because his homestead is out of town. The sheriff and Doc decided to redraw the city limits to include him, but since there's no such thing as a town map, the city doesn't really have limits. They're going to work something out over at the land office."

With a nod, Brand said, "Let's all go home."

His womenfolk made short work of setting Nell's shop to rights. Brand had his two horses waiting for them outside. The same as he'd always done it, only now there was a third tied alongside the pair. Nell had a horse now. A gray mare Nell had bought today from the smithy.

As they rode home, the warmth of the day seemed to bathe them all in peace.

"We got the addition to the house mostly done today," Brand said to Samantha. "It's a much finer building than before. And with Nell's homestead added, I now own twice as much land. And Becky brought over five cows and said they're our wedding present. She showed me how to properly turn them out to graze on my vast holding."

Samantha giggled. Nell, riding beside him, gently back-handed him on the arm that'd been shot yesterday. Brand noticed she'd aimed low, away from his wound.

When they got home, he found a ham in the oven, no doubt put there by Becky or Latta, or maybe even Clint. Potatoes and carrots were baking along with it. The family enjoyed a feast without anyone working too hard.

Afterward, they tidied up the supper dishes—Michaela bringing things from the table, Cassie washing, Nell drying, Brand putting things away. And without much urging, Sam agreed to take it easy for one more day at least.

When everything was all settled and clean, Brand went to where Samantha sat watching and helped her to her feet. He drew her into his arms. "I'm so glad you're all right."

She wrapped her arms around his waist. Michaela came up and put her little arms around them both. Then Cassie came from the other side. A family hug. Brand looked up and saw Nell watching them. He reached out one hand for her, and a smile broke out on her face. He pulled her into the family. They stood like that for a long time.

"Sam and I still have some healing to do, but tonight I feel good. Blessed. The Nolte family is as tough as they come."

Hero ran over and sniffed at Brand's feet. Brutus looked up from where he lay by the warm fire, obviously not feeling the need to join them.

The hug might not heal visible wounds, but it did a wonder on things inside. Fears and worries and dread.

When the hug finally ended, Brand said, "You can have the downstairs bedroom, Samantha, if you want it."

"I'll stay with my sisters for a few more days. Leland is building a cabin on his homestead, and it'll be done before we get married. Until then, I'd like to sleep alongside my sisters."

Brand didn't respond. He might accept that his daughter was growing up, but he was yet to be excited about it.

Nell said, "Good night, girls. See you all in the morning."

The girls went up into the cabin's loft.

Brand led Nell through the door to their own room some steps farther away from the girls. The sturdy room smelled of newly cut wood, with a dirt floor and one roughly built bed and a straw mattress. There, in the night, they became fully married. They committed themselves to a new life together.

And they did so joyfully.

Epilogue

Mrs. Blodgett struck up beautiful chords on the piano.

Nell sniffled into her handkerchief and clasped Michaela's little hand.

They'd held off the youngsters for two weeks longer than they'd hoped, but only because there was some upheaval concerning the Blodgett family.

Leland was building a more elaborate cabin than had been expected—four rooms instead of one. Then his brother Warren, who'd also homesteaded and helped build Leland's cabin, needed help himself with building. Warren, single with no prospects or, frankly, interest in a wife at this point, built one room measuring fifteen feet square. He had plans to add an entry room before the snow came, but he wasn't ready to build it just yet.

Then their sister Joy got the job as the new schoolmarm, with plans to live in the Blodgett cabin just outside of town. Though a woman living alone wasn't proper,

Warren's cabin was within shouting distance, so they decided it was proper enough.

One of her little brothers fought to be allowed to stay with Joy, but Mrs. Blodgett put her foot down about leaving four of her seven children behind, including one only fourteen years old.

Joy was hired because Mr. Betancourt had taken over the general store, left abandoned due to the deaths of its former owners, Peter and Henry Wainwright.

It was generally agreed that at sixteen, Joy was too young to teach school, but she was through all her books, and considering her classmate Samantha was getting married, which was a very adult thing to do, she was offered the job. She'd had many years of experience whipping her little brothers into shape. And besides, there was no one else around who was interested in the job. So no one looked askance at her age. Or maybe they did look askance, but they kept their mouths shut for fear of having to do the job themselves.

Mr. Betancourt had taught the school until the summer session had ended just recently. That meant Joy didn't need to start work until September. And the Blodgett family was moving away, and they had a good chunk of the children in the school, so the job wasn't quite so demanding.

It was all settled.

Yes, they'd held up the wedding, but now the day had come.

The ceremony was held after the Sunday service the last week of June. Clint had offered to cook a feast for the whole town, but Nell convinced him she could feed her close friends and family a sandwich and some cake and that would be all. Feeding the town didn't always have to land on his shoulders.

Besides, Latta Blodgett was helping, and the woman was capable of most anything. Nell was going to miss her.

The stagecoaches were running with six outriders on each route, and there'd been no more robberies of late. Not all members of the Deadeye Gang had been caught, but Nell hoped that the Wainwrights had been the ringleaders. Their deaths might break up the gang and end their murderous reign. Nell prayed for this as she sat with Michaela in the front pew of the church.

Latta Blodgett played a joyful tune on the church piano as Leland stood beside his pa, the parson. Leland gazed with pleasure down the center aisle, awaiting his bride. His brother Warren stood on the other side of him, while Cassie stood to Parson Blodgett's left. The parson clutched a Bible in his hands, a wide smile on his face.

The music changed then as Brand began walking Samantha up the aisle.

The bride wore a pretty pink dress that Nell had added more ruffles to than might be usual, for the dress needed to be beautiful for this special day. Samantha had on a matching bonnet with a wide brim. The bonnet didn't cover the scars on her face, but it cast them in shadow and made them less noticeable.

Cassie, Michaela, and Nell all wore new dresses, too. Brand was wearing a finely made, if Nell did say so herself, white shirt and a sharply pressed black suit.

She'd had her hands full talking him into a new suit. She was just grateful the man didn't want a pair of chaps for the wedding.

Brand and Samantha passed Nell. Michaela squeezed Nell's hand tight.

When Brand reached the front, he gave Samantha a kiss on both cheeks. He'd very deliberately kissed her on her scarred right cheek. It would continue to heal, yet the scars would almost certainly be with her for the rest of her life.

Then Brand took Samantha's hand and very gently placed it in Leland's. Leland nodded and smiled. Brand nodded back, then came and sat with Nell, Michaela between them. The little girl sniffled and held both their hands.

The parson did a wonderful job. The service seemed much nicer than Nell's. Of course, hers had been performed in a hurry in the doctor's office with Samantha badly wounded. So it didn't take much to be nicer than Nell's.

The young couple would be all right because Brand and Nell would see to it they were. But their marriage was done in such haste. Not unlike Nell's had been. Yet somehow Nell and Brand, two very grown-up people who feared for their daughters' lives, seemed to have made a much calmer decision.

Nell prayed for the couple as they eagerly made their vows. Then the music started up again, and the couple turned, arm in arm, and strode down the aisle, both smiling. Cassie followed them out, walking with Warren.

The small gathering of about fifteen people headed for the courthouse. Nell and Mrs. Blodgett had prepared it for the reception, including borrowing chairs and dishes from both their houses and a few from the diner.

Leland had shot a turkey. Nell had baked loaves of bread, and their main food was turkey sandwiches. Latta Blodgett had made a pretty cake with thick white frosting. The two families joined together, and there was much laughter and hugs and feasting. Even as they knew the Blodgetts were moving far enough away that they might never see three of their children and their new daughter-in-law again.

That made for some sadness under all the laughter.

Nell had a quiet moment when she found herself a few steps outside the circle of friends and neighbors. She watched everyone eating and laughing, embracing the young couple, and talking of recent events.

Mariah came to her side, slid an arm around Nell's waist, and the two of them stood watching without much talk. Before long, Becky came to stand on Nell's other side and gave her a gentle one-armed hug. The trio stood in a row, taking in the festive room.

"You're a mom now, Nell." Mariah rested her hand on her rounded belly. "You beat me to it."

"Probably going to be a grandma before you know it." Becky squeezed Nell gently.

"That never occurred to me. Good grief, I'll be a grandmother before I've become used to being a mother."

The three of them laughed.

"Oh, I think you'll be all right, Nell."

Nell watched her pretty daughters and, with much satisfaction, said, "Yes, I most certainly will be."

"We've had enough excitement for a while. I sincerely hope it's over." Mariah spoke the words Nell was thinking.

"A stretch of calm would be welcome. A peaceful countryside now that the Wainwrights are out of the stage-robbing business for good. Yes, let's hope and pray it lasts."

Wyoming Territory, a place where equality was practiced. The mountains outside Nell's window standing as sentries, placed there by God to remind everyone He would protect them all.

Nell gave it all a long thought, then hugged her friends. "I'm supposed to be hosting this party. I need to get back to work."

"And tomorrow you'll be back to work as justice of the peace." Mariah returned the hug. "I'm so proud to know you. To be part of the future."

Becky gave a firm nod. "The law in this town is in the hands of a woman. It's high time women made more of the important decisions around here."

"Whatever trials I preside over"—her eyes went to Brand—"I'm still a woman, and the main law I have to deal with is the law of attraction to my very handsome husband."

Mariah giggled and patted her belly.

Becky smiled and made a broad gesture for Nell to go be with her husband.

As she did, Nell marveled at how her life had changed. A wife, mother, judge, seamstress . . . she'd gone from being very much alone and liking it to being part of a new family and loving it.

She went to Brand's side. Their eyes met. He took her hand, and she read the impact of this day. Letting his daughter go. Giving her away. It hadn't come easy.

And now they'd go forward, together.

Mary Connealy writes romantic comedies about cowboys. She's the author of the Brothers in Arms, Brides of Hope Mountain, High Sierra Sweethearts, Kincaid Brides, Trouble in Texas, Wild at Heart, and Cimarron Legacy series, as well as several other acclaimed series. Mary has been nominated for a Christy Award, was a finalist for a RITA Award, and is a two-time winner of the Carol Award. She lives on a ranch in eastern Nebraska with her very own romantic cowboy hero. They have four grown daughters—Joslyn, married to Matt; Wendy; Shelly, married to Aaron; and Katy, married to Max—and seven precious grandchildren. Learn more about Mary and her books at

maryconnealy.com
facebook.com/maryconnealy
seekerville.blogspot.com
petticoatsandpistols.com

Sign Up for Mary's Newsletter

Keep up to date with Mary's latest news on book releases and events by signing up for her email list at the link below.

FOLLOW MARY ON SOCIAL MEDIA!

Mary Connealy   @maryconnealy   @MaryConnealy

maryconnealy.com

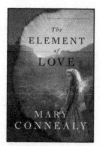

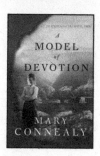